PRAISE FOR BARBARA O'NEAL

THE STARFISH SISTERS

"Barbara O'Neal is at the top of her game. *The Starfish Sisters* is a gorgeous, heartfelt story about two lifelong friends who, now estranged, must battle their way back to each other after years of betrayals and jealousy and misunderstandings. Suze is a famous, world-traveling movie star who seems to have everything but love—while her former best friend, Phoebe, does art and nurtures the people around her. O'Neal has written a deeply harrowing, suspenseful, and ultimately loving book that explores the nature of women's friendships and the lengths to which we all will go to protect those we love from danger. I read it far into the night, and, yes, I wept a few tears along the way."
—Maddie Dawson, *Washington Post* bestselling author of
Matchmaking for Beginners

THIS PLACE OF WONDER

"*This Place of Wonder* is a wonderfully moving tale about four women whose journeys are all connected by one shared love: some are romantic, some are familial, but all are deeply complicated. Dealing with loss, love, hidden secrets, and second chances, this stirring tale is utterly engaging and ultimately hopeful. Set along the rugged California coastline, *This Place of Wonder* will sweep you away with the intoxicating scents, bold flavors, and sweeping views of the region and transport you to a world you won't be in any hurry to leave."
—Colleen Hoover, #1 *New York Times* bestselling author

"Kristin Hannah readers will thoroughly enjoy the family dynamic, especially the mother-daughter relationships."

—*Booklist* (starred review)

"Barbara O'Neal's latest novel is simply delicious. Engrossing, empathetic, and profoundly moving, I savored every sentence of this story of several very different women who find solace and second chances in each other after tragedy (though not before facing some hard truths and, yes, a few rock bottoms). *This Place of Wonder* is one of the best books I've read in a long time."

—Camille Pagán, bestselling author of *Everything Must Go*

"I have never much moved in the elevated circles of California farm-to-table cuisine, but O'Neal makes me feel like I'm there. Rather than simply skewering the pretensions, *This Place of Wonder* pinpoints the passions. Some of these characters have been elevated to celebrity, some are newcomers to the scene, but all are drawn together by the sensuality, the excitement, and ultimately the care that food brings them. Elegiac but also forward-looking, this is a book about eating, but more than that, it's a book about hurt and healing and women finding their way together. I loved every moment of it."

—Julie Powell, author of *Julie & Julia* and *Cleaving*

WRITE MY NAME ACROSS THE SKY

"Barbara O'Neal weaves an irresistible tale of creativity, forgery, family, and the FBI in *Write My Name Across the Sky*. Willow and Sam are fascinating, and their aunt Gloria is my dream of an incorrigible, glamorous older woman."

—Nancy Thayer, bestselling author of *Family Reunion*

"*Write My Name Across the Sky* is an exquisitely crafted novel of three remarkable women from two generations grappling with decisions of the past and the consequences of where those young, impetuous choices have led. A heartfelt story of passion, devotion, and family told as only Barbara O'Neal can."

—Suzanne Redfearn, #1 Amazon bestselling author of *In an Instant*

"With its themes of creativity and art, *Write My Name Across the Sky* is itself like a masterfully executed painting. Using refined brushstrokes, O'Neal builds her vivid, complex characters: three independent women in one family who can't quite come to terms with their fierce feelings of love for one another. O'Neal deftly switches between three points of view, adding layers of family history into this intimate and satisfying study of how women make tough choices between love and creativity and family and freedom."

—Glendy Vanderah, *Washington Post* bestselling author of *Where the Forest Meets the Stars*

THE LOST GIRLS OF DEVON

One of *Travel + Leisure*'s most anticipated books of summer 2020

"A woman's strange disappearance brings together four strong women who struggle with their relationships, despite their need for one another. Fans of Sarah Addison Allen will appreciate the emphasis on nature and these women's unique gifts in this latest by the author of *When We Believed in Mermaids*."

—*Library Journal* (starred review)

"*The Lost Girls of Devon* draws us into the lives of four generations of women as they come to terms with their relationships and a mysterious tragedy that brings them together. Written in exquisite prose with the added bonus of the small Devon village as a setting, Barbara O'Neal's book will ensnare the reader from the first page, taking us on an emotional journey of love, loss, and betrayal."

—Rhys Bowen, *New York Times* and #1 Kindle bestselling author of *The Tuscan Child*, *In Farleigh Field*, and the Royal Spyness series

"*The Lost Girls of Devon* is one of those novels that grabs you at the beginning with its imagery and rich language and won't let you go. Four generations of women deal with the pain and betrayal of the past, and Barbara O'Neal skillfully leads us to understand all of their deepest needs and fears. To read a Barbara O'Neal novel is to fall into a different world—a world of beauty and suspense, of tragedy and redemption. This one, like her others, is spellbinding."

—Maddie Dawson, bestselling author of *A Happy Catastrophe*

WHEN WE BELIEVED IN MERMAIDS

"An emotional story about the relationship between two sisters and the difficulty of facing the truth head-on."

—*Today*

"There's a reason Barbara O'Neal is one of the most decorated authors in fiction. With her trademark lyrical style, she's written a page-turner of the first order. From the very first page, I was drawn into the drama and irresistibly teased along as layers of a family's complicated past were artfully peeled away. Don't miss this masterfully told story of sisters and secrets, damage and redemption, hope and healing."

—Susan Wiggs, #1 *New York Times* bestselling author

"More than a mystery, Barbara O'Neal's *When We Believed in Mermaids* is a story of childhood—and innocence—lost, and the long-hidden secrets, lies, and betrayals two sisters must face in order to make themselves whole as adults. Plunge in and enjoy the intriguing depths of this passionate, lustrous novel, and you just might find yourself believing in mermaids."

—Juliet Blackwell, *New York Times* bestselling author of The *Lost Carousel of Provence*, *Letters from Paris*, and *The Paris Key*

"In *When We Believed in Mermaids*, Barbara O'Neal draws us into the story with her crisp prose, well-drawn settings, and compelling characters, in whom we invest our hearts as we experience the full range of human emotion and, ultimately, celebrate their triumph over the past."

—Grace Greene, author of *The Memory of Butterflies* and The Wildflower House series

"*When We Believed in Mermaids* is a deftly woven tale of two sisters, separated by tragedy and reunited by fate, discovering that the past isn't always what it seems. By turns shattering and life-affirming, as luminous and mesmerizing as the sea by which it unfolds, this is a book club essential—definitely one for the shelf!"

—Kerry Anne King, bestselling author of *Whisper Me This*

THE ART OF INHERITING SECRETS

"Great writing, terrific characters, food elements, romance, a touch of intrigue, and more than a few surprises to keep readers guessing."

—*Kirkus Reviews*

"Settle in with tea and biscuits for a charming adventure about inheriting an English manor and the means to restore it. Vivid descriptions and characters that read like best friends will stay with you long after this delightful story has ended."

—Cynthia Ellingsen, bestselling author of *The Lighthouse Keeper*

"*The Art of Inheriting Secrets* is the story of one woman's journey to uncovering her family's hidden past. Set against the backdrop of a sprawling English manor, this book is ripe with mystery. It will have you guessing until the end!"

—Nicole Meier, author of *The House of Bradbury* and *The Girl Made of Clay*

"O'Neal's clever title begins an intriguing journey for readers that unfolds layer by surprising layer. Her respected masterful storytelling blends mystery, art, romance, and mayhem in a quaint English village and breathtaking countryside. Brilliant!"

—Patricia Sands, bestselling author of the Love in Provence series

MEMORIES OF THE LOST

ALSO BY BARBARA O'NEAL

The Starfish Sisters

This Place of Wonder

Write My Name Across the Sky

The Lost Girls of Devon

When We Believed in Mermaids

The Art of Inheriting Secrets

The Lost Recipe for Happiness

The Secret of Everything

How to Bake a Perfect Life

The Garden of Happy Endings

The All You Can Dream Buffet

No Place Like Home

A Piece of Heaven

The Goddesses of Kitchen Avenue

Lady Luck's Map of Vegas

The Scent of Hours

MEMORIES OF THE LOST

a novel

BARBARA O'NEAL

LAKE UNION
PUBLISHING

Published by Lake Union Publishing, Seattle

www.apub.com

Amazon, the Amazon logo, and Lake Union Publishing are trademarks of Amazon.com, Inc., or its affiliates.

ISBN-13: 9781662514920 (hardcover)
ISBN-13: 9781662514906 (paperback)
ISBN-13: 9781662514913 (digital)

Cover design by Faceout Studio, Amanda Hudson
Cover image: ©Olga Ilina, ©Sandra_M, ©Magic cinema, ©KDdesign_photo_video, ©Mark Borbely, ©savageultralight / Shutterstock

Printed in the United States of America

First edition

For my sisters, Cathy and Merry, who have always helped carry the load. Love you.

PROLOGUE

Dragon

Once upon a time, a dragon came over a mountain with a roar, spitting fire so fierce and hot that everything turned to ash in seconds.

Arlette had only stepped away from the porch a few feet to collect things for a dream catcher, specifically seeking the banded feathers of the great horned owl she'd heard in the night. Her daughter napped peacefully on a blanket on the porch, protected at head and foot by the family dogs—shepherd mutts, both of them.

By the time the dragon stomped away, nothing was left of that cabin or three more. Four people and eight pets were killed, and everyone said it was lucky it struck when it did, in the middle of the day, when everyone was out working or seeking work.

It didn't feel lucky to Arlette, who had been chased by the monster into the woods and emerged less than a half hour later to find her life in ashes. Why did it spare her? For what?

How could she bear to go on?

PART ONE: EARTHQUAKE

For he comes, the human child
To the waters and the wild
With a faery hand in hand,
For the world's more full of weeping
Than he can understand.
—W. B. Yeats

CHAPTER ONE

New York City

Five months and twelve days after her mother died, a painting ripped a hole in the fabric of Tillie Morrisey's life.

If it had not been an opening for her best friend's first show in three years, she wouldn't have even gone. It was pouring, the kind of Manhattan deluge that fills the gutters to knee height in ten minutes, so she was forced to wade to the subway, then splash the three blocks to the gallery. She would look like a drowned cat by the time she got there.

Two doors away from the beacon of the gallery spilling light from its big windows, an old woman tripped right in front of her. She was clearly unhoused, pushing a cart, her coat dragging on the ground. She stumbled, five feet ahead of Tillie, and practically somersaulted over, feet in the air.

Four other people were on the street, and not all of them were as clearly dressed up as Tillie, but none of them stopped. Tillie felt ashamed of herself for hesitating for even a tiny second—what did it matter if she got wetter or ruined her makeup?

She hurried over, holding her umbrella aloft. "Are you all right?" she asked. "Let me help you up."

The woman was a ball of cloth, layer after layer, her gray hair scattered down her back. "Bless you," she said in a craggy voice, allowing herself to be helped to her feet. "I can trip right over the air!"

"Take my umbrella," Tillie said.

"Oh, no, not for free!"

"Really, I don't mind. I'm just going right there." She pointed.

The woman peered up at her, and Tillie found herself pressing details into her artist mind, seeing the lady as an ancient little hedgehog, her hair caught under a knitted scarf, her nose red from the cold. She scrounged around in her pocket and came out with something she pressed into Tillie's hand. She imagined a germy rock, and wanted to drop it, but not until the woman was no longer looking.

"Thank you." Tillie handed her the umbrella, then dashed for the shining lights of the gallery.

A crowd had already gathered, impossibly polished patrons in cocktail dresses and suits, the monied folk you want to see at an opening. No one would mistake Tillie for one of them with her dripping hair and aging boots, but she wasn't there for them. Standing in the vestibule for a moment, she shook herself like a wolf and pushed her wet hair out of her face.

What had possessed her to give her umbrella away? Now she'd have to walk home in the rain. She looked at the thing the woman had given her. It wasn't a rock but a rather beautiful reddish crystal, and unexpected tears stung her eyes. It felt like a nod from her witchy, hippie mother, whom Tillie missed painfully.

The shoulders and heads of murmuring people hid any sign of him. Instead, her eye caught on a side wall, on a particular painting. It wasn't large, but the colors—many greens and slashes of pink, with turquoise and yellow—blazed into the room, loud as a siren. It drew Tillie across the floor.

She stopped in front of it, hair dripping on her shoulders.

It was of a little house in a nest of trees and bushes, with a porch and two figures without faces, and a pale cat licking a paw. The colors sizzled, blazed, those improbable pinks, the saturated lime and lemon. The figures wore turquoise.

Tillie didn't move, captured entirely by the scene, and even as she stood there, she didn't know what was so mesmerizing. It felt like a place she should know, and if she could just focus, she'd bring it in. The cat, licking a paw. The two girls.

A sound like a train filled her ears. Her chest was tight. Improbably, she felt tears running down her face, and could not seem to move away.

~

In his hotel room across the street, Liam Redfern had been staring through his window at the rain, feeling marooned and homesick for his own house, where his things were arranged the way he liked them and he could make himself a proper cup of tea. He'd drink that cup sitting in his favorite chair that looked out over a rocky cliff to the bay, where sailboats decorated the horizon. He hadn't been there in nearly five months, and he was very tired of life on the road.

It wasn't so much that he missed the room, the tea, that particular mug his mother had brought him from one of the Renaissance fairs where she sold her honey and soaps. He missed the simple routines of his life there, the simple beauties he'd chosen to be calming, such as his garden that he tended himself when he was home. He missed the meditation space and the kitchen where he cooked simple, good food.

The tangle of emotion, weariness mixed with longing mixed with resistance, was a warning that had grown more insistent over the past couple of weeks. He needed to talk with Krish about it, and sooner rather than later.

Below, he saw a woman hurrying through the rain, carrying a yellow umbrella. It was unexpectedly bright in the dark evening. He saw it tilt, and then realized that the umbrella was shielding a homeless woman and her cart of belongings. The woman with the umbrella helped her up and gave her the umbrella. Then she dashed away, entering the gallery below his windows. He'd noticed the gallery this morning, the window displaying abstracts in a palette of blues and greens that made Liam think of the sea. Now he was intrigued by the woman who'd left behind her umbrella.

A prompt rose, clear and strong. *Go meet her.*

A lesser voice argued that he might be recognized. Another said he should stay in and work on a new group of meditations they wanted to release in the near future. *They* being his business team, not Liam himself.

Which had become part of the problem.

He could see the woman pause by the door. She wore green stockings, and her hair tumbled down her back, dark as enchantment.

He grabbed his coat.

~

Tillie had no idea how long she stood mesmerized in front of the painting.

A hand touched her elbow lightly. "Are you all right?"

Jerking away from the stranger, Tillie slapped tears off her face, embarrassed.

The man raised his hands, palms out. "Sorry. I didn't mean to frighten you."

She blinked. For the second time in two minutes, she felt swamped by visuals. The man's face was straight from a Renaissance painting, with a high brow and eyes as clear as an angel's. The hair was pure surfer, sun-bleached blond, too long. The throat and hands showed the same long exposure to sun. But they were a long way from either Italy or surfing.

"Are you the artist?" Tillie managed, pointing to the wall.

"No. I'm not a painter, I'm afraid." The accent was from New Zealand. Maybe South Africa.

She looked back to the painting and walked up close to read the card: *Shiloh. Forest #21.* The colors blared, commanded her attention, and the buzzing started again, so loud, as if she were hearing some real thing that came from the world of the painting, something she couldn't identify. Birds? Insects?

She swayed.

"Steady," the man said, arm around her waist. This time she didn't protest. "Let's find you a chair, shall we?"

She allowed herself to be settled on a plastic chair near the coat check, out of the way.

"Breathe," he said. "I'll fetch you some water."

"Thanks." The noise in her head subsided as she took long breaths in, let them out. A part of her wanted to march right back and stare at the painting again, but she might fall flat on her face the next go-round.

Before the man came back, Jon appeared. He was her oldest friend from art school—a delicately beautiful dark-brown man with luminous eyes and the most elegant hands she'd ever seen. He'd fled a tiny town somewhere in Oklahoma and never looked back. They'd been roommates for years, sharing a terrifyingly cold space that was big enough for both to paint, with corners for sleeping and the bare bones of a kitchen while they tried to make their way.

He said now, "Tillie, baby! Are you okay?"

"Yeah, I'm good." She waved a hand, dismissing the weirdness. *Don't look at the painting. Don't look at the painting.* "Maybe I'm coming down with something."

"Do you want something? Some—"

"I've got some water here, mate," the man said, handing her a metal bottle. *A good voice,* Tillie thought, smooth and rich, doubly excellent with that accent.

"Thanks," Jon said, standing. He, too, appreciated the long limbs, the Renaissance mouth. He reached out a hand. "And you are . . . ?"

"Liam." Tanned wrist with scatters of bleached hair, four bracelets of natural stone and crystal around it. *Definitely surfer/hippie/New Agey something or another,* Tillie thought. No ring. Not her kind of man, but he would be worth a night or two of play. Those shoulders, his amiable expression.

"Liam. That's a name you don't hear too often," Jon said, giving his trademark grin, bright as a full moon.

"Not here, but pretty common where I come from."

Jon dipped his chin. "I stand corrected."

Liam shifted his focus—and Tillie thought it was as if he steered a spotlight, wide and deep, and shined it on her. It was hard to look away. "You all right?"

"I'm fine," Tillie said. "Thanks."

He raised a hand. "Take care, then."

Jon and Tillie watched him go, an athletic spring in his fit body. "Runner, you think?" Jon said.

"Mm. I'm going to guess surfer."

"Maybe." He touched his artfully thin goatee with one long finger. "Don't make 'em like that on the East Coast too often."

Tillie laughed, and slapped his arm. "Come on, let's see the show."

She carefully avoided the wall with the strange painting, keeping her eyes averted as Jon led her toward his abstracts, all modest in size with a spirit of melancholy or joy, phrased in unusual palettes. Two already showed the red dots that marked them as sold. "Well done," she said.

He wrapped his fingers in hers. "Thank you. That one reminds me of your eyes."

It was done in sea hues, with splashes of murky gray. "Really?"

"Yes." He stopped. "It took a month to get it right. All that light and all those shadows." He pursed his lips, considering. "I think I got it."

A ghostly shape lurked through the blues and greens, and something about it caused a return of the earlier disturbance. Tillie touched her belly. "Is there food here? I think I might be a little hungry."

"Jon!" a deep hearty voice said, the gallery owner. "I want you to meet—"

Tillie gave him a tiny push and slipped away, looking for the snacks that had to be here somewhere. Nothing too messy or hard to manage, somewhere near the back. A faint sense of dizziness followed her, muting the sounds of voices and music.

A gazelle of a girl with a long neck and yellow hair watched over the makeshift bar. Tillie pulled out her phone and snapped a photo, imagining the gazelle girl on an open plain, pursued by burly alpha lions.

She lowered the phone, narrowed her eyes, seeing possibilities in colors, in movement. The girl's long nose, long neck.

A flicker zapped the edge of her vision, the broken mylar that warned of an impending migraine.

Of course.

A migraine. That was what this weirdness was. She'd suffered from them for years, off and on, the remnants of a head injury when she was a small child. It was annoying that they could still surprise her.

"Do you have water?" she asked the gazelle.

Without a word, she produced a metal bottle, ice-cold. Working quickly to beat the growing size of the shimmering aura that would soon cover the vision of her right eye, Tillie filled an environmentally friendly plate with crackers and cheese and some wildly appealing raspberries. Water, food, rest. The magic cure. Sometimes. She couldn't lie down and have a nap, but she could address the other two.

A trio of chairs rested against the wall near the restrooms, and she gratefully sat down. The aura spread to the middle of her vision now, bringing a distant sound, a faint buzz. She opened the bottle and guzzled half the water. Maybe it would be only the aura. Sometimes, that was all it was. She closed her eyes and took long, slow breaths, pressed the cold bottle to her forehead.

"Try this," said the New Zealander, and pressed a cool compress into her hands. "Over your eyes."

She didn't question how or what he knew—the aura was spreading quickly, and she could feel the headache itself starting to build beneath her scalp. She lifted the wet, cold rectangle and pressed it over her eyes. "Thank you."

"Migraine?" he asked.

"Yes."

"D'you mind if I try something?"

"Go ahead."

He took her left hand and pinched a point between her thumb and forefinger. "Okay?"

"Mm." Nothing stopped the aura once it began, but it didn't really hurt, either. It was just blinding and strange. If anything could hold off the migraine itself, she was willing to try.

He kept pressing the skin on her hand. "Tell me if the pressure is too much."

The sensation was solid, a focus point, and after a little while—two minutes or ten?—the rumbling threat started to ease. The aura pulsed, true to its own schedule, almost twenty minutes to the second every single time. It covered her right eye in bright geometric rainbows—then ceased. She kept her eyes closed a moment longer, and Liam kept pressing the spot on her hand. She took the compress from her eyes. Waited. Nothing.

"Wow."

"Better?" he asked.

"Yes," she said with some sense of wonder. "Is that acupressure?"

"It is." His hands dropped to his lap.

"How do you know that?" she asked.

"Part of my job." He flashed a quick, rueful smile. So appealing, a little diffident, and she didn't think it was feigned. It offset the dazzlement of his beauty.

"You're an acupuncturist?"

"Not exactly."

"You don't want to say?"

A shrug.

"Okay. Well . . . um . . . thank you." She dipped her head sideways. "Twice."

He held her gaze. Such clear irises, somehow guileless. A disturbance rippled in the air, just out of sight, a soft shift in time, maybe, a shimmer of green and blue.

"Right, then," he said. "You good now?"

Tillie nodded. "Are you here with someone?"

"No. I ducked in to get out of the rain."

"Can I buy you a coffee or a beer or something?"

The smile was slow. "Yeah."

"Let me tell my friend."

They stood together. The quickest way through the room was through the narrow space by the painting that had captured her earlier. She could almost hear it, and planned to pass with her eyes averted, but as if it carried its own alarm, it called her attention. She slowed. Stopped.

Pinks and greens and turquoise. Blocks and shapes, almost abstract but not. "It's not my usual thing," she said. "Why can't I stop looking at it?"

"I like it," he said. "The children, the cat, the sense of the forest, lurking. Dangerous and inviting. The colors are great."

That sound returned, muted, a call, a faraway roar. The buzzy sense of disconnect crawled up her neck, and Tillie felt like she could *almost* see something, feel something, like she wanted to speak. No, she wanted to climb through the painting into that other world. "Ugh." She straightened, rubbed the back of her neck. "It just gives me such a strange feeling, like . . ." She shrugged. "I don't know. I can't call it in."

"It speaks to you."

Tillie laughed a little. "Literally." She shook it off. "Come on, we need to tell Jon we're leaving."

We. As if they were a couple.

CHAPTER TWO

Wulfecombe, Devon, UK

Clare Evely awoke to the smell of coffee and cinnamon and rain. A big warm hand fell on her back. "Time to wake up, love."

She rolled over luxuriously, bumping into a much-battered cat who was, by their best guess, at least seventeen. He croaked at her, then settled back down. Clare was finally rested after a three-week stretch of back-to-back ceremonies—weddings, a funeral, a handfasting, and her daughter's thirty-seventh birthday, a particularly precious thing now that Sage was pregnant. Clare had several grandchildren that she shared with Levi's children, but Sage had walked a difficult road, and this pregnancy was a blooming of a life that had been entirely too full of challenges.

"Good morning." Her voice was throaty. "Did you bring me a cinnamon roll, you wicked man?"

Levi rubbed her belly with his giant hand. "You've earned it." He kissed her forehead. "I've got to run. Nan Granger's mare is failing."

"Ah." She squeezed his hand. "It's never easy, but she loves that horse like a husband. I should bake her a cake."

He grunted in agreement, and Clare rolled over to watch him dress. He winked as he noticed, shedding everything to stand naked in the cold bedroom with its fading William Morris wallpaper. Light came in the dormers and skated over his big, solid form. He was a cheerful, lusty man, and it showed in his belly and thighs, weight he carried easily on his six-foot-five-inch frame. She had made a great many mistakes in her life, but Levi was not one of them. They'd been together for thirty years, and she thanked the goddess for him every day.

Reaching out, she brushed the back of his thigh. "Hurry home tonight, and I'll cook for *you* for a change."

He laughed and clapped her hip. "It's cooking you're wanting, is it?" After forty years in England, much of his Jamaican accent had been subsumed in the West Country cadence, but it came through now.

"Maybe."

"Mm. I'll get back as soon as I can." He finished dressing and bent to kiss her again, then made a little sound of pain and pressed a hand to his low back.

"Still bothering you?"

"Just gettin' old, I fear."

"Never!" She sat up. "Take some ibuprofen, will you?"

"Already done."

Clare watched him depart, noting the way he favored his right side, giving his walk a bit of a rocking limp. It had been bothering him for quite a while. Time he should see a doctor. "Don't overdo!" she called after him.

"You're the one! I'm not the one who hasn't had a free day in weeks. Take an easy day yourself, missus."

"I'll try. Liam's coming next week. I have a lot to do."

"He won't mind. Give yourself a day."

"I'll try if you will."

He grunted and was gone.

She scrolled through her phone, drinking coffee and nibbling the cinnamon roll. There were the usual texts from her daughters and the usual zero from her sons. Sage wanted the recipe for her seedy bread; her stepdaughter Meg reported back on a test for her youngest's bad throat—no strep. Meg's sister, Amelia, was always the chattiest. She lived on a nearby farm, and they shared the most in terms of interests. She reported that the daffodils were budding, and she had a great crop of lettuces already. Clare texted each one back, then texted the boys, too—neither she nor Levi had had any before they married, but the union gave them two, Ben and Arthur. An enormous brood of children, everyone said. She wouldn't have minded more, honestly, but time ran out.

She texted them in a group: Don't forget Liam will be here for Sunday lunch. Remember, no one but you and your families. No friends.

They were all a little swoony over their famous cousin coming to Sunday lunch out in the wilds of Devon, and Clare had had to crack down on the whole group of them. The girls remembered him, of course, but only as a boy, not the celebrated man he'd become.

Liam was her dearest friend's youngest. Helen had brought her brood home from New Zealand for a summer after the shocking, devastating death of her husband. The lot of them had stayed the season, healing in the sea air with cousins and good food and the ever-changing host of rescued animals that populated the farm. Clare had taken the broken Liam under her wing, patching him up with greenhouse experiments and the feeding of the limping, blind, and ancient pets. He'd proven to be a good correspondent, apart from a long stretch in his twenties, and they'd carried on a lively discussion of life, books, and the nature of spiritual pursuits for decades. She deeply looked forward to his visit.

Phone calls and laundry and garden tasks would wait. The lure of fresh air tugged her out the door and down the forest path she'd been walking since young adulthood, beneath branches just now swelling with the buds of leaves or flowers, still wet in the aftermath of last night's rain.

From the corner of her eye, she saw a flash of movement. A fluffy black tail was disappearing, gone. Her heart quickened. Surely it wasn't a wolf? She stayed very still, peering into the green dimness. The only sound she heard was the drip of water to the earth. No birdsong.

Without moving her body, she moved her eyes from tree to tree, looking up, looking left, looking—

Gooseflesh broke out over her entire body, and Clare whirled, yelling at the top of her voice. Into the depths of the forest dashed a big gray wolf, unmistakable. She could see his head and his big paws and, when he paused to look over his shoulder, his big yellow eyes.

She shivered in wonder and terror and, of course, the never-distant grief. No one had believed the tales of wolves in these woods, but here one was again.

Like an omen.

~

The Evelys had lived in the village of Wulfecombe for hundreds of years—over a thousand, according to some family legends, which stated that Thomas Evely had established a farm near the ford before the Conqueror came. Clare had her doubts about that, but she could feel the roots of her ancestors on every road and dale of the county, from Barnstaple to the sea. Her people had always been stewards of the land, raising sheep and growing corn—both the grain corn of old and the modern corn, and tending their needs from orchards and market trading.

She was rooted here, which wasn't always as romantic as it sounded. Her father, like many of the men of her line, had a penchant for drink, and when he drank, he was mean. Never physically brutal, which perhaps her grandfather had been, but a tongue could do a lot of damage. Her mother dealt with him in her long-suffering way, and Clare followed suit, ignoring him when necessary but mostly paying him no attention whatsoever. Her world was encompassed by the ways and rules of women—her two grandmothers, both long widowed; her aunts and girl cousins and their female neighbors; her two sisters, who had grown up and moved far away—one to Chicago, one to Vancouver. Many of her cousins flew away, too, leaving the village an echoey version of itself.

The only one Clare missed was Liam's mother, who'd followed a boy to New Zealand. They'd written letters sporadically, long missives that were a joy when they arrived in the post. Helen became a farmer herself on the North Island, a vegan, and a mother of six while Clare stumbled and stuttered, starting one thing or other, never quite finding her fit. She tried nursing school but longed for home, and returned to try her hand at a shop that failed. She married a man who proved to be meaner than her own father, but she left him in Barnstaple and returned to Wulfecombe with her children in tow.

Two years later, in the darkest moment of her life, Clare's maiden aunt Gillian had died and left Clare her house—a sudden and shocking surprise, as it was a house of some substance a couple of miles from the village on fertile land surrounded by forest.

It was both a blessing and a curse. Her aunt had lived in three rooms and left the rest to rot, which some of it had. Clare spent the first two years dragging things off to the tip—chifforobes and small tables, clothing from five generations, a trunk full of mildewed, rotting letters. It was good for her, giving her the focus and hard work she desperately needed.

She learned to love the process of clearing and remaking those old, dark rooms. One at a time, she gave them new life. A year on the back bedroom, two on the ancient kitchen. It would never be featured in *Country Life*, but she loved it.

The house had given her a place to offer Levi's children when they married, and space for their combined families to live together in relative peace. In those rooms, Clare had discovered her best life was as a mother, a wife, and a caretaker of the land her family had held for so many generations.

It was still a tumbledown mess most of the time, in need of one thing or another or perhaps twenty things. The entire east wing was closed off: three rooms that were never used, one with a fireplace the size of a plow horse. She fretted about it in the back of her mind sometimes, but not all of it could be managed at once. It was enough that the building stayed standing, that she looked after the small church and its graveyard by the river, that she was doing her small but significant part to make sure it didn't fall down.

Now she was getting it ready for guests on Sunday. Liam had been a beautiful boy, now a more beautiful man whose spirit shone as brightly as his hair.

This late afternoon, she kneaded bread on the old table in the kitchen. The light from the stark overhead fixture she kept meaning to replace was not the best at this time of evening, but it was enough to illuminate the task at hand—a big, seedy loaf smelling of ancient starter.

Levi came in through the back door, his heavy step telling her his day had been even longer than the hour suggested. "Hello," she said in as kind a voice as she could muster.

He nodded, stopping to hang his coat on the hook by the door, kicking off his muddy, knee-high wellies.

"Are you hungry? I've a chicken pie in the oven."

"I could eat." He washed his hands and arms at the big sink, and dried them with a tea towel hanging by the cupboard. She eyed his limp.

"Let me finish this last little bit, and I'll get it for you."

He was independent and didn't like being waited on, but tonight he only sank into the chair and rolled his shoulders. Not a good day, and hard on his body. She didn't want to rush his stories—he'd get to them as he settled—and she left him alone to watch her roll the dough, press, roll, press, turn, press. Sprinkle with a dusting of flour, knead again, until it felt like young skin beneath her palms.

As she kneaded, she offered soft, soothing samplings of her day, a feather coverlet under which he could rest. "I think I've finished the planting for summer. Cabbages are coming along nicely." She washed her hands, plucking off crusts of flour. "I saw Sage, and she let me sing to the baby." The pie she took from the oven was hot and crumbly, packed with carrots and potatoes and leeks in a savory white sauce she had perfected over the years. She placed it before him, touching his shoulder, and poured a glass of water.

Then she sat, apron gathered in her lap, and waited.

"The foal died," he said, and she'd known those would be his words. "Mrs. Granger howled like it was her own babe."

"The mare?"

"She'll be all right." He ate. She knew him well enough to know the small movements hid great pain. "It was all I could do to pull the colt from her." He put down his fork, rested his fists on the table.

Clare covered one of those fists with her own two hands. "It's hard work."

He nodded. "And I've grown too old for it."

"Maybe," she agreed. "Maybe a check with the doctor, just to see if there might be a slipped disc or something that could be fixed?"

He raised his eyes.

She sensed something more. "What is it?"

He turned his hand over and grasped hers. "They found bones at the new housing estate."

A chill ran down her body. "Bones?"

"An excavator dug them up, it seems, digging a cellar. A child's bones. They don't know if they're ancient or recent. That's all I've heard. I'm sure it's an old grave."

Clare felt the past open and howl. "Or it isn't."

CHAPTER THREE

New York City

The rain was still roaring down outside. Tillie wished for her umbrella, but Liam grabbed a big black one from the stand inside the door of the gallery and held it high enough to protect them both. She pointed to a diner down the block and shouted, "Coffee?"

He nodded.

They dashed for a red neon sign blinking "P-I-E." Liam dove for the door and held it open for her. She ducked under his arm, catching an alluring whiff of pheromones replaced with the scent of something baking as they pushed inside. It wasn't an old-school diner but a reasonable millennial imitation, with fresh red Naugahyde on the stools and booths, and pie safes on the counter. A young man came over to seat them. He was small and tidy, and Tillie thought of a cockatiel with a brush of white feathers on his head.

"Coffee, I assume?" he asked as they settled in a booth.

"Please," Tillie said, rubbing her fingertips over the vague whisper of migraine below her temple.

"Let me ask you, bro," Liam said, "can you get a pot of water *really* hot?"

"I got you," he said, pointing. "You want English style, with milk, am I right?"

"Yeah, that's exactly right."

His accent was not full New Zealand, with its pinched edges, or as deeply drawling as South African. Tillie decided he must have traveled a lot, and she wondered again what he did. Instead of probing, she bent her head to examine the menu. One side was burgers and eggs. The other was a list of pies and cakes. She felt a swift hunger and wondered when she'd last eaten.

The server returned with a fat steaming pot of water, a cup, a little metal pitcher of milk, and coffee for Tillie. "That looks amazing," Liam said, and the server beamed.

"Pies today are pecan, apple, peach." He glanced over his shoulder toward the glass-fronted fridge. "Mocha cream, banana cream, and everybody's favorite, lemon meringue. We also have honey cake. You need a few minutes?"

"Honey cake," Liam echoed. "Really?"

The server winked. "To capture the fairies."

"I'm not ready to order," Tillie said, taking a packet of sugar from the metal basket on the table.

"Nor I." When the man hurried away, Liam lifted the lid of the metal teapot and stirred the tea bags. "Promising. Could be a contender for the best tea I've had in America."

"You're nearly always better off with coffee."

"Yeah, no. I don't like the coffee here. No offense."

"None taken." Stirring a dollop of cream into her cup, she asked, "Have you been here awhile, then, in the States?"

"Awhile this time. Twelve weeks. I leave Saturday for Europe."

She inclined her head. "Work?"

He nodded but didn't elaborate.

"Do you travel here often?"

"Sometimes."

He still made no move to share what he did, and she let it go. Looked back at the menu. "I'm trying to decide whether to be healthy-ish and have a salad, or say to hell with it and dive into the pie."

"I'm going for the honey cake, myself," he said, tossing the menu down. "If that helps you decide."

"I don't know that I've ever had it," she said.

"A classic. If it's true honey cake, it will be soaked in honey syrup. I'm intrigued enough to give it a try."

"I'll look forward to your verdict," she said. "I'm going with the pie." She dropped her menu on top of his. Her gaze caught on the flesh of his throat, so golden (*like honey*, she thought), and her imagination gave her an extravagant visual of flinging her body over his naked one.

A slight smile curved his mouth.

Embarrassed, she thought, *Where did that come from?*

Except that it had been a while since she'd had sex with anyone, since she'd broken up with her fiancé five months before. She thought of honeybees buzzing around an open flower. She smelled honey.

Suddenly, as if a knife slashed open reality—

She stood in the dark, surrounded by trees and stars, hearing a roar of animal sounds, birds, and insects in a cacophony that swept her up, enveloped her entirely. She heard water nearby and the buzzing of bees or crickets or—

And then, just as suddenly, she was back in her body, in the booth, with Liam across the table. A sliver of the migraine aura edged around the outside of her iris.

"You all right?"

"Yeah." She literally shook it off, moving her shoulders and head. "Food will help."

She was glad not to be alone.

~

The coffee and sugar helped. By the time the waiter brought their food—the honey-soaked cake for Liam, peach pie for her—Tillie was feeling fairly normal.

Which, of course, meant her ex started texting.

I have been thinking about that trip we made to Colorado last year, he said. *Remember that moose we saw?*

Tillie sighed and turned the phone over on its face. The phone buzzed, buzzed again, and then again. She ignored it and took a bite of the indulgent pie. As the sugar, peaches, and crust hit her tongue, she widened her eyes. "Wow. This is amazing." She pointed with her fork. "Is yours?"

He'd admired the cake enough to shoot a photo. "For my mum," he said. "This is her big thing. Honey." Now, he was three bites in, almost wolfing it down. "It's the real thing, I reckon. No sugar. A little orange zest."

"Maybe you need two pieces."

Beside her on the table, Tillie's phone vibrated again. Once, twice, three times.

"You can answer," he said.

"No." She picked it up and put it under her thigh, where she could feel it but it wouldn't interrupt. "An annoying ex."

"Ex-husband?"

"Oh, God no!" But that made it sound like he was only an old boyfriend. "Fiancé, actually. We broke up a couple of months ago, and he's having a hard time with it."

Liam gave her his full attention, even setting down his fork. "Yeah?"

For some reason, the focus made her want to talk. Explain. Although, really, that wasn't exactly the right move with a guy you wanted to impress. And she did want to impress him. His lip shone with a brush of honey.

She said, "I should block him, but it feels mean." She plucked a sliver of peach and ate it with her fingers. "Has that ever happened to you?"

He watched her eat with her fingers. "A fiancée?" he returned with a slight smile.

"Maybe. Or someone you couldn't be with, even though you knew they loved you?" She heard the sentence and straightened. "Wow, sorry, that was really personal. I'm a little off tonight."

"I prefer personal and real to the superficial," he said. "I almost had a fiancée once. Turned out she was not as interested in the arrangement as I was."

"Sorry to hear that."

He shrugged. "That's life, as my friend Krish reminds me."

A little pain lingered beneath the shrug, and she wanted to follow the trail of it. Beneath her thigh, the phone buzzed again. Jared was drinking, she guessed, listening to albums on the turntable they'd bought to play the vinyl they'd collected. She could imagine him sitting on his couch in the rain, in the apartment they had planned to share, drinking beer and wallowing in the music they loved. It made her feel both really sad and really relieved.

The server paused by the booth, tilting his cockatiel head back and forth between them. "Would you like some more, handsome?"

Liam grinned. "Nah, bro. How about a grilled cheese?"

"You got it." He glanced at Tillie, his body still angled toward Liam. "You need anything, sweetie?"

She shook her head.

Liam folded his hands on the table—beautiful hands, long fingers with well-tended nails—only marred by the cluster of gemstone bracelets running up his wrist. Again, she wished he weren't such a surfer-hippie dude. "Working on your energies?" she asked, pointing.

"Ah, yeah, why not? My sister gave them to me when I started traveling. Reckoned it couldn't hurt." He took a breath, fingered the beads. "It's a challenging trip."

"Are you a model?"

"What?" He laughed. "No!"

"Actor? Dancer? Professional surfer?"

"I'm pleased you see me as a man of substance."

It was Tillie's turn to laugh. "Sorry. You're just so . . ."

He raised his eyebrows, waiting.

She was going to say *pretty*, but that wasn't it. Light skated along the bridge of his nose, his cheekbones, and she thought of Tam Lin, the knight stolen away by fairies. Following some instinct she'd learned to trust, she asked, "Would you maybe have time to let me sketch you?"

"You're an artist, too?"

She nodded. "I have so much work, I wasn't even going to come tonight."

"I'm glad you did."

She let the words skate around in her veins, awakening sleepy blood. "Me, too."

"I have time tomorrow." He paused. "Or tonight, if you'd rather."

An iridescent possibility rose between them. "I would," she said. "Rather. Tonight."

The rest of their meal had no weight. Liam ate his sandwich, and they dashed into the rain and miraculously caught a passing cab. Tillie gave the address and fell back in the humid car. His knee and hers touched. Neither of them moved. She smelled nutmeg on him, or maybe it was just his skin.

"I hope your coat is warm," she said. "It's going to be cold." She almost said *in the morning*, but was that what she meant? Why else would she be inviting him back to her apartment to ostensibly sketch him at 10:00 p.m. on a rainy night?

He took her hand and turned it over. "Shall I read your palm?"

His skin was warm, warmer than it should have been. Light from the street flashed over his hair, showed the faint shimmer of beard on his jaw, the growth of a day. She thought, *I will remember this.*

"Sure."

He spread her fingers open, stroked the center of her hand. Tillie was acutely aware of each brush of his fingers. "Long lifeline," he commented, then: "Hmm. A break early. Did you suffer an illness as a child?"

Was he *really* reading her palm? "I did have a fall when I was three or four."

"You don't know which one?"

Answering that honestly would mean getting into things about her mother that she wasn't interested in expressing to a stranger. To deflect, she tugged the streak of white in the hair over her temple. "That's when I got this."

"Head injury?"

She nodded. "I was out for several days, they say. I had to learn to speak all over again."

His attention sharpened, a contrast to his mild comment. "Interesting." He bent his head. "And this"—he slid his finger from the pad beneath her middle finger to the heart of her palm—"might be the breakup with the man who misses you."

The man who misses you. The words gave her a strange ache. "He does."

"Do you miss him, too?"

She raised her eyes. Shook her head.

Liam bent in and kissed her. He held her hand, and his other arm moved behind her shoulders, giving her a sense of protection. The touch of their mouths created a sense of light, and a fragrance of forest enveloped them. Tillie leaned in as if enchanted, pulled by something she couldn't name—

A bird cawed in her head. The porch from the painting emerged clearly on the screen of her imagination. Trees stood sentry around it, and the bird hopped down to the railing. A giant cat raced up the steps, and the bird flew away—

The lurking headache abruptly bloomed, throbbed across the bridge of her nose, and she felt suddenly sick to her stomach. Pulling away, she breathed in, then out. "Sorry," she whispered, trying to calm the nausea. "It's just—"

His hand fell between her shoulder blades.

Embarrassment mingled with the sudden, hard arrival of a full-blown migraine. She was trying not to barf in the cab when they pulled up in front of her building. "I'm sorry," she said. "I don't think I can—"

"Let me help you inside. That's all."

They ran toward the foyer in the deluge. Her feet and shins were splashed with water, her hair soaked before they reached the stoop. She paused for a moment in the foyer, thinking wildly that she should check the mail, but the blindness had spread over one eye, and she didn't even know if she could climb the four flights to her apartment. Sinking down on the stairs, she rested her head on her forearms.

"Do you have some medication to take?" he asked. "Can I get you something?"

She raised her head. His crown was surrounded with shimmering lights, like a halo. "It's four flights."

"C'mon. Lean on me."

Honestly, she was so grateful for his presence, she didn't think about anything else. Taking it slow, she held on to the railing. A whisper of regret moved through her—she wouldn't see him again after all this.

In a way, that made it easier. She didn't ordinarily take men to her apartment. It was too personal, too revealing, but without his help, she'd be sitting at the bottom of the stairs with her head on her knees.

Her loft, which sounded fancy but wasn't in the slightest, occupied most of the top floor. It was barely finished and cold as the tundra. The only reason she'd landed there was because she'd inherited it from a friend who had moved to Los Angeles. It was two thousand square feet of open space and windows. To counter the cold, she'd scattered space heaters around and grouped the living areas together. The rest was open for easels and supplies and stacks of canvases. Organized chaos. Liam looked at the painting closest to them, a nude female nursing a baby wolf, her hair wild and full of vines. He said nothing, but it made Tillie feel vulnerable. Too much of her was visible in this room. Far too much for a stranger to see.

When he said gently, "Let's get you settled," she nodded and took a step toward her bedroom—

And fainted dead away, like some Victorian heroine.

CHAPTER FOUR

When he was nineteen, Liam fell in love. The girl was called Opal, and she was as beautiful as her name, with iridescent eyes and silvery hair. He had read all of Tolkien as a young teen, and she made him think of Galadriel, the queen of elves. They met in a bar one July night during his winter break from uni, where he was dutifully and without excitement studying architecture. She was a restless backpacker from some suburb of Paris and had been on the road for nearly a year. She'd just landed in Auckland, and Liam was more than willing to play guide to her New Zealand travels. For a month, they wandered north and south, Liam leaning on a small stipend he'd inherited from his grandmother in Brisbane, Opal working in cafés and bars.

He was drunk on her. Her small, tanned breasts and musky scent, the lyrical song of her accent. She was aloof, ungiving, and it only made him work that much harder. They had a lot of sex, urgently and often in places where they risked discovery—bathroom stalls and gardens and once in a darkened doorway along a street in Wellington.

They smoked a ton of weed and drank way too much. It began to make him feel lost, unsure where he began and she ended. She absorbed him, and he was willingly sucked in, happy to become the sweat of her pores, the curve of her waist.

His best friend Krish grew increasingly freaked out. He showed up in Queenstown to try to talk sense into Liam, but he was too far gone. Krish stormed away, vowing he'd never speak to his friend again.

A year later, Opal abandoned Liam in Rishikesh for a deer-eyed Indian who swept her off to Delhi.

He was on the floor. Lost from the long sojourn into drugs and booze and love addiction, he wandered for another year, bouncing through one thing after another—a guru, a game, a lover, a promise.

Until he landed, quite by accident, in a Buddhist monastery. He was sick with withdrawal and despair, and they cared for him for three months, curing his physical ills, then curing his spiritual ones by teaching him the path of the Buddha and mindfulness.

Krish had found him there. Brought him home to Auckland, where Liam began teaching meditation, finding a large pool of hungry millennials. It was Krish who suggested the meditation app, well before apps for such things were common. As a result, they got in on the ground floor, and the app, with Liam as the host with his good looks and smooth voice, was a staggering hit. They'd hit a million followers within two years.

That had been seven years ago, and the business had grown into an empire.

Tonight, as he carried Tillie to her bed, he thought of what Krish would say about her. His attraction to her, more to the point. Her raven-black hair spilled over his arms. Her head fell on his shoulder. He thought she'd wake up once he got her on the bed and pulled off her boots, but she only murmured, a small noise of pain.

Her legs were clad in green tights. He lifted her knees and scooted her bottom sideways, then covered her with the duvet. She stirred, took his hand. "I'm afraid," she said.

"What can I do?" he asked quietly. Her lashes were dark against her pale skin, her mouth wide. She didn't seem to be in distress that he could see. Her respiration was even. Her skin wasn't too hot or too cold.

Again, he felt a ripple of recognition. He could swear he knew her, but he'd spent little time in the United States. How could they have met? Unless it was in another life, which many people in the world believed.

Her hand slackened in his, and he stood. Now that she was settled, he should go back to the hotel, get ready for his gig tomorrow. There would be nearly three hundred people waiting to hear from him, and he liked to spend an hour in deep meditation before such events. He owed them his best, most-centered self. It wasn't always possible, but he tried, always.

But he didn't want to leave her. He could sleep on the couch, nearby in case she needed help.

Her phone had fallen on the floor when she fainted. He picked it up and placed it nearby her on the bedside table so she wouldn't worry, then curled up on the sofa. The painting he'd noticed earlier kept watch, a naked woman and a wolf pup, savage and nurturing at once. This, too, triggered something just out of reach, but he couldn't draw it in. He closed his eyes. He'd just rest for a little while, then check on her and go back to his hotel.

CHAPTER FIVE

Tillie awakened with a dry mouth and rolled over on her back, taking stock. No migraine, despite the fact that she'd slept fitfully, too hot, twisting up in the covers. Every time she'd surfaced, something strange wove itself out of the painting she'd seen at the gallery—big leaves coming alive to form a bed she crawled into, a bird swooping through the air, sending out a call, tragic and enormous.

Over and over, it was the cat, grown to a giant size, its head coming up to her waist, its green eyes the size of baseballs. It purred. She rubbed her hands into its soft neck, cooing something.

She woke up, fell back asleep. She curled with the cat, its body warming her from neck to knees. Slept, awakened to—

Her bedroom. Reality. She sat up, thirsty and sweaty. Pulling from the metal water bottle she kept beside the bed, she pushed hair out of her face and stared into the dark. The scene from the painting returned, faint shapes coalescing, all of it coming alive with depth and sound, a starry sky overhead. The murmur of voices she couldn't quite hear, in a language she didn't quite understand.

She blinked, rubbed her face. A dream.

Just a dream.

Dawn peeked in the windows, washing the walls with pink. Only when she swung her legs out and saw her tights did she remember fainting. Liam must have put her to bed. It scared her that she'd been so vulnerable, passed out with a man in her apartment. He could have done anything.

Except—she could trust *herself.* She wouldn't have allowed someone she didn't feel comfortable with upstairs with her.

But didn't everybody feel that way?

Stop. Clearly, she'd survived his help.

Padding into the bathroom, she traded her tights and dress for yoga pants and a T-shirt, splashed water on her face, brushed her teeth. She moved her head, her neck. The migraine was gone. Barefoot, she headed down an open corridor toward the kitchen.

And there, fast asleep on her couch, was Liam. He was insufficiently covered by a thin afghan, and she grabbed another one from the back of a chair to make sure he wasn't cold.

His face.

In the soft light of dawn, she gobbled up the details—his jaw and cheekbones and brow. His mouth and throat. His hand lax in sleep, hanging beneath the blankets.

Moving quietly, she picked up a sketchbook and charcoals from a nearby table and sat on the floor. Long windows above the couch let in the pinkish, silvery light that touched the round of his shoulder, the tangle of his hair. She sketched quickly, reproducing the angle of elbow and wrist, hip and knee. On a fresh page, she captured his hands and close-ups of his nails—square and flat and clean.

New page. Eyebrows. Elegant, straight nose. Sharp jaw.

Mouth. She remembered kissing him last night, the sense of his shoulders offering a bulwark. The echo moved through her body. She reached for a wry sentiment—it had been a while since she'd had any-body in her bed—but she couldn't find any irony. He wasn't just some-body, some guy. He was . . .

She didn't know. Himself. Liam. Beautiful, yes, but unlike other men.

He slept on, oblivious of her attention. When she finished, charged by the pleasure of drawing him, she headed for the kitchen and set the kettle to boil, remembering he liked tea more than American coffee.

For herself, she measured coffee grounds into a French press, and leaned a hip on the counter as she waited. From this angle, she could see his long, fit shape beneath the afghan her mother had crocheted by the fire in her cottage.

Her mother. The now-familiar, entirely unwelcome pang burned through her gut. Tillie missed Arlette terribly. She'd died five months before without any warning, and Tillie hadn't managed to get it . . . what? In perspective? Was that even a thing if the person you lost was your mother?

It seemed impossible. She didn't know how to make peace with the fact that her strange and loving and reclusive mother was gone.

Tillie was alone. It had only ever been the two of them, living on a parcel of land tucked away upstate, where she raised goats for their milk and fine hair. She fed them with her garden, supplemented by visits to the health food store and the vegan café in Fox Crossing, the nearest town. Tillie grew up as feral as the cats who lived in the fields, home-schooled until she was nearly thirteen, when she rebelled and insisted that she wanted to go to a real school.

It didn't go as badly as it could have. In their little rural area, odd-ness was not unusual. Tillie had the luck of a long, muscular body and glossy hair and a vast talent for art and reading. When she realized what she'd missed, she gulped down everything in front of her, soaking up science, math, endless novels, and especially every art class available. Eventually, she won a scholarship to NYU for art. Her mother fought her on that, but she'd raised Tillie to be independent and think for herself.

In the end, she had to be at peace with her doing so.

And Tillie had hardly abandoned her mother. She loved being with her. Arlette's great love had been the old ways and old times. In one of her stories, she would have been the herbalist, called by some a witch, revered by others, who came to her begging for readings and spells and hope to cure broken hearts or bring back lovers. Tillie's friends had thought her odd. They didn't understand why Arlette didn't come to see her daughter's shows, celebrate her graduations, all the things a mother did.

But Tillie was more forgiving. Her mother had been wounded in some way that never really became plain, but she'd built a careful retreat in her farm and cottage, safe from the outside. Few places in the world had given Tillie the comfort the farm gave, even as she had to leave it to seek her own life.

There had never been anyone like Arlette, and now she was gone forever.

The kettle made a soft whispering sound, and Tillie pulled it off the burner before it could launch into a full whistle. Pouring water into the press, she inhaled the rich scent of coffee and felt it expand in her head.

The tiniest thread of pain, tinged soft purple, moved over the bridge of her nose. Echoes sounded from the base of her skull. Postdrome, it was called, the lingering wisps of the migraine episode.

Tillie was an expert, though she wished she were not. The headaches had begun long before she could remember, classic migraines that began with auras and progressed into brain-splitting pain, then receded a day or two later to disappear for months, sometimes even years.

As an adult, Tillie had sought treatment for the headaches, undergoing a battery of tests that revealed only that her brain was healthy, as far as they could see. Hormones, said one doctor; food sensitivities, said another. No one could make any significant difference, and honestly, they grew more and more rare, so she lived with them.

But since her mother's death, she'd had multiple episodes. Jared had blamed her grief, but he also blamed their breakup on grief. About that, he was wrong.

That reminded her of the text thread from last night, and her phone. Seventeen messages, all from her pining ex-fiancé. They followed the same pattern as always: *Remember when . . . I miss you . . . I love you, and we are meant to be together.*

The last message said, I don't know how to get you to understand this is the biggest mistake of your life.

A sharp annoyance pierced her, that he thought he knew better what was good for her than she did herself. It was part of the problem of the relationship—he pushed too far into her private self.

But truthfully, while there wasn't anything particularly wrong with their relationship—he would be an easy husband, a good partner, someone she could trust—there was also nothing particularly great about it. She had realized one morning as they drank coffee that she had no big feelings about him one way or the other, pro or con. That was no way to spend a life. At the very least, Jared deserved better.

Tillie's thumb hovered over the open message window, considering replies. Kind ones, thoughtful ones, ways to maybe make him feel better. It suddenly occurred to her that there was nothing *she* could do to make any difference to his pain. She was the source of it, and the only way to get over it was to feel it. Just as Tillie was struggling to feel and get through the grief of her mother's death.

She typed, This has to stop, Jared. I'm sorry I hurt you, but it wasn't a mistake that I broke up with you. I've asked you to stop texting, and you won't, so I'm so, so sorry, but I'm going to block your number.

Sorry.

Then she did it. Blocked him. A sense of relief poured through her, lightening the day. The cat from her dream suddenly popped into her imagination. She picked up her sketchbook and charcoals and sat down with a cup of coffee in her favorite chair—a big, overstuffed monstrosity that felt exactly like being cradled by a grandparent. Or what she thought it would feel like. She'd never had a grandparent.

Morning crept into the room, pouring golden light over the floor like a carpet. Liam slept on, shifting a couple of times. It seemed he would wake up at any moment, but he settled back in to sleep every time.

Whatever his work, it tired him.

She sketched the cat from her dream, big as a lion, then as a house cat with stripes around its face and a white back. Peering into the depths of her imagination, she spied a striped tail, too. The image was detailed—stripes up its legs, long white whiskers. A sense of love for the cat seeped through her, and she smiled to herself.

Liam stirred on the couch, sitting up abruptly. "What time is it?"

"Um . . ." She squinted at the clock in the kitchen. "Nearly nine."

He was on his feet instantly, blinking. "Damn! I'm going to be late."

"Do you want some tea?"

"No time." He stretched, long and lean, and she gladly eyed the length of him, the slice of flat belly beneath his shirt.

"Sure?"

He dropped to the couch to pull on his shoes but looked up with a smile. "Wish I could. How's your head?"

"Okay." She shrugged, embarrassed. "A migraine, that's all. You were really good to me. Thank you."

"No worries." He leaped to his feet and stuck his arms through his coat, patted the pocket, and made sure his phone was in hand. Then he paused. A ray of light struck his irises, and Tillie thought again of an angel. Her chest ached at his departure—it was so sudden and felt all wrong.

"Can I see you again?" he asked.

Relief swept through her. "Yes, please."

He smiled, deep and wide, and to Tillie's surprise, he bent in to kiss her. His mouth was as luxuriously plush as she remembered from last night, and tasted of possibility. Again, she felt something bloom around them, as if roses were opening, scenting the air.

"I don't want to go," he said, mouth millimeters from hers.

"I don't want you to."

"Damn. I have a gig at ten." He brushed the tip of his nose over hers, raised his head to meet her gaze fully and without hurry. "Pleasure to meet you, Tillie."

"Same."

And then he was gone. She listened to his feet running down the stairs and sent a whisper out to the universe.

Please.

CHAPTER SIX

The ballroom was full when Liam arrived through the back door. He could hear the murmurs and chatting as the participants indulged over coffees and teas served from giant dispensers along the back wall. In deference to the nature of his work, their work, the snacks were vegan and healthy—as healthy as a massive hotel could do, anyway, which was piles of grapes and bananas and hearty muffins (carrot or pumpkin or almond) and bowls of nuts and granola bars. Lots of coffee, and teas of every variety.

Krish, who was not only his friend but also his team manager, rushed over, a clipboard in his hand, an earpiece circling his ear. "Liam, where've you been? They're just about to get restless."

He smoothed the air with his hands, giving Krish his most calming smile. "It's fine, bro. Sorry. Time got away from me. Give me five minutes."

Krish gave him a look. They'd known each other a long time, since their school days in Auckland, way before all this started, which meant that Krish knew him a bit too well at times. "A woman, is it?"

"It's not like that."

He raised an eyebrow. "It never is, but here you are, late enough that I was afraid we'd have to cancel." His expression was not reassured. "Be careful."

"I'm good. Really."

"Go. Get yourself ready."

Liam clapped him on the arm and headed for the small dressing room. He donned a clean linen shirt and casual trousers, and pulled his hair back from his face, dampening his fingers at the sink to skim back the loose hair. It would fall free by the end of the first session, but as long as he started in a neat place, the participants didn't mind.

That finished, he sat for a moment and closed his eyes. Flashes played over his memory: Tillie's eyes, a greenish blue like the sea, fringed in heavy lashes he didn't think were fake, though he wasn't the wisest when it came to women's cosmetic enhancements. In the taxi, reading her palm playfully, he'd felt a frisson of connection, smelling the fragrance of her, something elusive and green.

And then, her dramatic fainting, that river of dark hair spilling everywhere, her legs in green stockings like a creature from the forest. This morning, her simple crossed legs, the calm in her rooms, the riotousness of her paintings, strange and compelling. He hadn't wanted to leave her yet.

Focus.

He took in a breath and mentally built a wall around any thoughts of Tillie. People had paid hundreds of dollars for the experience they hoped to have today, and he owed them his full attention.

More, he wanted to be present with them, and for himself. To do whatever he needed to do here, today, in this place. He allowed himself to empty, to clear his thoughts, his heart, and as much of his ego as he was able.

In a moment, Krish knocked. "We're just about to start."

"I'm ready." Liam rose and followed his friend's dark head through a small hallway to the stage. The lights had come down, not all the way, but to a more agreeable coral tone than the usual overhead brights. The participants were in mostly tidy rows, on cushions or mats or on the floor, most of them cross-legged, waiting. Many of them wore prayer shawls or sweaters. He scanned their faces, each one precious, every age and color and culture and sex, and love filled him. He looked at them, one by one, taking his time. The old woman with her thin white hair, embroidered violet blouse, and bare feet. The young man with a shaved head and enormous eyes. The two plump women with long dark hair, both dressed in red, perhaps sisters.

He rested his eyes on each one, seeing as many as he could before he began. Acknowledging them.

Years before, when he'd been stricken to his very soul by the devotion of the pilgrims at Varanasi, he could not have foreseen where his studies and practice would take him, but as he settled now, connected to himself and to them, and to spirit or presence or whatever terms felt right in a given moment, he knew he was exactly where he was meant to be.

Here. He was imperfect in his practices. Flawed as all humans were flawed, but imperfect practice was healing, anyway. *The more seekers in the world, the better,* he thought, and came onstage, barefoot and calm, raising one hand. Gentle, respectful applause rose. He took the tiny mic from Hanna, the stage manager, and tucked it into the neckline of his shirt, then sat on a cushion placed on a small riser. They'd started with the cushion on the floor of the stage, but it was hard to see the room from such a low vantage point, and hard for the back of the room to see him, so they'd gone to the riser.

As he settled, all the reasons and all his calm swirled in and filled him. "Hello," he said in a normal voice. "I'm so glad to see you all. Let's begin."

The world over, especially in the West, people misunderstood spiritual pursuits. Feared them. Liam had given up trying to name that benevolent force.

What he knew was that when it came time for this moment, the silence, the feeling of eternal connection with whatever it was that lived outside and *inside* of him, and the connections of the souls in the room when they meditated together, was a real thing.

Powerful. Important. For this time, for these hours, they were creating something calm and peaceful in a violent, chaotic world.

It wasn't until he was on his way back to his dressing room that he thought again of Tillie. A flash of her tumbling dark hair, the way she slid her eyes sideways to look at him.

Be careful, bro, Krish had said. Not be careful because a woman might try to use him for his position or status or whatever the hell. Be careful because his weakness was falling—falling hard. And yes, he felt that now, had felt it from the first moment he'd seen her in the gallery, but was solid, like *fated*, as if they were meant to meet, as if they were—

Don't say it, some voice in his head jeered. *Soulmates, right, bro? How many times . . .*

Disheartened, he sank onto the couch in the dressing room and fell back, closing his eyes. That was long ago, the pattern he'd broken after his pilgrimage.

Tillie was something else, something real. He felt it as solidly as his own hands.

He was sure of it.

CHAPTER SEVEN

Tillie was painting when the robot voice on her earphones said, "Jon calling. Answer it?"

"Answer," she said, and then: "Hey! How'd it go?"

"Never mind me!" he cried. "How did it go with *you* and Surfer Man?"

"Oh no, you don't." Tillie wiped her brush on a blue shop towel. "How was the opening?"

"I sold . . ." He paused for drama. "Out."

"What?" She spun away from the easel. "Jon! That's amazing! I'm so thrilled for you."

"Totally unexpected."

"Dude, that's great! You must be over the moon."

"It's a little unreal, honestly." He'd suffered a pretty substantial breakup and was only now emerging from the funk.

"I'm sure. I'm proud of you. You never give up."

"Thank you. Now you. What happened last night?"

She let go of a rueful laugh. "Oh, I was such a femme fatale. I got a blinding migraine. He saw me home, and I fainted."

"Tillie!" His voice was stern. "Girl, you need to see a doctor. I'm worried about you."

"Don't." She dabbed her tiny brush into a bubble of paint, and carefully edged a swoop of blue-ash gray into a shadow. "Remember how bad it was in college sometimes? It's just the stress of the new show."

She glanced toward a big paper calendar with red *X*'s over the days. One hundred four left to finish this set of paintings, and that didn't include framing or coming up with descriptions or any of the other stuff that so glamorously filled an artist's life.

"And," he said, "I don't know, grief?"

"Yes," she agreed impatiently.

"Don't take that tone with me. I'm your best friend, and it's my job to look out for you."

"Sorry." She straightened. "You're right. Of course you're right. I'm having trouble with my mom's death. It broke my heart."

"I know it did. Have you called your therapist yet?"

She shuddered. "I'm fine. Not everybody needs therapy at every turn."

"Mm. Not everyone, but you do, girl."

"Maybe." She looked toward the window made of tiny squares. "Hey, speaking of your show, do you know who painted the things along the back wall at the gallery?"

"Which ones?"

"They were sort of raw landscapes. Bright colors."

"No idea. Do you want me to find out?"

"That's all right. I'm going down there later. I'll ask myself—and crow over you!"

"Thank you, thank you. Want to go celebrate later?"

"Um. I have to pass. Liam is . . . maybe . . . coming back?"

"Oh, a *maybe* from him but *for sure* from me, and you choose him?" he said with mock affront.

"When you put it like that, it sounds pretty bad, but I want to thank him for taking care of me. He's only here until the end of the week, and then I'll be all yours again."

"Okay, but don't forget I'm leaving this weekend for Crete."

"That's right!" She dabbed her brush in a mix of phthalo green mixed with Hansa yellow, and leaned in to dot it lightly over the edge of a leaf. "I'm glad you're going."

"I still can't convince you to come with?"

They'd traveled a lot together. "You know I can't."

He sighed with exaggeration, but she knew he wasn't really upset. "I'm not giving up."

"How about this: Want to drive with me upstate to my mom's place tomorrow? I'm meeting a Realtor about what needs to be done to sell it."

"Knock it down," he said dryly. "I can't do tomorrow, but if you put it off a couple of days, I can make it work."

"Ugh. No. I have an appointment already."

"Well, call me if you need an ear."

"Will do."

Her coffee had gone cold, and she thought about running downstairs for a latte from the place around the corner, but first, another hour on the painting. She shook out her shoulders and rounded the studio, looking at the others in the series.

She'd sketched out a series of thirteen, a baker's dozen, a proper fairy-tale number. Four were mostly finished, five more were in various states of almost there, two were sketched and painted a bit, and four more still needed to be done. They portrayed a magical world of humans who looked like animals, or animals with the faces of humans, set in a forest where trees came to life. Wolves prowled the shadows. Mirrors reflected things that were not there.

Despite the fairy-tale spirit, they were not for children. Some of the themes were recognizable from children's literature—foxes and tortoises and clever talking birds—but there was a sharp undertone, a sexuality in the shapes and themes that would not do for children, a threatening evil that had once graced fairy tales but had been washed into the palest of grays by the misguided modern attempt to protect children from anything upsetting.

From her earliest memory, Tillie had drawn or painted some version of this kind of scene, likely taken from her mother's folk tales.

It had not made it easy for her to break into the fine-art world. She'd met a lot of resistance, and often despaired that she would be able to paint what she liked. In grad school, she'd caught the eye of a mentor who saw what she was trying to do, and helped her forge the connections where her work and fine art intersected.

Crossing her arms, she narrowed her eyes at a painting of a seagoing being, part owl and fish and mermaid, with streaming white hair, round yellow eyes, and the cheekbones of a girl Tillie had seen on West Twenty-Sixth Street. The creature looked at herself in a mirror, combing her hair. In the mirror, her reflection was a woman with wavy hair and abundant breasts.

A glimmer of the gazelle girl from last night tickled her brain. She sat at a table with a sketchbook to capture the image from memory. Only when she finished did she refer back to the photo she'd shot the night before.

And there, in the background, was Liam. His arm and the side of his face, his blond hair. A soft puff of yearning moved through her—she wanted to touch him, taste him, watch him laugh.

Watch him laugh? She scowled. It was one thing to be thirsty and want a roll in the hay. Quite another to start mooning over his laugh. He lived in *New Zealand*.

Tillie shook out her shoulders. Her mood was a little off from the migraine, and the only answer was to stay mildly busy. To distract herself, she pulled out a large pad of drawing paper and clipped it to a different easel.

Humming along with the music, she sketched an outline, the movement of the gazelle girl. It felt good to make big marks, the long line of her back, the limbs galloping gracefully. A sense of flow fell over her.

~

After the workshops were over, Krish popped his head in Liam's room at the hotel. "Got a minute?"

"Sure." Liam swung the door open, shirtless after a shower in anticipation of his evening with Tillie. As Krish followed him into the room, Liam splashed lime aftershave over a cleanly shaved jaw. "What's up?"

"I have an agenda for the rest of the week, if you want to take a look."

"Yeah, you sent it to me in an email." Liam combed his hair back from his face. It would dry on the way, more or less, but he was anxious to get going. "I'll read it later."

"I was hoping we could sit down over dinner and talk out some finer points of the rest of the tour."

"Sorry, bro." He flipped through the freshly laundered shirts, neatly tended and hung by an assistant. "I have plans."

"With the new woman? What's her name?"

Liam looked over his shoulder. "Tillie. I met her at an art show last night."

"Hmm." Krish flipped the pages on his clipboard, then crossed his arms. "Magical, is it?"

A burn spread through Liam's gut, both truth and resistance. He turned, buttoning his shirt. "Don't do that. I'm not the boy I was."

"Okay. Just . . . remember, this is your weakness."

"I haven't had a date in two solid years. I think I've done the work." Krish simply gazed at him.

A rare sense of annoyance rose. Liam said, "It's not your affair."

"It is if it knocks you off the rails."

"What rails? This endless train you've got me riding? I keep telling you that I'm tired, man." They'd been on the road for months, through Australia, then a stop in Singapore, three sites in Hawaii, each three days, then to North America—British Columbia and the West Coast of America, the Rockies, Chicago and Atlanta, now New York. They would go to Europe next.

"We've sold out every city on the schedule. That's making a fair sum of money, not to mention supporting at least forty people. Including me."

Liam turned toward the mirror, wishing only to be back with Tillie in her apartment, drinking tea, exploring the shimmering connection between them. Away from the expectations of his crew, the eyes of the people who awaited in those cities, hungry for answers they hoped he could provide.

Once, this had felt like important work. The world needed mindfulness, and the more he could help people discover it, the less suffering there would be.

Now, he wasn't sure. He felt imprisoned by the constant travel, the faceless hotel rooms, the lack of ordinary life to keep him grounded.

"It feels dangerous to live this way, Krish."

"Dangerous?" He twisted his mouth in a skeptical grimace.

"Yeah. No home ground. No ordinary pleasures." Liam couldn't quite express what bothered him—but it was more about the constancy of expectation, the hungry maw of ego that wanted more, more, more. "We're living opposite what we teach: simplicity and kindness."

"Yeah, I know. You brought that up in Oz. We've been working on the consumption angles. It's just a big task, and not all the hotels have systems in place. We've dropped the private flights and gone commercial."

"I know, I know." Liam took a breath, tried to settle into his patience, but it squished like a cloud, evaporating into discomfort and anxiousness. He felt both that he loved the attention of all those upturned faces, and that he was letting them down, that it was too much about Liam the Personality, and not enough about the path itself. "I just think I need a break."

"The tour lasts only a couple of more months. Let's finish it up, and see where you are then."

Liam sighed, unwilling to spend any more time on the subject now. He met his friend's eye in the mirror. "Everything good with you? Your dad's recovered?"

"He's all right. Thanks."

"Of course." Their friendship had become a bit off-kilter on this tour. They'd never had big heart-to-heart talks or anything like that, but since the age of seven, they'd spoken almost daily, which kept them both in the loop. Krish carried a lot of familial expectations—a sister with mental health challenges, a father who'd just had a heart attack and could not work at his former profession as a baker, a large working-class family who turned to him for many needs.

Neither of them had grown up with money, and the tremendous wealth spilling from the app, then the workshops, was surprising and welcome. It also came with challenges.

Like, how much was enough?

Krish said, "It'll all work itself out." He tilted his head. "Go with the purple. It's your best look."

Liam listened.

"Have a good time," Krish said. "Just don't be late. Gives me a bloody heart attack."

CHAPTER EIGHT

Wulfecombe

Sage Evely had learned to find pleasure in ordinary things. It was the thing that had, in the end, made life bearable.

Walking to work every morning was an ordinary thing. She loved her village, particularly on a spring morning when few people were afoot. Her terraced house crouched on the edge of town, and she followed winding streets down modern pavements to cobblestones, past the ford over the river that had been built by the Romans, and then the requisite castle ruin. It hadn't been much of a castle even in its heyday, only a tower keep and a wall that lay in ruins, but it was theirs, and they prized it.

History ran deep here. Wulfecombe had been a market town in the Middle Ages, raided by the Vikings in the Dark Ages, occupied by the Romans. Stone circles littered the fields with evidence of Bronze Age people, and it was possible to find archaeological bits from five thousand years of history. On the coast, fossils from dinosaurs littered the rocky beaches.

This morning, Sage took pleasure in the more-fleeting present-day beauty of flowers lining the gardens along the way—a competition of daffodils and narcissi of all sizes and shapes and incarnations, from standard yellow to white to ruffled white and peach. One border boasted white stars centered with apricot ruffles. It looked for all the world like an art installation of lady parts.

Sage's walk took her to Rosemary's Chocolates—her joy, her pride, the business she'd created and now run for more than six years. She'd learned her art in London and brought it home to her own little village, taking advantage of the tourist trade, visitors who came from many directions to the famed open-air market, or on their way to the coast.

This morning, it was only Sage and a fairly new hire, one who'd shown enough promise that Sage had pulled her from behind the counter to work in the back, making chocolate. Lexie was as skinny as an exclamation mark, her dishwater hair still straw-dry on the lower half, glossier on the new growth. She'd come to the shop through a council program designed to help find stable work for girls with a criminal background—almost always rooted in addiction or poverty and the wretched choices of partners the girls made. Lexie had a three-year-old daughter she desperately wanted to see regularly, and the motivation made her a reliable employee.

It would until it didn't. Sage knew firsthand how easy it was to suddenly find yourself awash in a mess again. She'd been clean for eleven years but didn't take it for granted.

The Wailing Jennies sang on the speakers, and rain tapped against the windows, sometimes admittedly leaking through the cracks in the ancient walls. The building had stood since the Middle Ages, always a place of hospitality, often run by women. An alehouse, a bakery, and various cafés over the centuries. Sometimes the staff feared the cellar below and avoided certain other areas—a dark stairway to the storage rooms overhead, a particular alcove near the alleyway, but she loved to imagine the ghosts were all women like herself, making their way in a world often more than a little hostile.

This morning, Sage and Lexie were working on ganaches to be flavored in various ways, then run through the temperer. She used a mandolin to slice ginger paper thin, ginger her mother grew organically in her greenhouse.

Clare grew carrots, too: purple and yellow, red Indian carrots, common English orange, which she'd promised to bring this morning. Sage would use them for dinner tonight at home, mixing the carrots with heaps of similarly shredded cabbage, red and green, with yellow and red onions, and then roast with olive oil and salt and pepper, a warm salad for a cold spring day. Nourishment for herself and the baby growing within.

"This good, boss?" Lexie asked, offering a pile of finely chopped walnuts, the sizes even and tiny.

"Well done," Sage said. "I'll start the jelly. Get the molds ready."

"Which one again?" Lexie looked at the stacks of molds in dozens of varieties stacked up on a pair of shelves that ran the length of the room. "I keep forgetting."

"That's all right. It takes time." She kept meaning to make a chart of which chocolates went into which molds, but there never seemed to be enough time. Paula had been nagging her to hire an admin assistant, but the truth was, it was hard enough to get and keep even a skeleton staff for the shop. Like everyone in the service industry, she struggled with staffing post-pandemic. It was the constant subject of conversation among small business owners, and it had put more of them out of business than the pandemic by far.

No one could figure out where all the people had gone. How did they live? *Where* did they live?

It was a mystery, and until it was solved, Sage would continue to hope to hire an administrative assistant to make a chart of the molds for her chocolates. "The round ones with lines on half."

"These?" she held up a pleated version.

"No, one more over. That's right. Make sure they're clean. No water."

"Right. I remember."

Sage poured water over finely chopped ginger and brought it to a simmer, inhaling the scent that mixed with the overt chocolate fragrance in the room. The ginger and walnut chocolates were one of her bestsellers, and she loved the mingling of flavors. She made a mental note to add them to the list of things she needed to be sure were stocked for her maternity leave, which would likely not be a long stretch, but she wanted to make sure this baby was well cared for, too.

A figure appeared at the back door, a tall woman with black hair cut short, wearing jeans and a peasant blouse below her raincoat. Her face showed the hard road she'd traveled, in deep lines along her mouth and around her eyes, eyes that looked older than her fifty-nine years.

"Hey, Mum. Did you bring my carrots?"

She held up a canvas bag with greens sprouting from the top. "Lots. They're very sweet."

Sage waited for what she knew was coming.

"Is she kicking?" Clare asked.

She laughed, turning to offer her belly to her mother, feeling a sweet little twist of love for grandmother and child as Clare's long hands cupped the six-month belly. As if on cue, the child in her belly shifted, pushed a fist toward the gentle voice she must surely be coming to recognize by now. "Hello, love," Clare cooed. "How's my darling girl today?"

Clare's hair had begun to sprout silvery threads, the shimmery strands coarser and wavier than the rest, and it roused in Sage a sense of tenderness. She passed a trio of gentle fingers over her mother's part as Clare spread her hands over her belly. A soft folk song played on the speakers. It had been Clare and Sage forever, before Levi, before her stepsiblings, Amelia and Meg, then their little brothers, Ben and Arthur. Just the two of them facing a world of trauma and sorrow. Sage had deserted her mother for a time, almost ten years if she was honest, but she was here now, and grateful.

"I'm so happy," Clare said, and kissed the belly.

"Okay, that's weird," Sage said.

Clare laughed. "Sorry. I got carried away. Liam will be here next week for a good Sunday roast. Can you and Paula come?"

"We wouldn't miss it." Sage had spent a golden summer long ago with her "cousin," technically not her blood but her mother's best friend's child. He'd been as lost as she that year, both of them grieving losses they couldn't speak aloud. She hadn't seen him since then, and looked forward to it.

"I've missed her while she's been on tour. How's she doing?"

"Great." Paula was part of a folk duo. They'd just returned from a tour of Ireland. "She's glad to be done with it before the baby arrives." She plucked a sliver of ginger from the pile and nibbled it. "What can I bring?"

"Would it be too much trouble to make the roast vegetable tart? Liam is a strict vegetarian."

Sage had spent many of her lost years cooking vegan in various places around London, eschewing meat in some strange offering of balance to her drug issues. "No worries. I love making it."

Clare nodded, and straightened.

"What?"

She hesitated, and Sage braced herself for bad news. Clare's eyes were the pale watery blue of a clairvoyant's, and they flickered now. "They found some bones at a construction site. Child bones."

Sage found a protective hand falling over her belly, felt her baby move, a tiny foot, a shoulder maybe. "Where?"

"Just outside the Roman villa, where the new development is going."

Bones. Sage looked toward the window, stirred the ginger, let the words rest in the air, and wondered if they had any meaning for her. A memory rose, struggling to bring itself into the forefront of her mind, but she shook her head. Not today. She pushed it back into its special box where it couldn't rake up the neat ground of her calm, ordinary life. "I don't want to talk about it."

"But, what—"

"No," Sage said. "I've asked you to respect my way of managing things. This is one of those times."

To her credit, Clare didn't push. She only nodded and took a small cosmetic pot from her enormous cloth bag. "I made you some salve for your belly. It will help with stretch marks, healing and preventing them."

Sage accepted the gift in the spirit it was intended. Her mother was what had once been called a wise woman—a leader among the women in the community, a healer, and in a more modern twist, an ordained minister with pagan roots. She was beloved in the town, and by her husband, and by her six children. Or, well, adored by five of them, anyway. Including Sage. "Thanks. I'll ask Paula if she's up for Sunday roast and let you know, but I'm sure she'll be as happy as I am."

"Take care, my sweet," Clare said, and kissed Sage's cheek, touched her belly once more. "I love you."

For a long moment, Sage rested the heels of her palms on the counter, watching her mother go, then looked down at the tattoo rounding her left forearm, a large, graceful dragon with green eyes. She'd had him done at the worst of her dark days, a reminder that there were things about your life you couldn't change, no matter how much you wished you could.

Then she pushed the thoughts away. Life was good now. A good marriage, a baby on the way, her famous, kind, and beautiful cousin coming to visit. The past could rest where it was, distant and unimportant.

CHAPTER NINE

New York City

Tillie surfaced from painting with a sense of awakening. She stood in front of her easel, but it was not the gazelle girl she'd started with.

It was the giant cat from her dream, who in turn had come from the painting at the gallery. She'd drawn him with oil sticks in deep indigo and amber, with long, long whiskers and pale blue eyes. Wise eyes, wise and kind, knowing. Human eyes but . . . not.

Her hands were covered with color, which happened with the oil sticks, but usually, she pulled on latex gloves. Not this time. Her arms were smeared with layer upon layer of color, up to her elbows.

At her feet were scattered multiple drawings of him, in many poses. They were tossed carelessly on the floor, one after the other. Tillie squatted and picked up a few of them. This one just his face, his nose as big as a building; a pose with him asleep, tail tucked over his paws. Always the bandit stripes.

She had no memory of drawing these pieces. The place where the memory should have been was as blank as if she'd had anesthesia. She frowned in confusion.

How many drawings had she made? She picked them up and stacked them in a tidy pile, counting.

Sixteen.

Her heart raced erratically.

An urgent need to pee suddenly overtook her, and of course, the buzzer rang from below. Dumping the drawings on the big table in the center of the room, she dashed over to the wall, pressed the intercom. "You can leave packages with the super."

"It's Liam," he said.

Liam. She looked down at herself, then at the room, but honestly, she had to pee before anything else. For one second, she considered sending him away, but her gut sent up such a huge roar of resistance that she said, "Come on up."

She buzzed him in, then dashed for the bathroom. In the mirror, she saw that she was a complete mess, hair yanked back into an erratic ponytail, smears of turquoise over her cheekbone and neck. Her hands would need serious scrubbing.

There was nothing she could do in the three minutes it took for him to get to the top of the stairs. Before she got out of the bathroom, he was knocking playfully on her door: *tap, tap, tap, tap, tap.*

"Coming!" she called, and looked around wildly for one thing she could do to make herself or her world more presentable.

There was nothing. She yanked the door open. "Welcome to the madness," she said, gesturing broadly for him to enter. "Sorry. I lost track of time."

He looked quite different. Cleaned up, as if he'd come from some hip, posh job. His hair was brushed back from his face and secured, and the scruffy five-o'clock shadow was gone. The shirt was high-end linen, patterned in light purple, and although he wore jeans, they were similarly expensive. She blinked. "Wow. You look fabulous."

"My disguise," he joked. "Looks like you've been hard at work."

A stab of terror bolted through her chest—how did she lose *hours*?—but she recovered. "Afraid you caught me as myself."

"I like it." His voice, as smooth and resonant as a long chord on a cello, worked through her skin, landed in her blood.

He waited outside the door, hands in his back pockets. "Sorry, come in," she said, flustered. "Sit down. Let me get you a beer—no, I don't have any. Um, how about coffee, or maybe—"

He closed the distance between them, hands landing on her arms above the elbows. "I've caught you at a bad time. Do you want to keep working?"

The scent of him filled her head, lime and clove and the promise of sex.

What she *wanted* was to lean in and wrap her messy arms around him, make imprints of her color-smeared breasts on that beautiful shirt, but instead, she took a breath. Shook her head. "I'm actually starving."

"Me, too."

"Uh . . ." She spread out her hands. "I *have* to shower. Help yourself to something to drink. Bubbly water or—" She shook her head. "That might be it."

"Truly, I don't need anything." He sounded like he meant it. "Take your time."

It was a little odd that he just settled in the big chair so easily and took out his phone, turning on the lamp, which cast a warm yellow light over him.

As if he belonged there.

~

As she scrubbed the layers of oil color from her body, Tillie tried not to think about the lost time, but the mess itself was part of the strangeness. Oil colors could stain the skin, and she did what she could to protect herself from them: gloves, long sleeves, a mask. She hadn't done so this time.

She didn't remember shifting from the charcoals she used to draw the gazelle girl to oil sticks. Didn't remember tossing drawing after drawing to the floor. Didn't remember any of it.

What the hell had happened?

Her mother always said there was a very fine line between madness and creativity. Arlette often fell over the line, disappearing into worlds only she completely understood.

As water poured down her face, Tillie worried that she might be developing her mother's illness, that this was the first volley in whatever undiagnosed thing she'd lived with, because she would never get treatment, even after Tillie left home and realized that Arlette really might benefit from some clinical intervention.

Would Tillie end up lost in a world of her own creation?

The world of the cat. Cat Land.

The phrase reverberated, as if she knew it, as if she could tell a story about it. *Once upon a time, there was a king of cats . . .*

She laughed. He seemed like a friendly enough fellow, after all, even if he was the size of a lion. A giant lion.

Some of her tension eased. Maybe she was being *slightly* dramatic.

Aware that Liam was in the other room, she kept her fussing to a minimum: simple makeup, her damp hair woven into a braid. Mindful of his outfit, she donned a black cashmere sweater and jeans. When she came out, he was still completely at peace with himself, reading on his phone.

"Hi."

He lifted his head. "Ah, the woman returns. When you first opened the door, I thought you were a crayon."

She laughed. "It was a deep day." She paused, glancing toward the stack of newsprint drawings. "An odd day, actually. Do you mind if we go by the gallery? I need to see that painting again."

"Sure," he said, standing. He slipped his phone into his back pocket. He pointed at the table. "Do you mind if I look?"

"Go ahead." She sat on the bench by the door to tie her short boots.

For a few long moments, he leafed through them, gently lifting one after another, and Tillie felt a faint dizziness—but she dropped her feet to the floor and grabbed her coat from a hook by the door. "Ready?"

"Am I allowed to comment? Or is it better if I don't?"

She shrugged. "I don't mind. I have no idea what they are."

"A cat, I'd say," he said with a quirk of his lips. "Made with energy and emotion and power. I'd pay substantially for one of these, mate."

"Yeah?" She crossed the room, boot heels knocking a rhythm against the wooden floor. Maybe this was the something she'd been looking for to give her work fresh energy. Setting aside the fear of the lost time, she allowed herself to really look at the drawings, and he was right. Fantastic energy. Joy. Fear. Intense colors and line work. "I just don't know where they came from."

"You will, in time."

"I mean—" She started to explain and then realized it didn't matter. Not right this minute. The scent of him filled her head, struck her limbic memory, and she was transported to the taxi last night, kissing him, anticipating something entirely different from a migraine. She was sorely tempted to take one more step and kiss him now, but it felt weirdly dangerous.

"Let's go take a look at the painting from last night," she said instead. "And get some food."

~

Settled in the taxi on the way over, she asked, "Now that you've seen my raw artwork, are you going to tell me what you're doing in town?"

He picked up her hand. "I lead meditation workshops."

"Um, what?"

He half shrugged. "You asked."

"It does explain the aura of calm." She waved a hand in a circle, indicating his body and head.

"Am I calm?"

"Yes." She inclined her head, thinking that he also felt safe, which was not usually the thing she was drawn to in a man. Though after Jared, she was pretty tired of drama. "What sort of meditation?"

"Mindfulness, and some visualization."

59

"Huh. Like, 'You're walking down a forest path and the birds are singing . . .'"

"More or less." His eyes glittered, and he made no defense nor took offense.

"I don't know that I've met a meditation teacher before. Is that why you're in the city?"

He nodded.

She plucked the bracelets on his wrist, rolled the beads beneath her fingers. "I should tell you I'm not in the slightest bit spiritual."

"We don't have to be the same."

When the taxi pulled up to the gallery, she got out first and stood on the sidewalk, waiting for Liam, but her eyes were already searching for the painting. She only could see Jon's giant abstracts, which practically hauled people in off the street. "Jon sold out last night, which if you don't know, is pretty incredible."

"Jon. That's your friend?"

"Yeah." She tapped her fingers against her thigh, bracing herself to go inside.

"You okay?"

She shrugged. "Maybe?"

He took her hand. Tillie looked up, grateful for the solidness of his hand. His presence. He was just tall enough that she felt appropriately small, a patriarchal bit of bullshit she nonetheless loved. Taking a breath, gripping his hand, she said, "Okay, let's do it."

A gallery worker greeted them as they came in. "Hello!"

"Just looking," Tillie said, moving like an arrow toward the back.

And there it was, the painting. Medium size, 11 x 20 inches. Still not at all the sort of thing she usually gravitated toward, but it didn't matter—her heart surged toward that porch, that cat, the figures. Did she want to buy it? She squinted at the price, but it wasn't that she wanted to own it.

She wanted to enter it.

Next to her, Liam was quiet, his hand solidly holding hers. Their palms were starting to sweat, and she was afraid she'd gross him out. She let go. "Excuse me," she said to the woman pretending not to hover. "Do you have any more information on this artist?"

"I'm sure we do. These six are the only ones we have, and they've only been here a week or so."

Six. She hadn't even registered the others. Another was clearly the same place, with the big rhubarb-looking leaves, and a road, and a house in the distance. None of them moved Tillie in the slightest. She liked the exaggerated color, but intellectually, not emotionally.

She looked more closely at the cat she'd connected with so deeply and saw that it had barely any details, just a shape in taffy and white. She'd supplied all the details herself, the whiskers and blue eyes, the stripes. "I don't get it," she said to Liam. "Objectively, I don't really like this style, but I want to be inside it."

"Does it remind you of something? Somewhere?"

She frowned, then shook her head. "I don't think so. I grew up on a farm upstate. We had cats, and even a porch, but none of these plants." She mined her memory for images from her travels, but nothing rose to match this house.

The woman returned with a single sheaf of glossy paper. "Not a lot of information. The gallery is the main contact, and as you see, it's just a single name. Shiloh."

"Do you know where she paints? Where she's from?"

The woman shook her head. "Sorry. I can find out for you, maybe."

"Will you?" Tillie gave her the number. "Text me."

"Are you interested in purchasing one of these pieces?"

"Maybe," she said, to be polite.

As she turned away, she caught sight of the cat in the painting again, and felt a swoosh of something, like wind, or a noise she couldn't quite identify. It made her dizzy, and Liam must have noticed, because he took her arm. She stayed still, waiting for it to pass. Terror rose.

What was happening to her? Was she going to succumb to a mental illness the way her mother had?

"Pie?" Liam suggested quietly.

"Too bright. Let's find a bar."

~

Liam settled with Tillie into an agreeably dark booth in a pub that smelled of a hundred years of beer. It boasted English favorites like shepherd's pie and fish and chips with mushy peas. Not vegetarian-friendly, but he was used to that. These days, there was always something, and on this menu, he found a mushroom risotto. Tillie ordered a pint of ale. Liam asked for water.

"Water?"

"I like it."

Her face captured him again, the simple oval, her indigo eyes. Her braid fell over her shoulder. Even in the low light, the white streak in her hair was quite visible. Her hands rested on the table, fingers folded together, quiet. He could imagine her as the wolf mother, the cat being, the owl mermaid from her art.

"You could be one of the characters from your paintings," he said.

"Feral?" She teased. "I've heard that before. I didn't get all the edicts about makeup and wearing certain things, all that. My mom was a total hippie."

"Seriously?" He spread a hand over his chest, weirdly delighted. "Mine, too."

"No kidding." She paused, studying his face. "That actually makes sense."

He grinned. "Like being a model?"

She had the grace to blush slightly. "Sorry. I mean—" She waved a hand. "We lived on a farm upstate, and my mom grew all of her own vegetables. Made kombucha before it was a thing."

"We were on the outskirts of the city, but same. No meat, no dairy, counters all covered with trays of sprouts and jars of sunflowers. She kept bees."

"Your own bees and honey. That's up there." She laughed. "I never had sugar until I went to a school Halloween dance in the seventh grade, but we bought ours. We didn't eat meat at all, but I was always trying to figure out ways to try it."

He chuckled. "Rebel."

"I was homeschooled until I was thirteen. You?"

"I never went to a public school. Homeschooled all the way."

"That's amazing. I *never* meet anybody with my background."

The waiter brought their food. "My mother would not have approved of this meal, I can tell you," she said, "but God that smells good. Are you still vegetarian?"

"I refuse to answer that question," he replied.

"So yes?" She grinned. "It's hard to eat meat if you've been raised without it."

"Yeah. I just . . . can't."

She sighed and touched her napkin to her lips. "When I traveled in my wild youth, I found it easier to let that go."

"Where'd you travel?"

"All over. Jon and I. At first, it was college holidays, you know, down to Mexico and Belize, and then after we graduated, we took a year and did the old-school backpacking thing." She enumerated the stops. "Started in Thailand, as one does."

"As one does."

"India, Sri Lanka, Croatia, Turkey, Egypt, Italy," she said, raising a finger for each place. "Germany, Norway, Iceland, then down to South America, Peru, Argentina."

"Impressive. Equal time in each?"

"That was the original plan, a month at each stop, but there were places we really liked and places we didn't care about. By the end, we were really ready to get back to New York and away from each other."

He laughed. "I did a gap year. Not as extensive as that. I didn't hear England on the list."

"We didn't go to the UK at all, or France, or Spain. It was a deliberate choice—those are the ones you'd visit anyway, right?"

"Fair enough."

"Now that we're sitting here, in a pub, I do wonder when I'll visit." She inclined her head and pointed above them, to where music came out of speakers. "I'm a fan of this kind of music, for one thing. Classic folk. I listen to this woman a lot when I paint. She sings the classics like this—" The song was a version of the story of Tam Lin. "But she also writes a lot of original songs that are in this realm, very dark fairy stories."

"Paula Davies," he said, leaning forward. "She lives in the town where my mum grew up."

"No way," Tillie said. Again. "She's my favorite."

For a long moment, he was quiet, only looking at her face. A sense of fate and fear mingled in his body, and he wondered if perhaps he should leave this connection alone, let it be. "I've never met anyone who knows her music."

"Me, either."

He stretched a hand across the table, palm up. "Give me your hand."

"Don't tell me anything scary," she said.

"No."

She reached over and placed her hand in his. Instead of reading her palm, he laced their fingers together, gauging the fit, finding it natural. Solid. "I think we were fated to meet, Tillie."

"I don't believe in fate."

"Don't you?" He held her gaze. A flicker moved there, a ghost.

She ran her thumb over the shape of his knuckles. "Would you like to come back to my apartment?"

"I believe I would."

CHAPTER TEN

The night was fresh and crisp. Tillie said, "Let's just take the train."

"Glad to."

The foot traffic was light. She peered shamelessly into the apartment windows facing the street, hearing snippets of conversation, televisions, clatters of dishes. She was deeply aware of Liam next to her, his loose-limbed walk, his curious air of calm. "How did you become a meditation leader?" she asked as they passed a yoga studio.

"The short version is that I found trouble young, and then . . ." He looked at her. "I found the opposite at a Buddhist monastery."

Something about this simple, clear story pierced her. "I've never found calm anywhere," she said. "I always feel like I'm looking for something that's right out of the corner of my eye." She thought of the cat suddenly, all the wild painting, the time she lost. "Can I tell you something?"

"Yes," he says, turning his clear eyes toward her.

"When I painted those cats today?" Suddenly, she lost her nerve. "I just . . . got kind of lost in them. Like, lost time, kind of."

"Like flow?"

She paused, crossing her arms. "No. Like, I—" She took a breath. "Never mind. It's too weird."

"You can tell me. I won't judge you."

"It was like a fugue state or something. I don't remember anything about the time I painted. Like I became someone else. Like . . . a split personality? Is that even a thing?"

He nodded, waiting to see if she would add anything. "I'm sure it's still a thing, but do you think you might have a memory hole from childhood, something you don't remember?"

"Oh, I know I have one. The head injury when I was four." She pointed to the white streak at her temple.

"You fell?"

"I think so?" She took a breath. "It's complicated. My mother was not always in the here and now, if you know what I mean."

"I do." He brushed his hand over her cheek. "I'm sorry about that."

"I hate saying that, honestly. She was so good to me. It was always just us, you know? Arlette and Tillie against the world. She felt safe at the farm, and I think having those boundaries really helped her stay relatively okay."

"My dad died when I was seven," he said. His hair shone in the streetlight, his nose casting a shadow over a cheekbone. "My mother was on the floor. She took us all to England, and we spent the summer with her best friend, on a farm. I had a bunch of cousins, and there were all these rescue animals, like a goat with three legs and dogs who couldn't walk very well."

Tillie smiled up at him. "That sounds beautiful."

"It was. The thing is, it really did heal my mum. She was always a farmer, but after that was when she got down with the bees and honey and all that."

"Nature heals?"

"Maybe." They were standing face-to-face, close to the wall. From somewhere came the sound of a band, and Tillie smelled the cigarettes of people smoking outside a bar. A triangle of light fell across the part of his hair, touched his lower lip, and it was all she could see. "Maybe it's just the thing of having things that have to be done. Simple things. Repetitive things."

"Mm." A honeyed sense of longing spilled through her. "Maybe I do believe in fate."

"Maybe I do, too." He leaned in to kiss her. The wall braced them, and the kiss went deep. His body was a million degrees, burning her at all the connection points, the palm of his hand on her neck, his fingers in her hair, her arm reaching up to pull him closer, their chests, their thighs. As if they'd rehearsed, their bodies slid into perfect alignment.

He lifted his head. Looked at her.

She looked back.

At some signal they both felt, they tangled hands and kept walking, not speaking.

After they walked for a little while, he stopped. "Close your eyes."

It said something about her trust of him that she did exactly as he asked.

"Do you smell it?"

She took a breath and grinned, keeping her eyes closed. Vitamins, patchouli, dried ginger, yeast. "Health food store."

He squeezed her fingers. "Let's go in."

They skipped down the steps to the basement store. It was well lit, with well-organized shelves, and a tidy row of bulk bins, half–Whole Foods, half–seventies co-op. The scent wrapped Tillie in a cozy hug, and from Liam's cheerful expression as he looked around, it was the same for him. He lifted a bar of soap, smelled it, offered it to her—honey and lanolin, studded with lavender, probably very nourishing, but not the greatest way to smell. She coughed a little.

He chuckled, bringing the soap back to his nose. "My mum made soap from goat's milk."

Tillie shook her head. "Not even gonna say it."

"Yours, too?"

"Of course. What was your mom's specialty?"

"Everything honey. Honey soap, honey balm, honey butter, bee pollen. All of it." They eased down the very slim aisles, past the Dr. Bronner's soaps and more modern Green Day products, through the lentils and beans and pastas and bulk dried fruit. She had a sudden yen for granola with raisins. "Hang on. I need some of this."

There used to be plastic bags on rolls, but of course, now they had paper bags of various sizes. Tillie filled a medium-size one, and suddenly thought of her mom, her sleeves and hair swaying, her jewelry clattering, earrings and a multitude of bracelets. Grief rose, wild and emphatic, and tears stung her eyes. She blinked hurriedly, trying to hide her sudden swell of emotion, but Liam noticed. Of course he would.

Instead of words, he handed her a handkerchief. "It's clean."

"Thank you."

"Do you want to talk about it?"

"My mom died not long ago. This place is making me think of her."

"I'm sorry."

"Thanks."

As they turned a tight corner, they passed a narrow endcap of incense. The fragrances mingled and swelled, and Tillie reached for a gold package that made her think of her mother. The scents of rose and patchouli filled her sinuses.

She was suddenly struck again by a sense of reality splitting, as if this were a stage set and everything real was on the other side.

She peered through the rent. *Faintly in the distance, a spark of light glowed, and she heard something like birds chirping, and caught a scent of roses. A road split a thick forest in two, the tree branches forming a tunnel overhead. In the distance was a house, and she could see a woman cooking at a stove—*

Liam grabbed her arm. "Steady there."

She swayed as if she would faint, but all at once, she was back in this reality. Here, in this world, with bright LED lights overhead and the package of incense in her hand. "Are you all right?" Liam asked.

She shook her head. "Um. Yes. I think that painting stirred something up. So weird."

"Is it?"

What she thought, looking up, was that she liked his face. His eyelashes. "I don't know. I'm off-kilter for sure."

"Let's get you home."

"Yeah."

Outside, she sniffed her sleeve. "We'll smell like this for days."

"A memory of home."

"Now I'm craving an avocado and sprouts sandwich on whole-grain bread."

He laughed. "Kumara soup with sunflower seeds."

"What's kumara?"

"Like a sweet potato, I think."

"Is your mom still alive?" Tillie asked.

"Definitely. Trying to run our lives at every turn."

"Lives? How many of you?"

He inclined his head. "Six, believe it or not."

"And where are you in the lineup?"

"Youngest."

"Mm," she said with some disapproval, reaching into the bag for granola as if it were popcorn, then held out the bag to him. "Spoiled."

"Quite," he agreed cheerfully. He accepted the offering, and tossed a cluster of oats and nuts into the air, captured it in his mouth and looked down at her, entirely pleased.

Tillie laughed. Some dark, heavy part of her dropped away.

The station was fairly empty. They stood together, close but not touching, and when they sat down in the sparsely populated car, he took her hand.

"Are you free tomorrow?" he asked.

"No. I wish. I have to drive north to my mother's farm to meet a real estate agent."

He looked genuinely disappointed. "Too bad. I have the day free before I start the next workshop."

"It's not very exciting, but you could . . . ride with me?"

"Yeah?" He smiled down at her. "I'd like that."

And then they were kissing again, as if they were fourteen and it didn't matter that there were other people around. Tillie fell adrift in the impossibility of him, and the iridescent bubble of this moment, and asked for nothing more.

This, now, him.

~

Her body hummed as they walked the two blocks to her apartment. Clouds obscured the moon, leaving only streetlights to illuminate the world.

But it wasn't so dark that she didn't see the figure on her stoop. "Shit," she swore under her breath.

"What's up?"

"The ex."

"Should I go?"

"No."

Jared saw them and jumped to his feet. He was a long-legged, very good-looking man, but Tillie noticed immediately that he was too thin, and by the uncertain, swaying stance, she could tell he'd also been drinking. Hard. "What are you doing here, Jared?"

"You wouldn't answer my texts."

"I told you I was blocking you. Please go home."

"I just want to talk to you." He looked at Liam with a sneer. "But I guess you're not all about talking, right?" He swayed, and she reached out to catch him.

"Let me call you a ride," she said.

"Fuck you. Fuck him." He sank down on the step, then raised his head and howled. Literally, like a wolf. She flushed with embarrassment, for him, for herself. "We are *soulmates*, Tillie. You know we are!"

Any hopes of having Liam in her bed tonight were rapidly shredding, but this was not okay. "You're free to sit here," she said, "but I—we—are going upstairs."

She took Liam's hand and led him past Jared, who leaned sideways to let them pass, both strange and utterly polite. He didn't move as she unlocked the main door, and when they got to the studio at the top of the building, she looked out the window. He was still there, his head hanging.

"Well, that was fun," she said. "I'm sorry."

Liam stood by the door. "You have a lot going on in your life right now."

She ducked her head. Nodded. "I guess you're going to go, then?"

He was silent a long time. "I don't want to. But I think I should."

Her heart dropped. "Okay."

"Can I still go with you tomorrow?"

"Oh, yes, please!"

"Good." He backed up toward the door. "I'm not going to kiss you because I won't go if I do."

She swallowed her longing to hold him back. "Okay."

"I'll see to your ex down there, too."

And then he was gone.

When she looked outside a few minutes later, Liam was sitting on the stoop next to Jared, who had his head in his hands. She could hear Liam's voice, calm and kind, and after a minute, they stood up together and walked to the curb. A car appeared, and Jared climbed in. She held her breath for a minute, hoping Liam would come upstairs. Instead, hands tucked into his pockets, he walked away. She watched until darkness and distance swallowed him.

CHAPTER ELEVEN

Wulfecombe

Sage's superpower was her extraordinary memory. It stretched to her very earliest days. Unfortunately, because she'd lived through a number of traumatic things and had then skulked around too long in the half light of lostness, she carried a load of unfortunate memories. She tried not to visit those things too often, but she was wise enough—now, anyway—that she didn't try to wall them off, either.

The upside of her memory was that she remembered good things, too, like the way her mother used to lean in to kiss her at bedtime, tucking her in with three kisses—one to her forehead, one to her nose, one to her cheek. She always took a breath on the last one, as if inhaling her daughter.

Sage also remembered the first time she tasted chocolate. She must have been three or so, and a neighbor had brought over a cake, layers and layers of chocolate—cake and icing, cake and icing, tiny layers of crumbly texture, and a drizzle of purest chocolate over the top. She was a fussy eater, always, but that cake had broken through every barrier she'd ever imagined.

She knew now that chocolate cake was not always the easiest to make, but the fine ganache icing and the drizzles had knocked her brain right out of her head, turned her into a being of pure sensuality. The adults had found her adorable, taking pictures of her licking her fingers, chocolate smeared over not just her face but also her hair and clothes.

At four, her life had been upended with a brutal and devastating twist that left Sage marooned in a lonely world. That loneliness had led her away from that sensual joy, down a long and crooked road. At fifteen, she'd discovered the cursed forgetfulness that addiction offered, and wandered away from the tethers of her mother and her village, lost in the city on her own.

But at the age of twenty-seven, at the bottom of one of her darkest days, she'd stopped in front of the shop of a chocolatier on a London street. It was a tiny place, tucked between two expensive boutiques, but the external wall was violet, and gold lettering proclaimed its purpose: *Madame Alain, chocolatier.*

The smell of it wafted out, rich and deep. Alive. Forgetting that she would not be welcome in her current state, ragged and unwashed, she allowed it to lure her inside. She had no money. She couldn't remember the last time she'd eaten.

And yet. She stood in the center of the tiny shop, surrounded by the textured scent of chocolate, and breathed. Breathed all the way to bottom of her soul. It stirred the shriveled parts, the pieces twisted and neglected, and they began to breathe with her, take on life.

A woman spoke from behind the counter. "Here you are, dear," she said. "A sample."

"Oh," Sage said, hauled back to reality. "I don't have any money."

The woman lifted a sanguine shoulder. "I have plenty of samples. You look like you could do with a little sweetness. Try this one. It has a little orange."

Sage accepted the gift, taking a small bite, the smallest she could manage so that it would last. It melted in bits on her lonely, starved tongue, and as if it were enchanted, it awakened her mouth, bright orange and sweet ganache and slivers of dark bitter chocolate. She savored it, tasting something for the first time in years. She was, for a moment, genuinely alive. Alight.

The woman smiled, as benevolent as a fairy godmother.

It didn't happen that day or even that week, but not long after, Sage found her way into a rehab to help her detox, and then into a halfway house where she worked at a vegan café for two years. When she trusted that her light was truly, completely flickering within, she went back to Madame Alain and asked to be her apprentice.

It was the most potent decision of her life, and no one would ever convince her that there was no magic in the alchemy of chocolate. It had healed her, that kiss of chocolate, awakening her to life as surely as the prince kissing the sleeping princess. Not that she'd ever wanted a prince, of course, though she'd found quite a pretty princess.

This morning, she'd come to the shop early, before dawn had fully broken the horizon. The town was sleeping, only the odd stray cat out hunting, and she'd let herself in to the old building to commune with the ghosts who'd not yet taken themselves to bed. She felt them rustling, reliving their times in these kitchens. She didn't mind their company as she pulled out ingredients, feeling a taste on her tongue, something elusive. Cream, of course. Dark chocolate, but not the darkest. Butter. Something popped, clear and bright. Yes, butter for caramel? No, toffee.

Hmm. She hadn't done much with toffee. Paula loved caramel, so she usually stopped there, but if the magic was urging her to make toffee, there must be a reason.

Toffee, it would be. Magic bites for someone who needed them.

CHAPTER TWELVE
New York City

The unfulfilled promise of sex after Liam left made Tillie restless and prowly. The work she should have done earlier was lost to the strange fugue state, for lack of a better description. She didn't know what else to call the lost time. Her stomach twisted in worry.

The best use of her restlessness was painting. To keep herself centered, she started Spotify on the Bluetooth speakers she'd installed in the corners of the studio, then changed into painting clothes. As was her ritual, she rounded the studio, looking afresh at each of the paintings, standing in front of each at a distance to check its impact and balance while also reminding herself what she was doing.

The woman nursing a wolf cub was one of the best this round—dangerous and moody, with what one critic called her "exquisite elevated sensibility." The others, too, had a spirit to them—the owl-mermaid girl was lost at sea, navigating home by the light of the moon. One showed an old woman offering food to the fairies, and in the shadows was a girl who'd grown too large for the world of the fey, chained to a tree.

Not all were dark, though most of them had an edge, but even the dark subjects held a reverence for nurturing. It didn't take an expert to interpret her longing for her mother. The woman feeding the fairies had

Arlette's face and body, a chubby woman walking toward a fantastical barn with magical goats trailing behind.

So far, so good. She needed four more. The series felt tapped out, as if she was ready to move into the next phase of work, but needed to finish this one first.

The table in the middle of the room was scattered with the cat drawings, and she leafed through them, suddenly intrigued by the possibilities. The wise, human eyes, the long whiskers. She often painted dogs and goats and little cats, but this one was very different. Curious, she picked up a thick stick of graphite and started to sketch—

Then she remembered the weird afternoon, the lost time. Sticking AirPods in her ears, she dialed Jon. He picked up immediately. "Hey!"

"Are you busy?"

"Recuperating after the big party last night, honey." He yawned. "No surfer boy?"

"I tried. Unfortunately, Jared was here when we arrived and spoiled the mood." Picking up a gessoed canvas, she placed it on a sturdy easel. She started drawing, tethering herself to her best friend. "How did you celebrate?"

"Drinks with Alexander, and then to Train. I missed you. I wish I could cure you of those damned migraines."

"That's nice of you." She picked up a burnt sienna oil stick and drew a broad curve, a back. Made a mark for an eye.

"Are you still going to your mom's place tomorrow?"

"Yes. The Realtor is meeting me."

"Sure you don't want to wait until I can go with? I've been a little worried about you. I mean, you don't know what happened to you when you were a child. Maybe you have trauma that's just now surfacing with your mom's death."

"Liam said the same thing, and while I appreciate your worry, I really do need to get the farm on the market. I can't stand to be there without her."

"I wish I loved my mother the way you love yours."

"I wish you'd had a mother who loved you the way mine loved me."

"Yeah," he said with a sigh. "Me, too. Anyway, let's talk about happier things. Guess who I saw last night?"

Tension seeped out of her body toward the floor as Jon launched into a gossip fest. It was exactly why she'd called him, his butterfly flittering through the world of humans. His art was solid and melancholy, but you'd never guess it from his chatter.

It served to keep her grounded as she worked. Sitting at the big table, she sketched the cat, then started painting, seeing a girl on his back, his ears tufted like a lynx.

Jon slowed down, and she heard him yawn. To keep him going a little longer, she said, "Tell me about the trip to Crete."

"I'm waffling." He'd broken up with his longtime partner almost the same week Tillie and Jared had split up. They joked it must have been a deep astrological shit show, but it really had been quite a bad month. They'd done a lot of whining over the past few months, Jon more than Tillie, since she'd initiated the break in her relationship, and Jon was the one devastated. "It just won't be the same without Reggie."

"It won't be," Tillie agreed, tilting her head to check the balance of values on the painting. "But it will be a celebration of your enormous career victory."

"Who wants to go on a vacation by themselves?" He sighed. "I'm not really all that comfortable on my own. You know, childhood judgment and all that shit."

"You've had too much therapy."

"Is that even possible?"

"Maybe not." She stepped back and brushed hair out of her eyes, feeling a streak of paint mark her jaw. "I think it would be good for you, but you're the one who has to live your life, so you do you."

"Thank you," he said with some irony. "Just think about going, okay?"

"I can tell you I will, but you know as well as I do that I can't take the time right now."

"I get it." He yawned massively. "I've gotta go, honey. I can tell you're painting and want company, but I'm falling asleep."

She half smiled. "It was nice when we shared a studio."

"See? People are good!"

"You're good."

"No, you're good. Good night."

She hung up. Music played from the speakers overhead and kept the worst of the silence from squashing her, but the room was open and echoey, and right at this moment, it made her feel small. She wished to be able to call her mother, who'd stayed up well past midnight, making soaps or reading her latest tome, and always welcomed a call from Tillie. It was easy to visualize her in the cottage, dressed in her favorite long-sleeve flannel pajamas, her feet bare, the long, wiry gray hair trailing down her back.

Longing burned. Tillie wanted desperately to be able to bend down and hug her. Arlette had been very plump during the past ten years, and her hugs were like sinking into a soft blanket. Standing in her studio, paintbrush aloft, Tillie fancied that she could smell her, that she was still with her. A ghost who would not abandon her.

~

After Arlette died, Tillie spent three days clearing out the farmhouse. She'd boxed up the kitchen and the living room, given away the aging furniture, the sparse artwork. Arlette had lived mainly in the greenhouse, amid the shelves and pots, the strings of peas growing to the ceiling in the winter, the tomatoes producing even in December. Tillie couldn't even enter it at the start of her clearing frenzy. She didn't know what to do with it, how to keep things going, or even if she should.

Arlette had died of a heart attack, which seemed sudden but turned out to be something she'd known about—she'd had one before, and was being treated, but she never told Tillie a thing. She'd dispensed with a great many of her things after that first one—as ever, putting her daughter first—and there had only been books and clothes to go through, a few papers, dishes and pans and aged furniture, most of which didn't even interest thrift shops.

Liam showed up at 7:00 a.m. with two paper cups of drinks: coffee for Tillie, tea for him, judging by the dangling paper tag. "Lots of cream, right? A little sugar."

"Yes." She was touched that he'd noticed. It was an aphrodisiac to be seen.

In the car on the way up, they listened to folk songs, singing along to Joan Baez and Eva Cassidy, the Lumineers, and Paula Davies, the lesser-known artist they'd realized they both liked. "She's married to my cousin," he said.

Tillie's mouth opened. "What? That's a weird coincidence."

He shrugged. "I'm sure we'd find other connections if we kept talking. The world is smaller and stranger than we know."

"True." Tillie passed a lumbering truck. "I thought your family was in New Zealand?"

"Yeah, first generation. My mum was from Devon."

"Is that north or south? My knowledge of England is pretty limited."

"West," he said. "Far west. Looking at your paintings, I'm surprised you haven't gone. The west is magical, full of legends and lore and fairies all about."

A yearning swept through her like a brisk wind. The forest from the painting wafted over her imagination, a forest filled with enchanted and dangerous creatures. "That sounds amazing."

"You should go."

It seemed suddenly odd that she hadn't, but she had no real reason other than always choosing somewhere else. "I've always traveled for the adventure, or really, Jon does. England seems . . . less of a challenge."

"Yeah, no. Americans think they know it, but . . . England is not America."

"What do you mean?"

He shook his head. Tillie was aware of the smell of him in the small space, that note of lime. "I dunno. It's just not the same country."

"Have you been back since your gap year?"

"Oh yeah." He sipped his tea. "We've done a few gigs in London. I haven't been back to Devon since I was a kid, but I'm going this time. I'm pretty solid with my mom's BFF. She lives in this big tumbledown house and has a bunch of kids. Her husband is a veterinarian, and they always have a handful of rescue animals. A blind goat, a hobbled dog, like that."

"That's kind of cool. Another old hippie?"

"Totally."

The day was bright and sunny, though winter hadn't entirely burned away. She loved the look of the March fields, empty with that glowing promise of spring. For all her worries about going back to the farm, she felt remarkably calm. Liam's presence was very peaceful. "Do you have more workshops or whatever before you leave here?"

"Two more."

"Would you be open to me coming to listen?"

"I don't know that you'd find it all that exciting."

"Meditation isn't meant to be exciting, though, is it?"

"No." He took her free right hand. "Truth?"

"Of course."

"Do you mind if I keep that part separate for now?"

A prickle of warning rolled like a burr down her spine. "Are you hiding something?"

"One thing," he said. "But I swear, it isn't bad. It's just that it might interfere. With—" He gestured between them. "Us. This. Whatever it is."

She narrowed her eyes. "Seriously? What does that mean?"

"Nothing bad," he repeated. "Promise." His thumb moved, sizzling over the long bone of her hand as if it conducted electricity. She felt it to her gut. It was enough to make her want to stop the car and make out on the side of the road. Just so she could touch him. So he could touch her.

She glanced at him, her skin rustling. "This," she repeated, "can't be anything, though, can it." It wasn't a question. "You live halfway around the world."

"I do," he agreed. "But this isn't my imagination, is it? There's something here."

She turned her eyes to the road, away from that burning blue, the earnestness. "It's not your imagination. But I still don't know how anything can emerge. Maybe we should just be here now." She grinned at him. "Isn't that what you guys all say?"

He chuckled. "Well, I don't know about all, but *I* might have said something similar once or twice."

The drive looped through a dark forest, to the cottage where she'd grown up. She parked and sat for a moment with her hands in her lap, looking at the porch, bare now but once populated with a wide swing and pots of plants. For a few beats, she saw the other porch, the one from the painting with the big leafed plant, the cat, the two figures in turquoise.

Shake it off. Literally, she shook her shoulders.

"You okay?" Liam asked.

She nodded. "Here we are." Her mother's vast herb garden was to the left, winter barren but tidy. At the edge of the fields was the greenhouse.

"I like it," Liam said.

As they climbed out of the car, the Realtor appeared on the porch, a slim woman with hair cut in a precise line at her shoulders. She wore muted red lipstick that made Tillie wish she liked makeup more. "Hello," she said, coming down the steps to greet them. "You must be Tillie. I'm Beatrice."

She didn't look like a Beatrice, Tillie thought, but the da Vinci painting of Beatrice d'Este suddenly showed itself to her. The Realtor could be her sister. She smiled. "Hi," Tillie said. "This is my friend Liam."

Liam gave her a polite nod, his attention on the farm itself. Beatrice stared at him for the barest second too long. He didn't shake her hand, just wandered toward the side lot, where hog fencing protected the garden from deer. Rabbits often managed to find a way in and have a feast, but Arlette never got mad, just reinforced the lower levels of fencing. "They have to eat, too," she said.

Tillie was fiercely glad that it was still so early in the spring that the garden was mostly fallow. She didn't have to see what Arlette had planted last year when she was still alive, for a harvest she'd never see. She spied a line of garlic shoots, and if she got close, she'd see the asparagus patch. Of course, the perennial flowers along the porch were popping tiny green heads through the earth, primroses and daffodils, which not even deer liked to eat. In a few weeks, they'd be dazzling.

One reason Tillie wanted to get it on the market.

"Shall we take a look?" Beatrice asked.

Tillie nodded. It still seemed impossible that her mom wouldn't be there. It was a relief to open the door to empty rooms, only a few boxes of paperwork remaining, which she'd drag home with her today. "It hasn't been professionally cleaned yet," Tillie commented. "But almost everything is out."

"Do you mind if I just do a walk-through?" Beatrice asked.

"Go right ahead."

Liam waited on the porch. "You can come in if you like," Tillie said.

He shook his head. "I'm just going to wander the gardens."

"Okay."

The house wasn't huge. The living room and kitchen split the main floor, and upstairs were three bedrooms of modest size. The floors were wide-plank pine, in need of a good cleaning and resealing, but solid. Tillie walked to the window over the sink and spied Liam squatting near the potato patch. He reached down to pluck what was likely an early violet, and the light caught his hair, shimmering.

Us. This. Whatever it is.

Beatrice's boots clopped solidly on the wooden stairs, and she made notes in the kitchen. "Obviously, the appliances need updating or maybe just removal. Let the buyers figure it out."

"Okay. That's easy."

"I had a walk around the land before you got here, and it's in remarkably good condition. Your mother must have had a lot of help."

"No. She did it all herself. She said it kept her young."

"Really? I'm impressed." She flicked through her notes. "Well, the house is not quite as appealing, but it has good bones. The barn is very well maintained, and there's plenty of land for a small farm. It's not always easy to find the right buyer for a place like this, but COVID brought a lot of young families out of the city. Some of them have stayed, building organic farms of all sorts. That's who I'm thinking will be the buyer here."

"Sounds great."

"All right, let me work on some numbers and a marketing strategy, and I'll get back to you in a day or two with a contract and a plan."

Tillie loved her efficiency and lack of small talk. "Excellent."

"Thank you so much, Tillie." She shook her hand again, a solid grip she trusted. "By the way, I am really an admirer of your work."

"Oh!" Tillie was caught off guard. "I'm surprised you know it, but thank you so much."

"You're too modest. It's not like a million kids go to Fox Crossing High School. You're pretty well known around here."

"I'm so surprised." She made a mental note to make something for her. Ink and wash, perhaps. Tillie saw her as . . . a black swan? Maybe. "Thank you."

～

The remaining boxes had come from Arlette's closet. Tillie had peeked into them when she first brought them downstairs—the usual detritus of a life: photos and mementos, paper tickets from trips taken long ago, a set of keys on a ring with a scribbled address that meant nothing to her. Most of it would end up in the trash, but Tillie didn't want to toss everything out without giving it the respect of a glance.

She wondered now if she could condense most of it into one box. She took the lids off the two top boxes and gauged the weight. Easy. Gathering sheaves of ephemera from one box, she transferred it to the other. A photo fluttered away and landed on the floor.

Liam knocked. "All right to come in now?"

"Yes." She transferred another handful of bits, then swept the last few things from the bottom of the box. Yellowed newspaper was stuck to the bottom, folded so she couldn't read it, and she used a fingernail to free it.

It was the *Los Angeles Times*, dated March 12, 1989, with the headline "Firestorms Kill Four."

"The *LA Times*," Tillie said. "That's odd. I didn't know she ever lived there."

Liam squatted easily beside her. "Maybe she didn't. Maybe it's just packing material or something."

She nodded, but put it in the box anyway. She opened the third box and found it only a quarter full. More detritus—an old map of what might be a park, a ticket for a ferry. Tillie looked at it more closely, seeking a destination. "Huh. LA to Catalina, June 8, 1989."

"Or maybe she *did* live there," he said reasonably.

Arlette had never spoken of her life before Tillie was born, not in any real way. Vague sketches, parents who died when she was young, making her own way in the hippie days, living on communes, trading her baking and cooking skills for a roof overhead. Of Tillie's father, she said only that many of them slept together at the farm where she lived—she didn't know which of the men were her dad, and it didn't matter. Arlette left when she was pregnant and went to the city to make money to raise her baby.

"When she said 'the city,' I always thought she meant New York. Maybe it was LA," Tillie said, and a sense of lostness filled her chest cavity. The bits of paper, the ancient mementos, made Arlette's life seem somehow lonely. "I wish I knew more about her life."

His fingers were laced together, hanging between his knees as he balanced on his heels. A shaft of light made his eyes look translucent. He waited.

"That's it," she said. "I just wish I knew more."

"Was she very private?"

"She was. But also . . ." Tillie frowned. "She had some . . . mental issues. Nothing particularly that interfered with her life or raising me, but she was reclusive, for sure. I sometimes wonder if she was abused as a child or something like that."

His brows pulled down ever so slightly. "Could it have something to do with the illness? Or was it an injury? That you can't remember?"

"Maybe." She shook her head. "Anyway, that's all a question for another day." She slapped the cardboard lid down on the box, and it suddenly gave way, two corners splitting. "Whoa," she said, staggering to her feet. "That made it a little bit heavy."

"Do you want some help?" He mocked a muscleman pose and gave a grunt.

"Yes." She smiled. "Please."

As he lifted the box, he said, "You've dropped something there."

It was the photo that had fluttered out. Tillie swept it up, turning it over to see a little girl, maybe two or so, in a Teenage Mutant Ninja Turtles T-shirt, sitting beside a swimming pool in a child-size chair. *T in Santa Monica,* it said on the back.

Not a child she recognized. She tucked it back into the box.

He carried it to the car, and she opened the trunk, shoving aside a blanket and a pile of junk she'd been meaning to get rid of. His forearms corded with appealing muscle, so he must not spend *all* his time in meditation. "How'd you get these muscles, Superman?" she asked.

He dropped the box in the trunk. "Yoga, actually."

"Really." Eyeing his arms, she wondered if the rest of him was that solid. She hoped she'd have a chance to find out. "I still want to sketch you."

"Better hurry. I'm leaving Saturday."

It gave her a pang, which she shoved away. "Come on. I know a place in the village you will love."

CHAPTER THIRTEEN

The Gentle Earth Eatery had been a fixture in the village as long as Tillie could remember. A gigantic geranium bloomed in the plate glass window, so huge it looked like it grew up through the floor, but it wasn't dusty or shedding. Someone took good care of it so it bloomed red and pink all year.

A bell rang over the door as she pulled it open, and the fragrance slammed her hard—cinnamon tea, baking bread, herbs, and spices. She halted so quickly that Liam bumped into her, his hands falling on her shoulders.

"Ah, this is the real thing, ain't it?"

"Yep." She inhaled deeply. "I feel like the scent alone could heal me."

The White girl behind the counter wore dreadlocks beneath a yellow-and-pink bandanna. Her nose was pierced between the nostrils, like a bull. "Hey, y'all, welcome. You can sit anywhere."

They slid into a booth by the window, and she brought menus over. Her arms were wound with flower-and-plant watercolor tattoos, and Tillie imagined her as the summer version of Gaia. "Special today is avocado and sprouts on sunflower bread with carrot-coconut soup for eight dollars. I'll give you some time to look at the menu."

"Mm, sunflower bread," Tillie said. "Bring us some iced tea, please."

Liam smiled, raising a brow.

"Trust me."

She headed for the kitchen.

"The sunflower bread is from my mother's recipe," she said quietly. "It was one of her best breads, and they begged for it."

"I was already set on the special, but now I'm really in, unless there's something better I should try."

She ran her eyes down the menu, thinking of her favorites over the years—the apple pancakes, the grilled "cheez," the seitan bacon. "My mother always liked a bean burger with guacamole, but I'm with you on the soup and sandwich."

The server returned with two tall glasses of iced tea. It was a deep reddish-brown color, even with the ice. "Ready to order?"

"I'm going with the special," Liam said.

"Cool." She smiled at him. "Are you Australian?"

"Close. Kiwi."

"Oh yeah? Whereabouts? My friend and I are going there next summer."

"You'll love it. Hiking?"

"Some. Camping. I want to sleep on the beach at Stewart Island. Supposed to be able to see the stars like nowhere else."

"Brilliant." He gestured toward Tillie. "What do you want, Tillie?"

She smiled. Charm surrounded him like an iridescent aura. She'd been slammed by it herself. "Same," she said. "Thank you."

"Of course." She smiled at them, but more at Liam, and clapped the menus together.

"Like a bee to nectar," Tillie drawled.

He gave her a half smile, acknowledging but not expanding.

She narrowed her eyes. "That happens to you all the time, doesn't it?"

"Sometimes. Does it bother you?"

"No," she answered, which was kind of a mistruth. "Well, I mean, I did it, too."

"The difference," he said quietly, holding her gaze and reaching for her hand, "is that I did it to you first."

"Oh." Light skated over the right side of him, illuminating the cheekbone, the straight nose, the edges of his lashes, the side of his throat. She itched to draw him, right now, in this moment. "Don't move." She pawed through her bag and came up with a Micron pen. Not her favorite, but it would do. She also brought out an Altoids tin of watercolors and a water-filled brush.

Luckily, the restaurant hadn't yet done away with paper place mats, so she flipped hers over to the white side and started to draw. Again, it was a way to channel the sexual energy building in her body, as well as a way to capture his likeness for her future self. There was something so grounding about really looking at a thing, without judgment pro or con.

"When did you start drawing?" he asked, watching.

"I don't remember," she said. "As long as I've been alive, I've been drawing."

"Cool."

His head was quite oval, the hair thick but a fine texture, all the colors of wheat. The brow was high, and maybe one day he'd lose that beautiful hair, but who would care? His eyes were not large, but the color—so bright and blue—made them more powerful. She studied the shapes, paused, studied the light, the angle of his eyebrows. His nose was Roman straight, his mouth—

Her skin whispered. Maybe she would have to skim over his mouth, giving the shape of upper lip, the swell of the lower one, without dwelling too much.

"So fast," he said.

"Lots of practice." She added a few defining details, the edge of his collar, an earlobe, and opened the watercolor box. "You can move now."

"That's a clever little thing."

"Yeah, I always carry it. Just in case." She plucked off the lid of the water brush and squeezed a few drops into each of the hard colors. While they soaked in, she picked up her tea and pointed to his. "You should taste that."

"Not a fan of iced tea, love. That's an American thing. We all think you're mad."

"Try it."

He picked up the glass and took a small sip, and his face changed. She drank deeply. The tea was the source of the cinnamon smell. It was orangey and very spicy and wildly refreshing. "They make it in-house."

"I stand corrected. I like it. A lot."

"You should always try the house specialties," she said, and dipped her brush. "I'm sure you've learned that over the years."

"Not really. I'm picky."

She laughed. "Really?"

He shrugged. "Yeah."

With easy swaths, she added color to the sketch, painting shadow on one side, highlights on the other, a little quinacridone magenta for his mouth, cerulean blue for his eyes.

"Oh my God," the server said, approaching the table with plates of food. "That's so good!"

Tillie smiled and moved the drawing aside to make room for the plates. The soup was steaming, the bread stuffed with crisp sprouts and perfect avocado. When her hands were free, Tillie gave the server the little watercolor. "It's yours."

"No way!" She gazed at it. "Will you sign it?"

"Sure." Tillie scrawled her painterly name with a cat face up the side.

And paused. The cat had been part of her signature for years, and now she couldn't remember why.

Shaking her head, she gave it back to the server.

"And you?" the girl asked Liam. "Will you sign it, too?"

"Nah," he said with a grin. "It's her work, not mine."

She was disappointed but so happy to have the sketch that she hugged it to her chest. "Thank you! Enjoy your meal!"

For a few minutes, they dug into the food. Quiet Indian ragas played on the overhead speakers. In the kitchen, the server and a male cook talked, but their words were an indistinguishable roll of sound. Tillie relished the flavors of the sandwich, thinking of her mother and the many, many times they'd come here together. It occurred to her that this would likely be the last time she'd ever visit. The thought gave her a sharp sense of loss.

It stung enough that she set down her sandwich and took a big gulp of tea, trying to cool the threatening tears. To distract herself, she asked, "What kind of meditation do you lead?"

"Pretty classic mindful meditation. Buddhist roots. Do you practice?"

"No. I mean, sometimes when I go to yoga or something, but not regularly." The pinch in her midchest eased. "Did you grow up with it?"

"Nah. I had a bit of a rocky period and landed in India in my twenties." He wiped his fingers on a napkin. "To be honest, it wasn't pretty. Strung out, exhausted, brokenhearted—all of it. I visited Varanasi and the Ganges." He pronounced it *Ganga*. "It changed things."

She imagined him, grimy and weary, sitting on the banks of the famous river. "The Mother River, right? Isn't that what they call it?"

"Right. It wasn't the river so much as the people. Like all these people believe in something so much that they sometimes walk hundreds of miles on bare feet. They make sacrifices to honor their pilgrimage." He held her gaze, and she felt the squishy discomfort of a nonspiritual person, afraid he would—what? Proselytize?

Instead, he said with a half smile, "It was humbling, and I realized I'd been a spoiled little shit."

It made her laugh. "That moment of growing up."

"Yeah. So I started wandering with a purpose, just to explore what I thought about. I mean, there are a lot of sacred sites all over the country, so I made my way to some of them—the Bodhi Tree and the spring of the Ganges. I read a ton. I spent some time in a monastery, learning to meditate, and since women had been a problem for me, I was celibate for two years."

"What does that mean? That women were a problem?"

A twitch of his shoulders. "I was given to falling in and out of love a little too much."

Tillie's body reacted to this, that it was easy for him to fall in love—and out. He wasn't quite meeting her eyes. An irritable adult in her mind argued, *For God's sake, it's not like it's going to be anything—he lives on the other side of the world.*

She picked up her sandwich. "So then what?"

"I went back home and made things right with my family and started trying to figure out where I fit. One of my mentors nudged me toward this work, teaching, and it's been good."

"Hmm." She realized she was enjoying the pleasure of the sandwich and the tea and the sight of his face across the table in equal parts. Something tense let go, but she couldn't really think of what to say to all that earnestness.

"It makes you uncomfortable," he said.

"Maybe." She shook her head, wiped avocado from her fingers. "Religion, spirituality, all of it feels a little . . . silly, I guess."

"And yet you paint fairies and magical beings."

She laughed. "So I do."

His slow smile was everything.

"Do you have time this afternoon for me to sketch you?" she asked.

He held her gaze. "I do."

"Let's get back to the city, then."

CHAPTER FOURTEEN

Her car was not huge. Liam sat right next to her, smelling of cinnamon from the tea. As the miles sailed by, she sang along with the music unselfconsciously, and he told stories of his travels, making her laugh but also offering moments of struggle. She told stories about hers. The unspoken agreement about what would transpire when they got back to her apartment hummed below everything, breathed in the spare touch he brushed over her hand on the gearshift, whispered in the sound of his voice. Tillie hummed with anticipation, feeling suspended in some magic spell he'd cast with his lively voice, his big hands.

When they pulled into the parking garage, she turned off the car.

"Finally," he said, and leaned in to kiss her. They were sweaty and disheveled in five minutes.

She surfaced, swallowed, smoothed his hair. "Let's go."

"I'll get the box for you."

"You don't have to. I'll have Jon help me."

"Jon, the artist at the show?" He sounded dubious.

Jon was many things, but it was true that strong wasn't one of them. "Okay. I just don't want you to think I'm using you as a pack mule."

"You can use me," he said, and kissed her again before he got out.

It was only two blocks to the apartment, but even Superman was huffing a bit by the time they got there.

And Jared was on the steps.

"Oh, for God's sake!" Tillie cried. "You have to stop this. I'm going to file a restraining order."

"I just want to talk to you!" he said. Again, he'd been drinking. Again, he looked like shit, and as a person who had loved him, she was sad for his pain, even if she was the one who caused it.

She took a breath. "I will talk to you tomorrow, okay? Go home, get some rest, and I will call you."

He stared at her, his red-rimmed eyes daring to hope. "Promise?"

"Yes," she said. "I promise. Now, let me call you a cab, and you can go home."

Standing a little unsteadily, he looked at Liam. "Are you a couple?"

Tillie glanced over her shoulder.

Liam said simply, "I'm sorry, Jared, but we are."

Jared nodded sadly and came down the steps, standing beside Tillie like a child while she hailed a cab. She poured him into it and gave the driver his address. "Promise you'll call," Jared said, grabbing her hand.

"I promise."

As the cab drove away, Tillie wondered if this would interfere again. But Liam, having set the box on the stoop, turned to her. "Was that all right?"

"Yes. Very."

"Good." He picked up the box. "Lead the way."

They paused on the landing halfway up; then Tillie was opening the door, holding it open. He tripped on the threshold ever so slightly, and the loose top of the box tumbled off, followed by a cascade of papers and photos and detritus spilling out. "Damn," he said.

Tillie pushed the papers aside with her foot. "I don't care."

Neither did he. In minutes, they were naked in her bed, kissing as if there would be a war tomorrow, their bodies hot and sliding, their hands exploring. Nothing else mattered but this overwhelming connection. Tillie felt enchanted, narcotically lost in the taste of him, the feel of his skin under her hands. He touched her as if he'd already memorized the manual to her body, and she discovered that he responded to her the same way, as if they were made to fit together. She cried out so long that she should have been embarrassed, but it didn't matter because he joined her, and they kissed, and kissed again, as if the act itself was an incantation, and they were now woven together, a single length of fabric.

She didn't think about how it would feel to tear that fabric apart.

$\sim$

"Do you want a glass of water?" she asked. It was late afternoon, and cloudy skies muted the light in the room.

"Not if you have to get up to get it." His head was tucked against her neck, his hand draped over her ribs. The duvet had fallen off the bed, as they nearly had more than once, and it was getting cold, but she hadn't wanted to move.

"I'm dying of thirst, though."

"Drink from my lips, my lady," he said, lifting up on one elbow to kiss her, and laughed. "I'll go."

"I have to pee, anyway." She looked for something to drape around her nakedness, but there was nothing close by, and honestly, she didn't feel self-conscious in the least. She swung her hips as she padded toward the bathroom, glancing over her shoulder to make sure he was watching. He was propped up on one elbow, appreciative.

Peeing away a UTI from so much sex, she washed her hands and face and tender vagina. In the mirror, her face was flushed, her hair tousled, and she thought she looked beautiful. Liam made it so.

He was on his back when she came out, golden and taut. Again, she glimpsed the Renaissance angel she'd first imagined when she saw him for the first time at the gallery. He held out an arm. "Come back."

"In a minute." She grabbed a long sweater off a hook for warmth, then poured two big glasses of water from the pitcher in the fridge. On the way back, she tucked a sketchbook and a box of charcoals under her arms and carried it all back to bed.

"Are you freezing?" she asked. "I can turn on a space heater."

"I'm all right."

"Can I sketch you? Like this?"

A tiny smile quirked the edge of his mouth. "Like one of your French girls?"

She tilted her head, confused.

"You've never seen *Titanic*?"

"Afraid not."

"That's just sad," he said. "We're going to watch it together."

"If you say so."

He rolled on his side, head in the crook of his palm. "Tell me what to do."

"Just like that," she said, already sketching. The newsprint was made for fast sketches. She did a handful of gesture drawings, capturing the length of his legs and the width of his thighs, his rectangular torso and the rounds of his shoulders. She drew quickly, looking without emotion or judgment, only trying to see what shapes were really there. After a few minutes, she switched to closer studies. His ribs, wound with tattooed script. *Set your life on fire. Seek those who fan your flames*, one read. And another, *Let yourself be silently drawn by the strange pull of what you love. It will not lead you astray.* She touched the second one. "That's how I feel about painting."

She captured the shape of his head, which made her think so much of an angel that she gave the suggestion of a halo, then sketched his knees and elbows, his hips and genitals, and then his beautiful, beautiful face.

Only then did she realize that she didn't see an animal.

"What is it?" He touched her leg. "You look stricken."

"It's just kind of weird." The charcoal was in her hand, paper at the ready, so she couldn't help but keep sketching—the angles of his ear, the shape of his fingernails. "I don't draw humans as humans. I always see them as animals."

"Like what kind of animals?"

"Everything." She gestured toward the easels and the paintings in shadow. "Wolves, badgers. Today, the Realtor made me think of a black swan, and the server was a fawn."

"Oh, that's quite good. But?"

She showed him the drawing. "I see you as an angel."

He laughed. "I think I've properly demonstrated that I'm mortal."

"Indeed." She shook her head. "It doesn't matter. It's just odd that I don't see an animal."

"I think I'm kind of sad about that, honestly."

She set the drawing materials aside. "Don't be." She pulled the duvet over them, cold in the gathering dark.

It felt completely natural to fall asleep with him. In some part of her brain, she knew that the whole thing was going to look really foolish in some future time, but this was now. She was enchanted, and she didn't care.

~

After such a long day, she fell into a deep sleep. At some point, the cat arrived and circled her feet, meowing not like a cat but a girl pretending to be a cat, and then he turned into a girl with big blue eyes and a laughing mouth. Tillie recognized her own face as they ran into a forest, dashing between trees. A dog romped along beside them, and they were all laughing and running, running and laughing, and then abruptly, Tillie tripped and fell, and the fall was long, falling and falling and falling—

Before she hit the ground, she startled herself awake.

Basking in the comfortable familiarity of her own bed, with the delicious surprise of a naked man next to her, his leg against hers, his hand flung over her hip. In the darkness, she saw that he was utterly asleep, like a child, and was pierced clear through.

In the reassurance of his company, she curled into her pillow, tucking her body closer to his, and fell back to sleep. This time, there were no dreams.

~

A tickle brushed her nose. She swiped at it, but it came back. She dreamed it was a butterfly and reached for the iridescent colors. A girl was with her, the cat girl, and she said, "Let's go back to the woods!"

A soft voice penetrated the dream. "Tillie. Til-lie."

At last, she surfaced, blinking at the light pouring into the studio. Liam was leaning on his elbow next to her, and she saw that he was freshly showered, and dressed. "Oh no! Are you leaving already? You should have woken me up. I would have made you some breakfast."

His smile was gentle as he swept hair off her forehead. "Nah. You were sound asleep, and it's early yet. I have a thing and have to get back to the hotel, but you don't have to see me out. I just wanted to say goodbye."

She reached up and pulled him into her, kissing him, reveling in the crisp cotton under her bare arms. He met the kiss; then her stomach growled. Loudly.

"That's romantic." She laughed.

"Everything about you is romantic."

"Don't get too corny, or I won't believe a word you say."

The lines along his eyes crinkled. "All right, you crass bitch."

"Maybe something in between."

He touched her cheek. "Can I come back tonight?"

She nodded. "Text me."

"It'll be around late afternoon. What if I take you somewhere fancy for dinner?"

"I'm down with that."

"Good." He glanced at his watch, stood. "Is there a luxurious vegetarian you like?"

"Dude. It's New York City. Of course there is."

He leaned in and kissed her forehead. "Make a reservation for after six, and I'll meet you back here."

"Okay." She sat up to watch him go. At the door, he blew her a kiss, and she laughed, but as the door closed, she thought, *How the hell did this magic fall into my life?*

"Get real," she told herself, getting up to start the day. It wasn't magic. It wasn't some fairy tale. He was leaving in two days, and she would never see him again. Passions born during trips abroad never lasted.

But she could enjoy it for now.

CHAPTER FIFTEEN

Wulfecombe

To help bring in the funds it took to keep the house running, Clare had started a small farm. The learning curve had been tremendous. She'd been raised in town and didn't know a turnip from a cabbage, but the land had always been rich in these fields, and it made sense to at least try to fund the repairs by reviving the farm.

The first years, she'd been wretchedly unsuccessful. The cabbages went in too late and bolted before they matured; she'd lost all the chickens to a raid by a fox, then faced one of the hottest summers in a decade, which burned all but the sturdiest plants. She'd had a marvelous crop of tomatoes, however, and she'd been lucky to grow some heirlooms that set them apart, so she sold those gold, deep-red, and enormous purple-black-red varieties to a handful of restaurants.

It wasn't enough to even cover the cost of the garden, but it gave her hope. Before the next season, she and seven-year-old Sage had learned some carpentry skills and built a better shelter for the chickens, then made charts of when to plant what and how to rotate them for the highest number of yields. With the profits, she built two long greenhouses and put peas in early, and started other green crops for the restaurants, providing them with a wide array of salad greens for their high-end dishes.

It was never her main source of income, but she had found healing and hope in digging, in tending the little flock of hens, in fresh air and hard work. It saved her sanity at a time when life had seemed very dark indeed.

This morning, she collected a basket of peas, saving the best for Sage and keeping the rest for the gathering on Sunday. A pale-colored cat wandered through the aisles, seeking her attention, and she bent down to give him a pat. "You're looking pleased with yourself," she said. "Been out policing the mice?"

He meowed, twirling his tail about her knee. His eyes were blue and ever so slightly crossed, the legacy of a bunch of cats in the area. She'd had several of his line over the years. In fact, she'd met Levi when one of them had developed an abscessed paw, and Sage couldn't stop wailing over him. Levi didn't ordinarily bother much with house pets, but he'd taken pity on the sorrowful little girl, drained the abscess, and given the cat an antibiotic. The next day, he came around asking Clare if she wanted to go for a tea.

A figure appeared at the doorway. Sage, holding one hand over her belly as if to keep her baby safe, said breathlessly, "I had nightmares about the bones. The ones they found at the new estate."

Clare straightened. "I heard they think it was a teenager."

"I dreamed it was an angel."

An old, old pain rustled, and Clare knew enough to tamp it down before it got up and started stomping through her life. With more calm than she felt, she crossed the space between them and slid an arm around her daughter's shoulders. "They're doing all the tests to find out who it is. It might be a Roman or a Viking or some medieval milkmaid. Let's just wait and see, shall we?"

Sage sank hard into her mother's embrace, clinging as if a storm had blown up and the winds would take her with it, tear her away.

Clare held her tight. "It's all right. It's going to be okay."

CHAPTER SIXTEEN

Although she wanted to lie around and moon about Liam, Tillie had a show to finish. To get herself into the right mindset, she set a primed canvas on one of the big worktables under the north skylight and layered it with a glaze of darkest ultramarine mixed with just a tinge of phthalo green, then left it to rest while she showered. Starting the day as she meant to continue had been her practice for a decade.

After the shower, she made herself a smoothie of slightly wilted spinach and frozen strawberries, along with a cup of coffee, and carried them to the easel. Her sketch of the cat with a girl on his back was there, and she suddenly remembered the girl in her dream, in the woods. Letting it surface, she used a soft focus on the painting, allowing trees into the background, a shaft of sunlight. The girl was not quite right, and she tilted her head, took a sip of smoothie, and picked up a black oil stick. Over the flying brown hair, she drew tendrils of black. Better. She smiled.

It suddenly occurred to her that the girl was Tillie's imaginary friend, Sunny. Of course.

Her phone buzzed. Jon. "Hey, what's up?"

"You need to call your boy. He's blowing up my phone."

"My boy?"

"Jared."

"Oh, shit. I forgot I told him I'd call him. Sorry, I'll do it right now."

"Why did you open that door, baby? You're just stringing him along."

"That is *so* not fair!" she snapped. "He has been texting me constantly, and when I blocked him, he showed up *twice* on my stoop. I'm trying to be kind, but he's making it pretty hard."

"I'm sorry. I take it back. Just call him so I can get some sleep."

Something in his voice was a little . . . off. "You okay, dude?"

"I'm good. Just want to sleep some more."

"All right. I'll call you later."

For a moment, she stood in the midst of her paintings, thinking. Dropping the oil stick in the cart where it lived, she held her phone next to her chest and paced through the room, end to end, thinking about what to say, how to . . . ease his acceptance. Nothing came. But to honor her promises, to both Jon and to Jared, she unblocked him and dialed.

He picked up on the first ring. "Tillie?"

"Yes. Are you in your right mind this morning?"

"Hungover," he said with a hint of ruefulness. "Which is to be expected. Look, I'm sorry I keep playing the same record over and over."

This was a surprise. "Yeah, it's not that much fun for me."

Silence. "I just don't know how to let you go."

Tillie started pacing, anxiety rising at the pain in his voice. "I know," she said, and sighed. "And I don't know how to help you. But we are not together anymore, and we aren't getting back together. I would like it if we could be friends someday, but that's not right now."

"I hear you."

She stopped. "Do you?"

"Yes. I've already called a therapist, and he'll see me this afternoon."

"Good."

"Just . . . don't block me, Tillie. I can't stand it."

For a moment, she stared up at the rectangular windows showing her a cloudy sky. "Okay, but if you text me, I'm going to block you again."

"Fair."

"And if you show up on my doorstep again, I will get a restraining order."

"What? That's a little extreme."

"No, it isn't. I'm done with this."

"Fine." He was much less conciliatory. "I just wanted to talk."

"About what?"

He paused. "I don't know. Just—"

"No more talking. We're done." She paused. "I am sorry. I didn't mean to hurt you."

She hung up.

A wild energy swelled through her body, anxiety and anger and weariness with the situation. She threw the phone on the couch and, fueled by too much emotional energy, stomped toward the pile of papers by the front door, still lying where it fell when Liam brought it in. She started scraping them up, dumping them back into the box. A flash of Liam's mouth came to her, his hands on her body as they left the mess yesterday and twined themselves together. Her skin rippled. If she hadn't let Jared go when she had, this whole thing would not have been possible. What a relief!

Live for today, she thought, and scraped the last few papers into a stack. One had sailed all the way over to the wall, and she walked over to pick it up, turning it over to organize it with the others.

The words on the paper penetrated her emotional storm. A chill wound through her body.

It was a death certificate, dated March 9, 1989. For Matilda Magdalene Morrisey, age three.

Matilda. *Tillie.*

Her skin rippled, cold then very hot, and a buzzing filled her ears. This death certificate was for *her.*

CHAPTER SEVENTEEN
New York City

Tillie stared at the death certificate in blank horror, then spread her hands out in front of her, heart racing. Wildly, she thought of *The Sixth Sense*. Maybe she was dead and just didn't know it?

Don't be an idiot.

She was very much alive, sitting on the battered wooden planks of her loft floor. The clouds of earlier had cleared, and bars of sunlight fell on her thighs. A scent of coffee mixed with gesso perfumed the air.

She was alive.

And yet, this death certificate had her exact name: Matilda Magdalene Morrisey. Not exactly *Jane Smith*.

Who was she? And if it wasn't her, then who was this Tillie?

Anxiety invaded her body, making her heart race, blurring the edges of her vision. She leaped to her feet to pace, reminding herself to breathe in, breathe out.

In, out.

She rounded the room, end to end, breathing, trying to calm the anxiety she felt.

She looked at the paper in her hand. Matilda Magdalena Morrisey. Died age three.

She wished she could call Jon, but he'd clearly been in sleep mode.

In the meantime, there was Google. She sat down at the laptop set up on her kitchen table, called up the search engine, and typed in the name. Her own name. The name of this child who'd died.

And there, on the first page, was an obituary from the *Los Angeles Times*, dated March 12, 1989. It featured the same photo of the little girl that was in her mother's things. A chill ran down her spine.

Matilda Magdalene Morrisey, age three, died on March 9, a victim of the Valencia firestorm. She was survived by her mother, Arlette Morrisey.

Arlette was Tillie's mother.

Tillie stared at the article for long moments, her hands shaking. She had to rub them against her thighs, trying to calm herself. "Mom!" she said aloud. "What the hell?"

She ran a search for *Valencia firestorm* and found that it had blasted through a canyon in Los Angeles in 1989. It had started in a nearby open area and, fueled by Santa Ana winds, roared through a small residential area, burning so hot and fast that it killed four people, two seniors, a young mother, and Tillie's namesake. They couldn't get out in time. Three people huddled in swimming pools. Most of the other residents were at work or school and returned to the ashes of their homes.

Horrific. The black-and-white photos showed the now-familiar moonscape left by devouring fires.

Tillie thought urgently of her imaginary friend, who'd kept Tillie company throughout her lonely childhood. Could this be her? A sister who died? A shivery sense of loss moved through her, and unconsciously, she reached for the scar on her head, where her hair grew white. Was this fire the trauma that marked her? Was it the thing she couldn't remember?

Filled with a tangle of emotions, she shoved away from the computer and stood, pacing away to the far end of the studio, then back to the kitchen for fresh coffee.

While the water boiled for the French press, she headed for the table in the studio and looked at the girl riding the cat. Her black and brown hair, her smile and exuberance, arms up in joy. The photo in her mother's things was in black and white, but this could be her.

Maybe.

What she did know was that she'd long had an imaginary friend who had been very real to her. Her name was Sunny, and they had a secret language so adults could not understand them.

The kettle whistled, and she headed back to the kitchen, aware of a thread of genuine panic winding through her lungs. She poured hot water into the press. Across the room, the box stood open, yawning. More answers were there, she suspected, but how could she reach her hands into a cavern of dragons?

None of this made sense. How had Arlette survived when this child died? And if the girl was Tillie's sister, where was Tillie at the time?

Why did Arlette call Tillie by her sister's name? What point was there to that?

And why hadn't Arlette ever told her about living in Los Angeles? About the child she lost so tragically?

Electrifyingly, she thought, *Do I have other family?*

Her childhood had been deeply lonely—just Tillie and her mother at the farm, the animals, and nature, all good company but no substitute for friends or family. She'd read novels filled with sibling sets and cousins swarming, aunts and uncles and grandmothers, friendly neighbors who dropped by for tea, and ached for them.

What if she did have family somewhere? How could she find out?

She thought suddenly of the painting at the gallery. Could it be that it reminded her of something from that time? If she could talk to the artist, maybe it would help jog something.

The panic started to grow, and abruptly, she donned her apron and her gloves and turned toward painting. It was the only thing that would keep her sane today.

Putting music on the speakers, she forced herself to leave the cat painting alone and instead addressed finishing one she was very fond of, which would go in the show. It was a fairy-tale rendering of Arlette as a wise woman hen, her long hair depicted in gray-and-brown feathers, her face beaked with Arlette's bright eyes. A raccoon and a rabbit sat at her feet. In the tree branch overhead was an owl. Tillie added very tiny details that forced her brain to focus—the nearly invisible black line along the owl's feathers, brushstrokes to thicken the raccoon's fur, layers to her mother's feathers.

But while it was helpful, it wasn't as therapeutic as she'd hoped. She kept thinking about her mother having an entirely different life she'd never told Tillie about. A life with a child who had her same name.

Why? Why hide this?

The image of the cat walked across her imagination, inserting itself insistently between her eyes and the painting. Walking beneath a gigantic leaf, and Tillie following behind, hiding in the shadows as the feet of another child ran past. She held the cat close and giggled—

She blinked.

The painting before her was entirely transformed. "No!" Tillie wailed. "No!"

The rendition of her mother as a hen was now dark and menacing, her hands turned to claws, her hair in black raven wings, her soft figure carved into the wasp shape of a young woman, bosom and bottom divided by a tiny, tiny waist.

Tillie stared, unable to fathom what the hell she had done. She'd worked on this painting for months, and now, it was a completely different thing. She wanted to cry. She wanted to fall down and howl. She wanted to—

Picking up her phone with a shaking hand, she called Jon. Voice mail picked up, and she texted: Something is going on with my brain, and I'm scared. Call me.

The phone rang immediately. "What's up, baby?"

In a wavering voice, she told him about the painting, about the fugue state in which she painted without remembering anything, and she couldn't help a little catch in her voice. "There's more, but I want to tell you in person. I'm really scared. Can you come over?"

"Give me twenty minutes."

"Thank you."

CHAPTER EIGHTEEN

While Tillie waited for Jon, she paced, wishing that she smoked so she'd have something to do. She'd smoked briefly in her early twenties to gain an aura of hipness she sorely lacked, but gave it up soon after. Instead, she rounded the studio: the living areas, the kitchen, one after the other, touching this canvas and that, stopping to look at the series to make sure she hadn't altered any of the others. Evidently, her alternate self only wanted to ruin her favorite. Whenever she passed it, she wanted to wail. It had been so perfect! A tribute to her mother!

She could paint it again, but it felt sullied now.

When Jon arrived, he was carrying Chinese takeout and bottles of good root beer. "I was fairly sure you hadn't eaten," he said.

"Wait." She realized the sky was full-on twilight. "What time is it?"

"Just after five. But I'm going to bet you haven't eaten since yesterday."

"True." She thought of Liam. Was he still coming over? She hadn't seen anything from him on her phone. A crest of disappointment rose, crashed into the confusion she felt over everything else, dissipated. Really, didn't she have enough going on without worrying about a guy?

Jon dropped the bag on her counter. "Show me the painting."

She gestured toward it. From this distance, she could see it wasn't objectively ruined. The dark bird was quite interesting, and details marked her as Tillie's creation—the jeweled tones in her eyes and rings, the sumptuous fabrics, the hint of elf in her ears.

"This is the painting of your mom?" He moved closer. "How did you do this in a day?"

"I don't know." Gooseflesh broke on her arms. "I don't remember it."

"It's really gorgeous work." He leaned in, looking at the brush-strokes, and then smiled. "Hey, I like the cat."

She hadn't even noticed it, but there it was, the white-and-tan-striped cat in the background. It hid beneath the leaves that had been trans-formed from roses to the enormous rhubarb leaves from the painting at the gallery.

Tears pricked her eyes, rising in response to an emotion she couldn't even identify.

Next to the cat was the child who had been tied up, too big for the land of the fey, now an ordinary-size girl, sitting cross-legged, hiding under the leaves.

She swallowed. "What is going on?"

Although he presented a frivolous front to the world, Jon was quite solid in practice. "Let's sit down. Tell me everything."

She grabbed the sheaf of papers she'd found that morning and shoved them toward him. "This is the other thing."

He sat on the couch, head bent over the death certificate. "I don't understand."

"Me, either." She sank down beside him. "I'm obviously not dead, though I did consider the *Sixth Sense* possibility for a minute."

He grinned. "You're definitely not dead."

"But what is this, then? I had a sister? Why did my mother give me the same name?"

He shook his head and looked at the certificate again. "It's really strange. Did you know she lived in LA?"

"No. I knew we'd lived in New Hampshire, because that's what my birth certificate said when I had to get a new passport." She frowned, recalling. "Remember, I applied so we could do our tour, and I had the expired passport but not the birth certificate. It took a couple of weeks to get it all straightened out."

"Yeah! We were freaking out because we were afraid it wouldn't get here in time."

Tillie nodded. "But nothing about LA."

He looked grave. "Maybe the episode was your brain trying to get you to remember something."

Something dark wiggled in her gut. "I'm scared."

"I get it." He straightened. "Did you look up the story online?"

"Yeah. It's all true. Nothing else to go on, though. The firestorm killed four people, one being Matilda. Who I think"—she stood, grabbed the photo of the child from the top of the box, and handed it to him—"is this little girl. Same picture."

"So sad," he said. "What a cutie."

Tillie folded her hands in her lap, as if she could make sense of things by creating order in her body.

"I'm not getting the timeline here," Jon said. "You saw the death certificate and the other articles, and looked them up, and then you started painting?"

"Yeah. I was trying to get out of my head."

"And then what? Blacked out?"

"Kind of? I don't know. It's not like passing out. I . . ." She couldn't sit, and stood up to pace again. On the table were the original sketches of the cat. "It happened a couple of days ago, too. I drew this cat, over and over."

His face showed no expression as he leafed through the group of drawings, looked at the dark rendition of Tillie's mother. "Same cat."

"Yeah."

"But what happened, exactly?"

"I started painting, and then when I came back to myself, I had done all this work and had no memory of it."

His soft dark eyes were sober. "Do you think you might be having an emotional breakdown, maybe over your mom's death? You did take it pretty hard."

"I don't know!" she said with exasperation. "Not really. I took it hard because I loved her, and she was my mom, and I'm going to miss her terribly. That feels normal, and she died five months ago. This just started."

"What triggered it?"

She sank down beside him. "That weird painting at your show."

"Weird painting? One of mine?"

"No, no. It's in another part of the gallery, in the back. Did I not tell you about it?"

He frowned. "Not that I know of."

"Sorry." She told him the whole story, seeing the painting, feeling so weird, getting the aura, meeting Liam. "And then I got a migraine that night and just went to bed. I thought that all the weirdness was the headache."

He'd been around her long enough to understand how her migraines worked. She was luckily not a person who often suffered for days on end, but they could be intense while they lasted. "What did Liam do that night?"

"He got me into bed and slept on the couch."

"Seriously?" His eyebrows rose.

"Right?" She shook her head.

"So you haven't slept with him yet?"

"Oh, he came with me to my mom's farm yesterday and . . . well." She shrugged. "He stayed last night."

He tilted his head ever so slightly, like a border collie trying to make sense of something. "He went with you to your mom's place?"

"Yeah. He had some free time, and I couldn't cancel the real estate person, so he offered to drive with me."

"Huh. That's different."

"I know. I really like him. It sucks that he lives so far away."

"Mm." He took her hand. "But maybe you've got enough going on without adding in a romance."

She looked down, taking strength from his grip. "You're right. Just a fling."

"Good girl." He slapped her thigh. "C'mon. Let's eat. Everything will be better after a meal. Then we can make a plan."

~

He'd brought her favorite black pepper tofu and white rice, which she gobbled in such a rush that she realized she'd barely eaten anything in twenty-four hours. "Maybe I'm hallucinating because I'm starving."

"You never eat right when you're painting hard." He slurped drunken noodles with chopsticks and eyed the work lined up around the studio. "I know you're worried about it, but the show is shaping up really well. And I know you had something else in mind with the fairy godmother hen or whatever that was, but this is better. Dark. More emotion."

Tillie saw what he meant—the other was more sentimental, her tribute to her earth-mother mom—but she was still sad.

And scared. "What do you think is happening?" she asked in a hushed voice.

"I don't know." He measured her for a long minute. "Maybe it's past-life memories."

She rolled her eyes.

"I mean, why not?"

She shook her head. "Or maybe I'm just—losing it."

"What if it's PTSD or something, from when you were little? You don't remember the head injury that gave you the scar, so maybe it's connected to that?"

She fingered the white streak. The idea had a ring of possibility. "Maybe."

The buzzer rang, and both of them startled a little.

"I forgot! It's Liam!" She realized she was still in her messy painting clothes, and her hair was tied in a knot at her nape. "Shit!" She touched her apron, then leaped up, heart suddenly buoyant, and pressed the speaker. "Hello?"

"It's Liam."

She glanced over her shoulder as she pressed the button to let him in. Jon set his meal down on the coffee table and delicately wiped his mouth, his fingers. "You look amazing, doll. Don't worry."

It was too late to make any changes, anyway. Tillie heard his footsteps ascending the stairs and opened the door with a swell of new-lover eagerness, her entire body springing forward the instant she saw him, his beautiful face, those long limbs. He caught her in a hug, a low sound in his throat. He smelled of aftershave and his skin, and as they crushed together, their arms looping hard around the other, she was wildly glad to kiss him.

"I missed you," he whispered.

"Me, too." She held on a moment longer, then released him. "Come in. My friend Jon is here. It's been . . . a strange day." She realized, stricken, that she'd never made a reservation, and now here she was, eating. She turned toward him. "I didn't make a reservation. Jon brought takeout. Which we can share, or—"

Jon stood. "Or we can get some more." He held out his hand, which Liam accepted. "How you doing, man?"

"It's all good," Liam said, then looked between them. "Is everything all right?"

Tillie took a breath, then offered the truth. "Not really."

He paused. "Should I go?"

"No!" Tillie cried. She took his hand and brought him back to the couch. "Although you might be running away when you hear it all."

"No," he said. Rubbed her hand between his two. "Tell me."

So between them, Jon and Tillie recounted all of it—the death certificate, the weird painting.

He listened with care and quiet. Tillie found herself wanting to lean into him, let him put his arms around her. Cry, maybe. Saying it all aloud, she felt the weight of it.

"Are you willing to play with questions a bit?" he asked.

She looked at Jon. He shrugged.

"Sure," she said. "Why not?"

"Answer as fast as you can. Don't think."

She nodded.

"Who is the cat?"

"Sunny."

"Who is Sunny?"

"My imaginary friend from childhood."

"Was she a real person?"

"Maybe?"

"Why didn't your mother tell you about this history?"

"She has something to hide." A pinch twisted her heart. More quietly: "She has something to hide." She took a breath. "How am I going to find out what it is?"

"We'll figure it out," Liam said, and drew a line encompassing the three of them.

"We got you," Jon added. "Maybe you need to go back upstate and talk to some of her friends. See if anybody knows anything."

"That's a good idea."

"I'll go with. Tomorrow?" Jon said.

Tillie nodded.

"Tonight, you two do whatever. I've got plans."

"You didn't tell me that."

He kissed her cheek. "You didn't need to be alone. And now you aren't. I'll be by in the morning to pick you up. We can drive my car."

He drove a ridiculously beautiful old-school MG, on which he had done all the work.

"Yum. I'll love that."

After Jon left, Tillie realized that all she really wanted to do was take Liam directly to her bed. It might have been avoidance of the hard things she faced, but maybe it was just that he cast a spell over her whenever he arrived. "How hungry are you?"

115

His smile was slow. "Depends on the menu."

She wondered if she needed a shower after the long day at work, but he was already standing and taking her hand, and they stood by the bed in a bar of fading light and took off their clothes. She took her time, tracing the lines of poetry tattooed around his ribs, the tai chi symbol on his inner wrist. He kissed her throat and gently tugged her into the unmade tangle of the bed they'd only vacated this morning. They made love slowly and easily.

Lying together after, naked skin to naked skin, Liam rested a hand on her belly. "I have an idea if you want to try it, about your memory and all this."

"Ugh. I forgot about it."

He nodded. "You don't have to."

His eyes were as calm as a lake in midsummer. Tillie never trusted anybody, but she trusted him. "No, I have to keep working at this before I get an ulcer."

"Close your eyes," he said, and something shifted a little in his voice. It was softer, deeper, maybe. "Take a deep breath, and let yourself sink into the bed, heavy and comfortable."

She followed his instructions, taking pleasure in the weight of his hand on her body, his leg against her own. As she lay there, he pulled the comforter over them, and it gave her a sense of protection.

"Imagine the scene in the painting that started everything. Really see it, as many details as you can."

Easy enough, since she'd been obsessing.

"When you've got it clear, let it get as big as a room, and imagine that you can step into it."

Something quickened in her blood, but she did as she was told, feeling herself step into the world of the artist.

"Look around," he said quietly. "What do you see?"

A porch. A stone house, a step.

"No hurry. Take your time."

It allowed her a moment to breathe, and she felt a tension draining from her body, giving her space to look around. A road led to a deep forest of pines and mixed deciduous trees, as thick and mysterious as a fairy-tale wood. The word came to her clearly, a *wood*, not a *forest*.

A garden surrounded the stone cottage, a classic style, pinks and blues and fluttery leaves. Roses. She didn't know the names of the others spilling over a little stone fence, but the big plant along the porch came to her. Rhubarb. Cut it and eat it, sharp and piercing, or cook it in a pie pan with sugar. *Crumble.*

As she stood there, she saw that the weather was gray and misty, and she was wearing a thick sweater. She looked down at her body, touched the hand-knitted garment, the skirt beneath it. She saw rubber roots on her feet, muddy and battered, but she felt a swell of love for them. Puddles and mud.

A girl appeared. Her imaginary friend, Sunny, with dark hair and bright blue eyes and freckles on her nose. *Where have you been?* She asked. *Let's play fairy tale.*

Abruptly, Tillie fell from the vision into the bed, as sharply and abruptly as if she'd been torn out of that world. She fell hard, gasping, her eyes on the stained ceiling. She clutched Liam's hand fiercely, as if he alone would keep her from tumbling into a void.

"Easy," he said. "You're safe." He brushed hair from her brow. "You're safe."

She took in a breath, felt her body recognize where it was in time and space.

"Did that give you anything?"

"I think that the girl who died might be the imaginary friend I've had all my life. I call her Sunny. My mother used to tell me that I had talked about her from the time I could speak."

"Do you think she was imaginary?"

She fronted. "I don't know. She doesn't feel imaginary in that visualization." She called back the image. "I could see a lot of detail about her, about the house." She thought of the sweater she was wearing, the boots. "It doesn't seem like Southern California, either," she ventured. "Rainy. Colder."

"That's good."

Next to her thigh, his was bare and warm. His eyes were calm and beautiful. "Thank you," she said. "Bet you wished you'd found somebody easier to have a New York fling with."

He waited a beat, his thumb on her cheek. "Is this a fling?"

She looked at him, unsure of her answer.

"That's not what it feels like to me," he said.

A swoop of longing moved in her body, surging toward the places their bare skin touched. "No," she admitted, "but I know better."

"Do you? What do you know, Tillie?" He swung down to kiss her, looked at her mouth, kissed her again, lightly. She loved the feeling of his lips, as if it they were cut to fit hers. "That love is an illusion? That we're all jaded and no love is real?"

An unexpected sting of tears rose beneath her eyelids, and she looked away. "Maybe." But more than that, she thought, *This just doesn't happen, not like this, some beautiful being dropping into your life, falling in love with you at first sight, and then it comes to something. It can't come to anything.* "You live very far away."

"I do. They have invented this thing called planes."

She shook her head. "That sounds awful. Being with you like this and then—"

"What? Longing for each other?" He smiled, and she saw the slightly crooked canine tooth that made him seem so human. "Imagine what the reunions will be like."

Wishing she could believe, she turned into his chest, breathed in the smell of his skin, the crispness of hair against her forehead. "I just wish you didn't have to go so soon."

"Me, too."

"When is it?"

"My flight is Saturday morning, at seven a.m."

She wanted to ask him to stay a little longer, but that was a suggestion that should come from him. Instead, she curled closer. "Are you hungry?"

"I will be, but I'm not right now."

"Let's nap."

He gathered her close, and that was just what they did.

CHAPTER NINETEEN

Wulfecombe

During the tangled days of her addiction, when all else was lost and she had no sense of who she was or how she would keep living, Sage had taken refuge in kitchen work. The ordinary business of cutting carrots into rounds, slicing mushrooms into slivers, and chopping cabbage gave her hands something to do, her mind a place to rest, if only for a moment. The smell of dill, pungent and sharp, or the more luxurious depth of garlic brought her body into the moment, into the now, where she was.

At that time, she was too broken and full of shame to return home, so she chopped and learned to stir and fry and combine, learned that bits of this and bits of that, unremarkable on their own, could create something beautiful and nutritious. Sometimes, the dishes gave her an appetite of her own, and sometimes she could even eat them. In this way, little by little, she was able to heal.

When she'd healed enough, she returned to find the woman at the chocolate shop, who seemed unsurprised that Sage had returned. She apprenticed to her, all the while cooking at cafés and restaurants. When at last she could face her mother, she made a box of the most beautiful chocolates she was capable of creating, got on the train with her meager belongings, and went home.

In the box had been a selection of her own inventions and some she'd learned from the chocolatier, who had shown Sage the layers and science and timing required to produce beautiful chocolate.

For her return home, she'd made strawberry rhubarb and coconut lime, robed caramel in her own secret recipe, dipped cherries and mangos in dark chocolate, and formed thin crunchy bars studded with chips of almonds. Things she remembered her mother loved.

Clare, being herself, accepted the gift in the way Sage meant it, as an expression of her remorse. Each chocolate contained her tears. Each contained her hope. Some held her losses and her sorrow.

In a household where lame rabbits and broken birds, blind dogs and three-legged cats, were enfolded without comment, Sage, too, was embraced. She took up residence in her old bedroom, overlooking the fields of carrots and cabbages, and there saved enough money to buy her own equipment and open her own shop.

She'd cooked herself straight, and brewed chocolate to bring herself alive. This morning, she'd assembled treats for her father while the baby in her belly turned somersaults and gurgled most uncomfortably. They'd chosen not to find out what the sex was, though Sage assumed the child would be a girl. They all did. What else would two women bring into the world but another?

Which made her sister Meg laugh. "Careful! You'll have a boy just so the universe can balance things out."

This morning, she was bringing a care package to her father. Technically, he was her stepfather, as her mother had left her biological father when she was quite small. She didn't remember him.

Levi had entered their lives when Sage was seven. He was a widower, sad and lonely, having come to the west to take up a farm veterinary practice where his sad children, missing their mother, might breathe fresh air and grow vigorously. Amelia was seven, same as Sage, Meg fourteen and the most resistant to Clare, who had mothering to spare. Meg had kept herself aloof until a few years ago, but Sage and Amelia took to each other like litter mates, tumbling through the countryside and the farms with their father, doing chores around the house with Clare. A few years later, the boys were born, two in three years.

Sage let herself into the gate, taking care not to let out the animals, the goose who couldn't fly, the hare who couldn't hop, the dog who couldn't see but greeted her with a howl, nonetheless. He stood at the top of the steps that led up from the road, his entire black end wagging, the house rising up behind him, much grander outside than it was inside. Tulips bloomed against the gold stone.

"Good morning, George," she said, patting his head.

Levi was in the garden, scattering feed for goats and chickens and whoever else. The lame hare, nearly two feet tall, followed the big man, along with George, who'd come around with Sage. "Hello, love," he said when he saw her. "Look at you—that baby is growing like a melon!"

She chuckled and patted her bump, rolling her hand down and up. "Vigorous, too. She's been kicking me for hours."

Levi kissed her head. "That's a good sign."

"I bought you your favorite potatoes," she said.

"Mm. Did your mother tell you I've had a bad week?"

"Of course she did." Sage inclined her head. "Arthur will be all right. He's just exploring."

Father and son had been fighting about his education. Arthur wanted to travel instead of finishing at university. Levi wanted him to wait. "It's only two years. He'll still be young."

Sage shrugged. "Either way."

"You didn't come all this way to give me potatoes when you'll be here tomorrow, girl. What's on your mind?"

Sage set the basket down on a table they used to drink coffee. "Is it possible that a wolf really lives in the wood? Maybe the old legends are true?"

He lifted his head, surprised. The legend had been woven through the stories of the village as long as he'd been here, and many centuries before that. A great black wolf, creeping through the woods, pet of the Green Man who ruled the trees.

But that wasn't what she was asking. "It's most likely a dog, of course, but . . ." He shook his head. "Could be a wolf. Mountain lions have been spotted in the West Country. Why not a wolf?"

"My mother said she saw one."

He nodded, gazing at the uneven line of trees at the edge of the property. "Is this about the bones they found?"

Sage nodded, a hollow echo of memory and terror reverberating through her middle. "I've heard they're not historical."

"Well, they won't know that for a bit. A bone is a bone. You know, they find these things every second Tuesday." He clapped a palm around her upper arm. "Don't fret, love."

"You're right." Sage sighed. *Accept the things you can't change.*

"Let's go in, have a cup of tea. You can tell me why I shouldn't bother Arthur about a gap year."

CHAPTER TWENTY

New York City

Tillie was dreaming. She was curled up in bed under the eaves of what she somehow knew was an attic room. A cat stretched the length of her body, chin to knees. His purr was low and comforting, and when she bent her face to his, he licked her nose. She kissed him back, his fur as soft as down, his nose just slightly wet as it touched her skin. She was awash with love and murmured words in some nonsensical language, and—

She awakened. Human arms held her.

Liam was asleep, as deeply as a child. Closing her eyes, she gave herself over to the heat of his skin against hers, the soughing sound of his breath. It was lovely for a long moment, but he ran uncomfortably hot, and she had to pull away, slipping into her yoga pants and a sweatshirt to go to the kitchen for water.

Where the other dream had unsettled her, this one had left behind a fragrance of sweetness. She could feel the cat's head against her face, the low, rumbling purr against her fingers. Drinking water, she thought it was a strange amount of detail for a dream.

That cat again.

On the horizon was a faint hint of dawn. Tillie wanted coffee, but she was afraid it would wake Liam, so she carried the glass of water with her into the studio and looked at the renditions of the cat she'd drawn. His striped face, his blue eyes, his enormity. A giant of a cat, touching her body from chin to knees.

From where she stood, she could see Liam sleeping. Again, her fingers itched to capture his image, and since he'd given her permission before, she felt he wouldn't mind if she sketched him now. On the same tablet of newsprint she had used for the cat, she employed charcoal to outline his form, the length of his legs, his hair scattered on the pillow, his jaw.

Then another, wilder, with wings against his back, slightly unfolded as if in rest. Another with the wings in a slightly tighter shape. A feather had escaped and fallen to the floor.

Another of him standing with that little smile, arms crossed, the wings just visible over his shoulders.

No. Scowling, she tore the paper from the pad and tossed it aside. *Silly.*

She looked back to the drawing of his sleeping pose with folded wings and tried it again, drawn to something elegant in the shape of the feathers, long and white. Using a sharply pointed colored pencil, she sketched tattoos with asemic writing tattoos around his belly and ribs, wondering what words she would actually use. It would be too personal to use the poetry that wound around his torso, and whatever the words were in the painting should support the idea of the angel. Angel of mercy? Messenger angel? Angel of death?

Angel of the forest? The skies? The lost?

She didn't know.

With tiny strokes to create texture, she filled in details on the sizable wings, then looked for the oil sticks she'd been using so often lately. When she found them, she layered white, dove gray, and a very smeary bit of cerulean for depth. The color was excellent, sending a flutter of approval through her body. She stood back, tilting her head sideways. *Better.*

When she looked up, Liam was propped on one elbow, watching her.

"You were asleep. Is it okay?"

"Can I see?"

"Yeah."

He flung the covers away and reached for his boxers on the floor, tugging them over his nakedness. She watched him move, admiring the curve of his buttocks, the shifting length of his quads. It was comforting that he was not a social media brand of perfect, that he had slight love handles, and his belly could easily go from slightly soft to chubby.

She liked every single detail of his body. His hair, straw-colored and messy in the morning light, the glittery sheen of new beard, his beautifully cut jaw. It felt impossible that she had never seen him in her life before the gallery, and he'd taken up so much space in her mind so quickly. Up close, he smelled slightly of sweat and sex. She touched his back, the place where the wings would sprout.

"Whoa. I love the wings, but that's not what I was expecting."

"It doesn't mean I think you're angelic."

"I get that. More like—" He shook his head. "Fallen."

A quickening brightened the space of her imagination, and there was the heart of it. The sketches were no longer a portrait of Liam, but the start of a new painting. "Yes!" She used a thumb to smear the edge of a wing. "I'm going to paint this, I'm afraid. Will you sign a model release?"

"You mean for your show?"

"Probably. Is that okay?"

He reached for her, one hand on her lower back, their thighs touching. "I might have to ask my business manager if it's okay."

"Really?"

"Really." He nodded. "If it was just me, I'd say go ahead, but there are probably things related to images of me that will require some hoops. It might be too much trouble."

"I'm crushed!" she cried honestly. "Are you a commodity or something? I *knew* you were a model."

"It's not like that, not a model," he said. "I have an app, and it's connected to my name and likeness, and these workshops are a big moneymaker. Not just for me, but for the people running the company."

Her sense of him shook itself, rearranged. She thought of him dressed in fine business casual, imagined him before a podium, talking with humor and depth. "Are you famous?"

He hesitated. "Maybe. A little."

Light skated over his brow and tumbled down his nose, the shapes so compelling that her fingers itched again. "Can you find out? I mean, if you don't mind." She glanced toward the drawing. "I just have this sense that it might be really powerful."

"Yeah," he said. "I will definitely try."

For a moment, she sat there, touching him, wondering if the only thing she'd wanted was to paint him. It happened sometimes.

But no. A thrum of yearning ran up and down her legs, pooled in her belly. She leaned in to kiss him. "Do you need to get somewhere?"

"Not that soon," he murmured, and she lost herself entirely—again—in his body.

One more time.

~

After Liam left, Tillie reluctantly set the drawings aside, set up her phone to play a folk-song list, and tried to immerse herself in the work at hand. Whatever else was going on in her life, she had a show coming up and needed to be ready.

The one good thing about all the upheaval was the sense that something was stirring, something that would be a good addition. As Jon had pointed out, the painting of the dark raven had a lot of power, even if that wasn't where she'd begun.

If she'd learned anything about art, it was that the head knew very little. Paintings came from . . . somewhere else, and her best work always emerged when she let go of control and gave herself up to the process. She sketched the cat and the girl in her dream, the porch and the girls, the giant cat and the woods in a loose way, her way, however they showed themselves to her. There was definitely something there.

Jon would be arriving midmorning, so she took a break to wash charcoal and sex and strange dreams from her body. Stomach growling, she looked for something to eat, but the same thing happened that had been happening every time she looked recently—the cupboards were empty. She made do with another coffee and told herself they could get lunch somewhere on the road. But really, she ought to order groceries. She opened the app and started making a list of things to order when she was actually going to be there long enough for them to be delivered.

Then, to distract herself, she looked up the website for Jon's gallery and scrolled down to the painting that had obsessed her. And of course, there it was.

Why hadn't she done this before?

Never mind. The painter's name was Shiloh. The text was the blue of a live link, but when she clicked on it, all it said was, *Shiloh paints her travels around the world.*

Not much. Why was she so reclusive?

She ran a search for *Shiloh, painter*, and all that showed up were a couple of galleries and the same information. Frustrating. What if Tillie were some big-time buyer and wanted all of her stuff? What, then?

The thought was so judgy, she had to laugh at herself. Shiloh was not obligated to be online for Tillie's pleasure. And who knew? Maybe her way was better.

At the bottom of her very plain website was a Yahoo! address. Not expecting much, she opened a fresh email and typed:

> Hi, Shiloh. I'd love to talk to you about one of your paintings in Tillerman's Gallery in NYC. It's kind of important.
>
> Thanks,

Tillie Morrisey

Almost immediately, an email came back: Thanks for your inquiry. I'm out of the country and checking email sporadically. I'll get back to you when I can. Shiloh

Reading it, Tillie felt frustration rising, tangling her mind. When would she ever get answers?

And then she heard herself. Honestly, what was the big deal? She'd been losing her mind over a painting that wasn't even to her taste. Maybe Jon was right, and she was just fixated on all this stuff because she didn't want to face how much she missed her mom.

Just in that moment, she missed her even more. Wished that she could rest her head on her mother's shoulder and let her soothe this roiling ball of emotion.

And yet, even that little fantasy was complicated by the questions surrounding the news story and the little girl.

Mom, what did you hide from me?

CHAPTER
TWENTY-ONE

Jon arrived, looking shiny clean and rested in a green activewear hoodie and expensive jeans.

"You look good," she said.

"Thank you."

She picked up her coat but dropped it on the floor. Picked it up, then dropped her keys; picked them up, but a lipstick rolled out of her bag. "Damn it!" She grabbed it before it could disappear under the couch.

"Are you sure you want to do this?" he asked. "Maybe it's better to let sleeping dogs lie."

She gave him a look. "If it was you, would you let them lie?"

"Girl, I'd poke them until they woke up and started barking, for sure. But I've also never had anxiety so bad that I almost ended up in the hospital."

"Fair enough." She tucked everything in her purse and shoved her arms through her coat sleeves, pulling hair out and flinging it over her shoulders. "I have to find out what she was lying about. Why. Maybe that's the whole reason I'm screwed up in the first place, that she had some dark secret she never told me."

Solemnly, he nodded. Touched her shoulder. "Let's go, then."

When they were well underway and out of the Manhattan traffic, he said, "It *is* weird that she never told you about this other girl."

Tillie chewed her lip. "Maybe it was just too hard for her to talk about?"

"So she just never told you that you had a sister? That's a stretch."

"Yeah, that's a lot." She sighed. "But there was a lot that was not exactly . . . ordinary about her."

He touched her hand. One of the things that made them friends was being able to make space for the weird parental baggage they each carried. His very religious single mother was 100 percent sure he would burn in hell for being gay, but she wrote him letters every week and wanted him home at holidays. Tillie's mother had been utterly devoted and supportive, but she wouldn't travel, ever, and she had what she called her "fits," periods when she didn't seem to be completely in contact with this world.

Trees along the road were glazed with green, and they passed a field with a pair of frolicking lambs. Tillie felt a whisper of recognition, a flash of déjà vu before it evaporated. The music on the stereo was very mellow jazz that unwound her nerves, and she let the tension go.

Jon said, "By the way, did you know your boy is a rock star?"

"My boy?" She echoed. "You mean Liam? He's a meditation teacher."

"Yeah," he agreed. "A *rock star* meditation leader. Google him."

She frowned, thinking of when she'd asked permission to paint him, and he had been unwilling or unable to give it. He'd also requested that they keep their connection separate from his work. "I don't want to. It's not like he's a serial killer or something."

"You really haven't googled him?" Jon looked askance. "Who just goes in uninformed these days? And why *would* you?"

She didn't want to admit that he'd asked her not to. That was what someone would say when they had something to hide, and it suddenly made her feel like the star of a bad horror movie, trusting where she should not.

And yet . . .

She thought of his gentleness when she was sick with her migraine, the way he'd come with her to her mom's farm. Tentatively, she offered, "I just feel like there's something here. With us."

He looked at her, then back to the road. "Like what?"

"I don't know." But she did. "It's like I've been waiting for him. Like all roads lead here. To him."

"I love that you're feeling that, sweetheart. I do."

"But?"

He shook his head. "You know the buts. I'm gonna respect you enough to trust you. If you trust him, I trust him."

"Thank you."

"But google him anyway. Right now."

"No! I don't want to. It might change things. It might change how I see him." She plucked at a loose thread on her sleeve. "I have been planning a painting of him, but when I asked him to sign a model waiver, he said he couldn't without asking his businesspeople."

"Yeah. Not surprising."

Her curiosity was killing her now. "How famous?"

"The app is Quiet. It has over a million reviews."

"Huh." She'd heard of it. "Does he lead the meditations? Because you have to admit, he has a great voice."

"Yes, on both counts. He also has books. Think Brené Brown famous."

Her stomach flipped. "No," she protested. "I've been with him in public. People don't recognize him walking down the street."

"Well, it's a pretty specific group of people, right?"

She covered her ears. "Don't say any more. I don't want to know."

"Okay." The word was layered with a sense of *You're being ridiculous*, but Tillie ignored him.

When they got to the village, he said, "Where to?"

She drew a blank. It wasn't like her mother had a ton of friends. "She used to spend a lot of time at the quilt store with Calla. Not that they were exactly friends, but she's been around as long as I can remember. Maybe she'll remember something."

"As good a place to start as any."

The quilt shop was in a quaint building with apartments over the shop and a display of fabric snippets in the window. Only snippets, Tillie knew, because sunlight would fade bolts of cloth. They walked to the door, but a sign read CLOSED. It wouldn't open for another hour. "Damn," she said mildly, then looked down the street for other ideas. The natural-foods store was around the corner. "I have an idea."

Mother Earth Foods was open and thriving, judging by the number of people going in and out. It had originally occupied a former small-town grocery store, the old-fashioned kind with wooden floors and a butcher counter in back. They'd expanded since the last time she was there, taking over a shop next door to add a bigger produce section. She stood just inside for a moment, smelling the air, but it no longer carried the pungent quotient of nutritional yeast and patchouli and freshly baked bread. The recognition made her a little sad.

A young woman behind the florist counter smiled. "Hi. Can I help you find something?"

It seemed foolish to ask now that she realized it was no longer a funky little hole in the wall, but what did she have to lose? "Yeah," Tillie said. "I'm hoping to talk to the original owner, May Paulson?"

"Oh, sure. I just saw her." She straightened from her task and peered down an aisle. "Yep, there she is. By the canned goods, end of aisle seven."

"Thanks."

They headed in her direction. She looked up as they approached, her gray hair woven into a braid that fell down her back. Her sinewy arms showed beneath a Life Is Good T-shirt featuring a tent and a dog. "Good morning," the woman said as they approached. "Tillie, isn't it?"

"Wow, good memory."

"How are you, dear? I was sorry to hear about your mama's passing."

"Thank you. I'm okay. I actually wondered if you had a minute to talk to me about her, about when she came to town."

She glanced at her watch. "A little time."

"Do you remember when she first came here?"

"I do. She lived right across the street with you for the first year. She was looking for a farm, but it needed to be just right."

"I didn't know that we ever lived in town."

"You were the cutest little girl, all hair and eyes." She tugged off her gloves.

"Thanks. Where did she come from? Do you remember?"

Her gaze sharpened. "Do you not have any family?"

"Not that I know of."

"I'm sorry. That must be hard." She straightened a can of pears so the label faced outward. "I always thought she was from New England somewhere. I can't remember why I thought that. Maybe an accent or something? It's been a long time."

"It has. Not California?"

She frowned. "No, I'd remember California. It was one of my dream places."

"Did she work around here anywhere?"

"No, she seemed to come from some money. Or she had enough that she didn't work."

Tillie smiled. "Thanks. I appreciate it."

"Sure, honey. Anytime."

Jon lifted a hand, and they fell in step, heading out to the street. The sun was out in a brilliant blue sky, and it was hard to feel dejected in the face of such relentless spring cheer. "New England," she said. "First I've heard of that, too."

"The mystery deepens. Did you run a Google search on her name?"

Tillie looked at him. Blinked. "No. It never occurred to me."

"Let's get some coffee and do that."

But a woman was at the door of the quilt shop. "First, Calla."

They hurried down the street. Tillie called her name before she went inside.

She turned. Unlike the owner of Mother Earth Foods, Calla had not aged well. She was stooped, with a mild dowager's hump and entirely white hair. "Tillie!" she cried. "How are you, honey?"

Sweetheart, honey, dear. "I'm good. How are you?"

"Been better." She cursed softly. "This damned lock. Will you get it for me, young man?"

"Of course. These old locks can be sticky, can't they?" He opened it and stepped back. "If you have some WD-40, I can spray it for you."

"Well, that's really sweet. I do have some somewhere. Come on in."

Tillie touched his arm in thanks for his kindness.

The store smelled like fresh laundry. Calla pointed to a door in the back. "Look in the cupboard over the toilet for the WD-40, son."

He winked at Tillie.

Huffing a little, Calla swung her enormous fabric bag on to the counter. "What brings you to town, Tillie? I heard you're selling your mom's farm."

"Yeah. I just don't want that life, I'm sorry to say, and it seems a waste to hang on to it and let it go to seed."

"Good choice. It's a hard life."

"I found some papers my mother had," she said without preamble. Calla was a straightforward person and expected the same of others. "They made me wonder about where she came from. Do you remember her talking about her life before?"

"It was never reliable." She shook her head. "That was always the thing, wasn't it? She sometimes said she was from Maine, sometimes California, sometimes New Hampshire. It was like she couldn't remember herself, which . . ." She raised her brows and let Tillie fill in the blanks.

"She might not have."

"Right. I'm glad to see you're okay. Doing really well for yourself."

Tillie was surprised anew, but of course, it was a small town, and people talked about each other. "Thank you." She paused. "Did she ever talk about a daughter that died?"

Her eyebrows shot up. "No. Did she have one?"

"I think she did," Tillie said. "I'd like to find out more if I can. Was she close to anyone else in town that you can remember, maybe when she first got here?"

Calla looked toward the window, peering back in time. "She had a boyfriend for a while. Eddie Johnson."

"Is he still here?"

"I haven't heard about him dying. You can find him on the old mill road, on the other side of the lake. He's got about thirty acres or so."

It was quite a distance to the other side of the lake, but she made note of his name. Maybe she could track down his phone number. "Thanks, Calla."

"You take care of yourself, sweetie."

She nodded.

Outside, Jon said, "I think you need to eat."

"Yeah. Let's get some burgers and look up my mom's name."

When they'd settled at a small table in a local café, Tillie said, "I've been in so many restaurants the past few days! I just can't seem to remember to get groceries."

"You've had a lot going on." He tapped her menu. "Eat something hearty. I need you to take care of yourself."

The simple phrase almost shattered her. She closed her eyes, willing the sharp, sudden emotion away, but tears welled up beneath her eyelids and seeped out. She covered her face with her hands.

"Oh, baby." Jon scooted from his side of the table over to hers and looped his arms around her.

"I'm sorry." Tillie breathed. "This is all . . . I just hate that I have to think about her in a new way now, when she doesn't have a chance to defend herself. I love her. I don't know how to be in the world without her, and I don't want to be upset with her."

He rubbed her arm, leaned his head into hers.

In the safety of his presence, Tillie let the bubble of grief rise. She saw Arlette last summer, picking tomatoes, her hair grown thin the past few years, but still long and woven into a skinny braid. She'd offered Tillie a perfect, deeply red tomato. *It's like a jewel, isn't it?*

After a minute, the bubble dispersed. She took a breath, leaned into Jon's shoulder. "Thank you. I don't know what I'd do without you."

"You're strong. You'd be okay." He kissed her head and moved his chair back into place. "Let's get some food in you."

~

Once they'd eaten, which brought her flying emotions back into her body, she said, "Okay, let's google my mother."

"Sure?"

She nodded. Together, they bent over her phone as she typed *Arlette Morrissey.*

There wasn't much. The first three results were her obituary, which she'd written herself before she died.

> Arlette Morrisey passed away peacefully in her
> home in Fox Crossing, New York, after a long ill-
> ness. She is survived by her daughter, artist Tillie
> Morrisey.

Tillie always wondered why she'd left it so bare, but she would never have dared change it. Arlette would have risen from her grave to haunt her.

The next result was a hair salon. A lawyer in New Hampshire. An obituary for a woman in South Carolina in 2009.

Nothing else.

Jon said, "Google her name, the year of her birth, and the town she was born in."

Nothing.

On impulse, Tillie googled *Valencia firestorm* and her mother's name. The same story she'd read in print came up, but so did three others. Two led to a story obviously written in the first days after the fire, where she was listed as one of the victims, the mother of a toddler killed when the fire swept through her home. The family also lost two dogs.

Tillie repeated this aloud. "'The family also lost two dogs.'" She shook her head. "But no mention of another child." Something crept up her spine, dark and unidentifiable. "Where was I?"

"Are you sure you want to keep going down this road?"

"No." She read the short story again. "But I can't leave it now, can I? I have to find the truth."

"Do you?"

"You know I do." She clicked on the final result, which was a story about a list of plaintiffs who'd brought a lawsuit against a construction company that was liable for the initial fire. "Listen to this." She read it to Jon. "The money was substantial."

He googled the construction company and the lawsuit. "And it was settled for millions."

Tillie divided the number of plaintiffs into the settlement. "My mother ended up with just under two million dollars."

"A lot more then than it is now."

"There's the money she used to buy the farm," she said. "But where was I? How do I find out?"

"Maybe you have to go to LA, talk to people there."

"Ugh." She pressed her face into her hands. "I have a show to finish. I can't afford this right now!"

"You're in good shape. You could take a few days, fly out there, see what you can find out . . ."

"Or maybe I can do it online. Find numbers of people and just call them or something."

"Yeah, that could work."

Tillie was suddenly depleted to her very bones, as if the center of her body had been scooped out and left on the counter, like a squash without seeds. "I think I need to go home and rest right this minute. I'm not sleeping very well."

"Good idea."

On the way out of town, she asked Jon to stop at her mom's farm, just to see if there might be something she'd missed, but a cleaning crew had scoured the place. There wasn't so much as a button left anywhere inside. Her feet made hollow echoes as she crossed the kitchen floor. It made her feel lonely. In memory, she saw her mother in jeans and a tank top, her feet bare and strong, stirring something on the stove. The stereo played her favorites: Crosby, Stills & Nash; Joni Mitchell; Led Zeppelin. Tillie thought of her, young and pretty, living in California, with a daughter.

Who had died.

The woman at the stove became a paper prop, hiding a truth she desperately needed to unravel. Where was Tillie?

Where was she?

Everything she'd ever known about her sole parent had shifted completely, and she had no idea what to put in its place.

"Why did you lie to me, Mom?" The rooms were silent.

Outside, she paused. She probably wouldn't be back here again, and she pressed the visuals into her mind carefully—the fenced garden and the barn and the woods. How many hours did she spend in those woods, with a cat or a dog or herself, making things up, drawing the trees and acorns, and imagining little fairy homes beneath the brambles?

Could these woods be the source of her dream?

No. These were deciduous trees. The ones in her dream were pines. She let the image of them rise—tall, thin pines, with undergrowth below. And—she noticed it for the first time—a creek.

For the first time, she felt the deep truth she'd been avoiding. The dreams were memories.

She just had to find a way to unlock them.

CHAPTER TWENTY-TWO

After the workshop, Liam met with his team in a borrowed conference room. The day was soft outside the windows, luring his attention toward the budding trees and soft breezes, the promise of greenery just out of sight.

Without preamble, he said, "I called this meeting today because I need some time."

"Time?" echoed Yolanda, a brown-skinned woman with impressively shiny black hair she wore cut in a line so straight it could slice peaches.

"Time off."

"What are you on about? We're booked out."

He shook his head. "I need some downtime. Cut everything for a couple of months."

"Two months!" Yolanda slammed her hands down on the mahogany table. Her rings and bracelets added emphasis, banging against the wood. "Nah, no can do."

Krish glanced between the two of them, raised a hand. "Hold on, hold on. What's up, bro?" He smoothed his beard with index finger and thumb, his dark eyes piercing. "This about the woman again?"

"A sheila?" Yolanda blustered. "Not again!"

He scowled at her. "Out of line."

She glared but apologized. "Sorry. But you've got an empire here. It doesn't turn so easily."

Liam shot a look toward Krish, who was responsible for this attitude. It made him angry. Two years ago, Liam had been sideswiped by a breakup from a woman he really had expected to marry, but it had been a normal kind of breakup between two adults who hadn't wanted the same things. Only Krish had seen it as the same as his previous breaks. No one else knew his history.

He looked at Krish for a long moment. He looked right back, unapologetic. Liam felt a surge of uncommon anger.

He took a breath. "I never wanted an empire," he said calmly.

"Well, it's bigger than you now. It's all of us." Yolanda indicated the people around the table. Mike, a muscled man from Adelaide who ran the security team; Penny, a fragile-looking blonde fresh out of uni who was Krish's assistant, planning and executing logistics; Alan, Yolanda's second-in-command, a pale Scot with a shock of curly red hair. Their eyes were all fixed on him. Worried.

There it was, the conflict. He looked at each of them, feeling a need to avoid letting them down. They had pinned their fortunes to his star, and he was mindful of his responsibility to them.

And yet, he felt the peace of Tillie's apartment echoing through him, lying in her bed this morning, watching her paint. Her energy and passion called to him, the way her arms moved, the tilt of her head. He felt he'd known her before, maybe in a hundred lives.

"We've been on the road almost all year," he said now. "I think we can safely take a break for a few months. The world won't end."

"Hold on, hold on," Krish said. "How about a few weeks instead? Not now, but when we finish the European loop." He flipped through notes on his phone. "End of June. You could take the rest of the summer."

Resistance rose in his belly, his lungs, and he listened to his body for a long moment before he spoke. "No." He would have lost her by then. Lost any chance of seeing what it was. "I need it now. Three months."

"You just said two," Krish said.

"That's all of Europe!" Yolanda cried. "We've been working on this for a year. It's a growing market, and they like you."

"I know, Yolanda, and you have done a great, great job with this. Can we just push it off until next year?" He steepled his hands and exhaled. "I'm tired, man."

"You don't look tired." Yolanda pushed back. "You did look tired, but now you look reenergized."

Krish said to the group, "Give us the room."

They rose, exchanging looks, and filed out. Liam knew what they were thinking, and it made him defensive. When he was alone with Krish, he said, "I told you, it's not like that."

"Look, bro, I'm on your side, remember?"

Liam shook his head. "No, I don't think you are."

"Who knows you better than me, bro?" Krish leaned forward. "I've seen this a hundred times with you, this thing where you always think you're in love. You chase her, find out it isn't what you thought, and everyone ends up crying."

His uncommon anger grew molten. "That's reductive. I am not the boy I was in school."

"I get that. But some patterns are more difficult than others to root out." He shook his head. "I gotta tell you, this feels like that pattern."

Despite himself, Liam felt a faraway flicker of doubt. It was sudden. He'd been lonely and off-kilter for a few months. He thought of Tillie last night, the way she laughed, the softness of her lips. "I've done the work, man. I haven't slept with anyone for two years!"

"Maybe that's the problem. Just because you sleep with somebody doesn't mean you're meant for each other."

"Stop." Liam glared at his friend. "Give me some fuckin' credit. You're always thinking about Opal. But I was young. We all fall hard at that age."

"It's not just Opal. Look, I'm not trying to disrespect you, but you're a love addict, and you know it. Every woman you fall in love with is going to save your soul or something."

"I've done the work. Two years, man. Two years to go through my shit and get my act together."

Krish looked away. His tone was softer when he said, "What's her name again?"

"Tillie. She's an artist."

"Tillie," he repeated. "You've known her only a few days. And if you haven't had sex with another person in two years, it's bound to feel powerful."

Liam waited. A thumping of fury pounded his temples.

"A lot of people are depending on you here, and you've made commitments. Why can't you just accept the end of June, and see how it goes?"

Again, that pulse of resistance. This morning in meditation, he'd felt the prompt to clear his schedule. "She's in trouble, I think. She's going to need someone in her corner."

"She doesn't have anybody else? You appeared to save her?"

When he heard it like that, it sounded ridiculous. "It's not like that." He let the moment they met rise in memory, the fall of her dark hair, the electrifying connection when he looked into her eyes.

Like he knew her. Not in some other life or in a dream, but in life, in this life. He just hadn't figured it out yet.

"If it's real," Krish said, "it'll stand the test of your wild schedule. That's something she's going to have to deal with, anyway."

The thought of spending his life like this, on the road constantly, one city to the next forever, felt like a prison. "I hate this, bro. I never wanted it, not like this."

"I know. But here it is."

Liam thought of the team, hopeful faces around the table. He thought of the rooms full of people who paid princely sums to meditate with him in person. It seemed ridiculous, and it always kind of had, but he'd been rooted in the practice itself, in the teaching, and the joy that gave him, so it was all right. Better than all right.

Good. Deeply fulfilling.

But now it wasn't.

"Maybe just think on it for a night," Krish said.

Liam nodded. "One night."

"Good." Krish clapped him on the shoulder. "I'll tell the others."

"Will you meet her?" Liam asked.

"What will that do?"

"Maybe a lot. Maybe you'll see what I see."

"I always see what you see, bro. You have good taste in women, aside from Opal."

Liam smiled. "Try."

"Sure. Name the time."

"How about right now?"

CHAPTER
TWENTY-THREE

After Jon dropped her off, Tillie fell face first into her bed and pulled the covers around her, exhausted. Comforted by the scent of Liam in the sheets, she slept and, for once, didn't dream of cats or girls or anything else. She simply slept, hard, until the buzzer rang. Jumping up, she saw it was nearly six, and staggered over to the speaker. "Hello?"

"Hello," Liam said. "It's me."

She buzzed him in and glanced in the mirror to make sure she didn't look too wild. Just once, it would be nice to be ready for him rather than being a mess. She smoothed her hair and her shirt and waited for him to knock. One, two, three, with energy. It lifted her out of her fog. She flung open the door.

"Oh."

He was not alone. A gravely handsome man stood beside him, his dark eyes unreadable.

"Tillie, this is Krish, my oldest friend and now my business manager." He presented her in return. "Krish, this is Tillie, my . . ." He looked back to her, vulnerability in his eyes. It touched her. "New friend."

She accepted the outstretched hand. A dry, firm grip. He was prepared to dislike her, she thought. "Come in."

Liam touched her waist as they came in, then bent to kiss her cheek. So polite. "I'm afraid I have only water or black tea or coffee to offer. I can't seem to get myself to the grocery store. There is literally almost nothing in my cupboards."

"We're fine," Liam said. "I wanted Krish to meet you and see the work you're doing because he's the one who can give permission for using my image."

"Uh . . ." It knocked her off-center, and she felt unpleasantly ambushed. "I'm sorry, I'm just sort of—" She touched her forehead. "I had a big morning, and I fell asleep when I got back here."

Krish nodded, his hands folded in front of him like a deacon's.

"If you mind," Liam said, picking up on her discomfort, "he can come back. Or I can come back, too."

"No, no." She took his hand without thinking, and he smiled gently, his fingers curling around hers. Their team, solid.

"Over here," she said. "These are obviously just sketches, and they'll be less on the nose when I finish." She pointed to the gazelle girl and the crow woman. "Like those."

"Jesus!" Krish exclaimed. "These are really good. I wasn't expecting an artist of . . ."

She waited.

He had the grace to finish. "Such power."

"Thank you."

"Do you mind?" He gestured to the other paintings curing on rails along the wall.

"Go ahead."

As he followed the paintings, stopping at each one with the kind of attention that let her know he had some knowledge of art, she looked at Liam. "You could have warned me," she whispered.

"I tried. It went to voice mail every time."

"Oh." She'd been asleep for at least a couple of hours, and honestly, could have gone for the rest of the night. She couldn't remember when she'd been so tired. Empty. Thoughts of her mother wafted through her mind, and she pushed them away, tightened her fingers around Liam's. He glanced down, pleased. Light came through the upper windows, fading now with the day, but it washed his face with something like holiness, and a spot beneath her ribs ached. She wished he didn't have to go so far away.

Krish rounded back to the sketches of Liam as an angel. "What's the plan for this work?"

"The painting, or the series?"

"Both, I reckon." His arms were crossed. Closed position.

"I have a show in four months at the Helen Appleward gallery in Manhattan. This painting will be . . ." She almost squinted into the distance, as if the painting in its finished form hung out there somewhere. "I'm not sure, but in this vein."

"His face will be recognizable?"

"His face is kind of the point."

"Do you know who he is?"

"Krish," Liam said.

"It matters, don't you think?"

Tillie stepped in. "I didn't know. But my friend Jon told me today that he's—you—are, as he said, a 'rock star' meditation teacher. With, like, an app and workshops around the world, right?"

Liam looked sad. "Yeah."

"And you had no idea before this?" Krish demanded.

"No." She crossed her own arms. "This isn't an attempt to exploit his fame. It's just . . ." She looked at the sketches, the wings. "What came to me. It's how I see humans, not as themselves but other things."

Krish gestured toward the gazelle and the owl being, side by side. "Like that?" He looked down his nose at her, and she suddenly saw a Belgian Malinois. Most dogs were hostile or eager to please, but a Malinois knew he was better than you.

"Everyone. I'm seeing a Belgian Malinois when I look at you."

One eyebrow rose in disdain. "A dog?"

"Lean, smart, loyal," she countered.

Liam said, "Bro." The word carried layers Tillie couldn't decipher, but the top notes were annoyance and maybe a request.

Nodding, Krish said, "You must see what the connotations are, his face as an angel, representing himself as divine."

"I see your point in a way. In a big way, actually." She pursed her lips. Disappointment rivered through her limbs, along with a rise of anxiety. If she ditched this, she'd be even more behind, and it was feeling like a core painting. "I might be able to—" She broke off, knowing the whole point was the visual of his face. "I don't know. If it won't work, it won't work."

"Permission is not technically required, though, is it?" Liam asked.

She turned, surprised. "Not for something like this, actually. Art is considered free speech, so as long as I'm not using your image to sell something, it's fair use. And because you're a public figure, the rules are even more lax."

"But you'd be selling the painting," Krish said.

"I mean, yes. But it wouldn't be considered commercial." She shook her head. "Never mind. I don't want to cause you trouble."

"Thank you," Krish said. "The optics would be terrible."

She shrugged her agreement. "I hear you."

"I'm going to get out of here, then." He shook her hand. "Good to meet you." He pointed at Liam. "See you tomorrow morning, bright and early, yeah?"

His face was stony. "Yeah."

"Last one."

"Here," Liam returned.

Krish let himself out.

Tillie scowled. "That was really weird."

"Sorry. I thought it would help if he met you."

"Help what?"

"Get the release signed," he said, but his gaze shifted away, and she sensed that wasn't the whole story.

"It's all right." Her phone buzzed somewhere across the room, and she realized she hadn't checked it since she got home. She moved to pick it up from the nightstand. The new notice was a message from Jon, and a long line of other notices scrolled down the screen. She should deal with them, but it felt exhausting.

"Have you eaten?" she asked. "I'm starving, but I don't want to go out."

"Takeout?"

"Or I could order some groceries, and we could cook. Nothing fancy, maybe just some omelets and toast?"

His expression lightened. "That's sounds amazing. Red onions, maybe. And avocado?"

She nodded in happiness. "And some crazy seedy bread."

"Sun-dried tomatoes."

She opened the grocery delivery app on her phone and started adding items. The vegetables and eggs and bread. "Anything else?"

"Hot chocolate and milk."

She laughed, adding them. "Done." She ordered and set the phone down without opening the messages or email or any of the other things tugging at her attention. Instead, she crossed the space between them, lifted her arms around his neck as if they'd been together a hundred years. "Hi."

He exhaled and rested his forehead against hers, his hands on her waist. All at once, the world outside fell away, and she was standing in a circle that felt like home. *Him, her, this.* She couldn't possibly speak that aloud, so she simply rested there, forgetting everything but right here. Now.

Her phone buzzed again, and she reluctantly pulled it out of her pocket. Jon again. "Sorry, I need to look at this. I've been out of touch for a few hours."

"Go ahead. I'm going to wash my hands."

"Oh, look," she said with a smile. "Three voice mails from Liam."

"Told you I tried." He grinned and disappeared into the bathroom.

Jon's messages were straightforward. At 4:07: Checking on you. Doing OK?

At 4:55: Checking again. LMK when you get this.

At 6:12, just now: Worried. Text me, or I'm coming over.

She typed: I'm fine. Just fell asleep. Liam here now. Will call tomorrow.

His reply was swift. Good. Have fun, baby, punctuated with an emoticon of a face with a tongue hanging out.

She laughed, carrying the phone to the couch, where she looked at the other notices. Nothing enormously important. Texts from a couple of acquaintances, headlines from news apps, an email from her gallery inquiring over her progress. Flicking open the app with her thumb, she started to respond that all was well when another one caught her eye. It was from Shiloh, the artist who painted the work that started all this madness.

> Tillie Morrisey! I know your work, woman!! How amazing to hear from you. I'd be glad to help, but I'm not sure which painting you're talking about. There are a few locales in that series. Which one did you mean?
>
> I'm getting on an overnight train so won't have much service until tomorrow (Vietnam time), but I'll keep an eye out for your email.
>
> Can't get over it! I love your work!
>
> XO
>
> Susan Heever a.k.a. Shiloh

Tillie's hands started shaking. She typed out a fast reply:

Susan! So pleased to meet you this way. Sorry
about that—I should have said the number. Which
now I've forgotten. It's a porch against a forest, with
two figures (maybe children) and a cat. A plant with
big leaves. I can get the actual number, but that will
be tomorrow.

Thank you so much.

Tillie

"What's up?" Liam asked, returning. He sank beside her, body
angled to give her his full attention. She loved the way he listened with
his whole being.

"It's the painter. She got back to me, but I forgot to include the
number of the painting, like an idiot."

He shook his head. "Don't talk about my lover that way."

She smiled. "I'm glad you're here."

"Me, too."

The food was delivered, and they cooked beautiful omelets and
avocado toast with hot chocolate. "It's not sunflower bread," Liam commented, "but pretty good."

Tillie nodded in agreement, glad to be at home, to be eating ordinary food. "I love that bread. I used to make it all the time when Jon
and I lived together. We were poor as hell, and the bread got us through
a good many months."

He smiled. "He's a good friend to you."

"The best."

Quiet acoustic indie music played on the speakers, and as if to add
the exact perfect note to the scene, rain pattered against the skylights.
Sated, they pushed their plates away. Liam picked up a deck of tarot
cards from the table. "Do you mind?"

She held out her hand, mock scowling. "Don't get your energy all over my cards, man."

"I thought you liked my energy all over you."

"This deck was my mom's," she explained. The cards were as soft as an old pair of jeans, and she shuffled them easily, once, twice, again.

"Did you find what you were looking for in Fox Crossing today?" he asked.

"Not really. It would be easier if I knew *what* I was looking for, but all I know is that my mom was lying to me my entire life."

He said nothing. Lamplight spilled over his pale hair, picking out sparks of gold, and she imagined adding gold to the painting she wasn't going to paint. *The Listening Angel.*

She shuffled the cards again. "What are you hiding, Mom?" she asked capriciously, split the deck, shuffled again.

"Mother card," she said, declaring the meaning she sought, and turned over The Empress. Her lips quirked. "Daughter." She pulled The Fool and laid it down. Card three was their relationship, The Moon.

"Secrets," Liam interpreted.

"Surprise!" she said, laughing, then drew the next card. The Chariot. A card of movement and power.

Liam whistled. "A lot of Major Arcana there, love."

Challenges: The Tower. "Of course," she said, rolling her eyes.

The final card was The Hierophant, which represented the need to seek the help of a spiritual mentor, a need for perspective. Tillie frowned, trying to think who that might be in this case. Who could help her sort this out?

"Draw one more," Liam said.

"Why?"

"Why not?"

She turned it over, and they both laughed. Knight of Wands. "That must be you."

He spread his hands with a grin. "Ta."

She absorbed the arrangement, moved the cards infinitesimally, touched The Empress. "This is the wrong card for my mother," she found herself saying. "She was soft-spoken and kind of . . . timid."

"Maybe The Empress is you."

She glanced at him, then spoke more honestly than she would have to almost anyone but Jon. "Maybe one day, but not now. I do feel this is right for me, The Fool. Fresh new experiences." She searched her mind for a powerful woman mentor but couldn't come up with one.

Abruptly, she scraped the cards into a pile. "The last thing I need is more introspection." She stacked them together, shuffled, shuffled again, then again. "Tell me about your day."

His expression had been open and cheerful, but the expression slipped, so classically a face falling. "It was all right."

"Doesn't sound like it."

He touched her thumb, pulled her hand into the cradle of his palm. "I tried to rearrange things to get some time off." His eyes were a shimmery pale aqua that seemed unreal. She wanted to paint that color, the layers of depth in them. "To be with you a little longer."

She swallowed, curled her fingers around his. "Doesn't sound like it worked out."

"If it was just me, it'd be a breeze, but a lot of people are counting on me."

"I didn't go look you up, by the way. Jon told me about you, but I wouldn't let him keep going. I wanted to respect your wishes."

"Thank you."

"It sounds like you're pretty famous."

"Must not be too famous, because you didn't know me."

"Not really my world."

"Fair enough." He traced the edge of her thumb. "Not really mine, either, to be honest. I didn't really plan for any of it."

"How did it happen?"

He tugged her hand. "Come here, and I will tell you."

"I'll crush you."

"Nah." He kissed her fingers, and she allowed herself to be pulled into his lap, straddled his thighs. A hand slid under her shirt at the back.

"Tell me," she said, and ran her fingers through his hair, loosening it.

"I chased a woman to India," he said. "It was a bad idea. We did a lot of drugs, and I made a disaster of the good life my mother gave me." He lifted the hem of her shirt, urged her to raise her arms. She did, and he tugged the shirt over her head. "She left me in Rishikesh, and I spent a year sinking as low as I could go."

She slipped her fingers under the collar of his shirt to feel the heat of his skin. "Then you found a teacher. Mentor?"

"Teacher. I was lucky that he turned out to be a good one, a man with principles and lineage, and he took me in. I studied with him for five years, then went home to Auckland." He traced the scoop neck of her bra with his fingertips. "I was teaching there for a couple of years. Getting some traction."

"Mm-hmm." She leaned in to kiss his neck, his warm throat. His hair brushed her nose.

"And then Krish said we should make an app." Her bra fell to the floor. "And it took off."

"Took off?" She stood and pulled him to his feet, walking backward to the bed. He shed his shirt, paused to step out of his jeans, followed her to the bed where she, too, was clothes-free. Their skin met.

"A million followers in two years."

"Holy shit," she said, and then he was kissing her, and there was no more conversation.

CHAPTER TWENTY-FOUR

Wulfecombe

Heartburn was the price Sage paid for pregnancy. It made it impossible tonight to lie down, so she paced back and forth between the sitting room and the tiny kitchen of the flat, back and forth to keep her legs from getting twitchy, back and forth to keep her anxiety down, back and forth to be a peaceful incubator for her child.

She felt haunted, ever so slightly off-center, and she couldn't pinpoint why. The bones had unsettled her, bringing up memories of Rosemary, that terrible loss so long unsolved, but it felt like more.

On impulse, she opened the book of recipes her mother had given her upon her wedding to Paula. It contained all the family favorites—Clare's cottage pie, and her grandmother's apple crumble; Levi's fried dumplings. A quarter of the way through, she found the sunflower bread, and although she didn't bake as often as she cooked other things, she'd learned this bread at Clare's side when they were both sad and broken. The smell of baking bread, her mother said, could heal anything.

She assembled the ingredients, most of them ordinary enough, and was pleased to find she even had flaxseed in a sealed container. Humming quietly, starlight shining through the window, she blended yeast and water, flour and flax, a little vinegar and the sunflower seeds, then left it to rise, donned a sweater, and went outside.

The moon had set, leaving behind a star-bright sky. When she lived in London, this sky had been one of the things she most desperately missed. Out here, away from the city lights, the night sky could be astonishing. She paused to step out into the little box of garden they enjoyed, and looked up, taking a deep breath of air, salty and fresh from the nearby sea.

"Do you see that bright one?" Sage asked, one hand on her belly. "That's Venus. Or maybe Mars. I get them mixed up, but we'll make sure to look it up properly when you're here. I hope you love the sky as much as I do." She smoothed her palm over the round of baby, up and down, feeling a swish, a bump, a gurgle.

She'd never imagined that she'd be a mother. Even at nine, she'd known she only liked girls, not boys, and even then she'd known that boys were required for babies. Not even for a baby could she imagine doing *that*.

But as time passed, as she fell into addiction, then climbed out of that pit, she'd felt a longing to know what it was like to generate life, to bear a child. Her arms ached for the shape of a small body, her nose for the smell of a baby's neck. When friends had babies, she played with their little bean toes and volunteered to babysit as long as they needed, singing to them in her low voice, a singing voice she was secretly proud of. Her own mother had sung to Sage, and she knew all the songs, the old songs.

Folk songs had led her to Paula. She'd heard her playing in a café in the nearby holiday town of Cloverly, a voice as pure and clear as a winter morning. It called Sage right out of the kitchen store where she'd been browsing and into the café, where a crowd clustered around the small dais where Paula sang and played guitar. She wore a red scarf over her magnificent, wavy blonde hair, and her cheeks were rosy red. She sang a ballad about the Green Man giving help to a lost child.

Sage had been in love once or twice, but when Paula caught her eye and winked without missing a beat, she was swamped with a sense of the future unfolding, a happy future.

With children.

And so it had come to pass. Sage thought it would make a good fairy tale. They'd both navigated tests and troubles, sought the advice of wise women and mages, and fallen to the darkness of a curse—Sage to drugs, Paula to an emotionally abusive relationship that had left her battered and torn. Paula adamantly wanted to raise children. They would have one from each of their gene pools, and then adopt lost children, too.

It took longer than they'd hoped to get pregnant, and the pandemic had delayed them even further. They'd winnowed down their wishes, and Sage had finally gotten pregnant. And she loved it.

Now, the past was seeping out of the woods, a miasma smelling of helplessness and sorrow. The thought of the child's bones they'd found haunted her. Had Rosemary been dragged away by a wolf?

Or was it something worse than that?

She didn't want to let it in. Didn't know how to keep it out.

"What magic is in the sky tonight?" Paula asked, behind her.

"Venus . . . or maybe Mars," she said, and chuckled, leaning back as Paula embraced her from behind, her hands circling the mound of baby. "I'm really going to have to find out."

"Mm." They stood in the starlight a long time. Finally, Paula said, "Come to bed, sweetheart. You both need rest, no matter what the future holds."

Sage allowed herself to be led, stopping to tuck the bread into the fridge to rise overnight, and allowed herself to be held. Allowed herself to let go of the past and future and just curl into the now.

CHAPTER
TWENTY-FIVE

New York City

"I don't want to sleep," Liam said, nestling into her. "Let's talk and talk. All night."

She laughed. "You'll never get up in the morning."

"I don't care. It's my last day. I can wrap up, talk to people. They'll be happy."

"I hate to hear *last day*."

He kissed her fingertips. "Yeah."

"I'm dying to see you in that world," Tillie said.

"It's not really me. Not anymore."

"What do you mean?"

He rolled onto his back. "It wasn't supposed to be . . . this. I like helping people, and I mean, I guess this does that, but I don't like the celebrity aspect. That makes it more about me than about the meditation, and that's exactly the wrong angle."

She wanted to practice listening as he listened. She waited.

After a long moment, he continued. "I don't think it's good for me."

"In what way?"

"I'm trying to be human and in the middle of humanness, and this gig takes me out of that."

"Maybe you should stop."

"Right." He shoved hair behind his ear. "I mean, obviously. But there's a whole team wrapped up in these appearances, and people have paid good money for the workshops. In some places, they've been waiting for three months to get to one."

"I can see why that might cause some pressure."

He looked so sad that she crawled up close and curled over his chest, forcing him to cradle her. "Do we have any time tomorrow?"

"A little." He brushed hair away from her face, his fingers lingering near her ear.

"Are you going back to New Zealand?"

"No. The tour isn't over. We head to England, then . . ." A hand spread out into the room. "Europe."

A pain pressed the air from her lungs. "I hate that."

"Me, too."

"Then let's talk all night, and I will take you somewhere I love tomorrow. How about that?"

"Good."

"I don't know why, but this does feel—"

He nodded. "I know." He kissed her. "I know."

~

They did talk, but at some point, they both fell asleep. He was bending over her when she woke up, already dressed. "I should be done by noon."

She reached for his hand and kissed his palm fervently, then tucked it beneath her cheek. This was the last time he would be in her room in the morning, and the idea made her whole body hurt. As if he sensed it, he knelt on the covers and gathered her naked into his fully clothed embrace, then kissed her hair, forehead, nose, and mouth. "I promise I'll be back as soon as possible."

"Okay," she whispered, and reluctantly let his hand go.

He kissed her one more time, lingering, and then with obvious effort, pushed himself away. "Eat something."

Then he was gone, and she was alone in the apartment, in the silence, aching at the loss of his company. Rolling onto her back, she stared at the ceiling. "Tillie Morrisey," she said aloud, "you are a fucking idiot."

Instead of lying there, pining, she forced herself to get up and shower, make coffee and an actual breakfast of a fried egg and toast. It was remarkably fortifying. Habit kicked in, and she donned an apron and headed for her easel.

The angel sketch waited. Almost alive, with an energy she found difficult to ignore. She couldn't use it in the show, and she really didn't have time to be messing around with something that wasn't directly *for* the show, but she couldn't resist doing just a *little* work on it. While he was fresh in her mind. As she started to paint, she realized that she didn't have any photos of him, and she needed to rectify that tonight. What if she never saw him again?

What if? Her cynical side sneered. *Get real. This is it.*

Which she couldn't think about. Enough time to have a broken heart after he left. She didn't want to pre-break it.

Going with the vision she had last night of his hair, she used a tiny brush to paint very small lines of metallic gold through the length of his locks, adding more across the crown of his head. Touches along the wings, so subtle they almost couldn't be seen. A minuscule bit in his eyes.

Good. She stepped back and admired her work. It was a very solid sketch, and she could make an actual painting from it, but for at least a couple of hours, she needed to keep working on the show.

Gazelle girl was excellent, and Tillie chose her, changing the color of her fur to a pale turquoise to match the ombre in her hair, with a block of the same color over her nose. She had an urge to add horns, and had to look up whether the females had them. They did, so she outlined them in a sienna shade.

It was a good morning of work, and she was glad when her timer went off. Sticking to her wish to be cleaned up and dressed when Liam came back, she took a second shower to wash her long hair and blow-dry it perfectly straight, and even added a little makeup. It was never a lot because she'd never really learned, but some lipstick and mascara to accent her best quality—thick, long lashes. If she were to paint herself, she'd choose a llama for those lashes.

Just after noon, she was ready. And immediately restless. She couldn't sketch, or she'd get drawn into her practice, and then her good jeans would be a mess. Her new sweater made the most of her meager curves, and it cost a fortune, so no painting.

A text came in from Liam: Sorry. I have to sit down for a minute with an important donor. Will be leaving in about 20.

Which meant it would be another hour before he got there. She made another cup of coffee, taking her time with each step, then sat down at the table with her back to the studio, and opened her laptop.

All the questions about her mother came rushing back. Who was she? Who was the dead child to Tillie? It was unsettling that it seemed as if Arlette had used Tillie to replace that lost girl. Why else would she keep the same name?

And they were the same age. Which was impossible, really, unless she was a twin or something, and no twin had shown up in any report of anything. It seemed that there would have been a report of the twin surviving.

A rustle moved through her at that thought, a flash of hiding beneath the covers with somebody, speaking in a language that wasn't English. She leaned into it, closing her eyes to see if she could gather anything else.

Nothing.

She sighed. One thing she should be wary of was the real possibility of manufacturing memories because she so desperately wanted to find answers.

Facts. Stick with facts.

The one piece of information she had picked up yesterday was the man who might have been Arlette's boyfriend when they'd first arrived in town. She clicked open her notes app, scanning down the various tidbits she'd collected yesterday to find his name. Eddie Johnson.

She googled his name and the words *phone number*, and there he was. Eddie Johnson, 2397 Old Farm Road, 518-555-9865. He must still have a landline, which was not surprising in the country, especially since he was likely in his seventies or better.

Taking a breath, she called before she could talk herself out of it. The phone rang six times. She was about to hang up when a man answered, sounding much younger than expected. "Hello?"

"Hi. My name is Tillie Morrisey, and I'm looking for Eddie Johnson?"

"Why does that name ring a bell?"

"I grew up in Fox Crossing. Maybe that's why?"

"Who are your people?"

"Only my mom, Arlette Morrisey."

A silence. Then: "I'm sorry for your loss. She was a good person."

"Thank you. Is this Eddie?"

"It is. How can I help you?"

"You sound so young," she commented.

He laughed. "Hard work keeps you healthy."

"I guess it does. Listen, I was in town yesterday, and Calla at the quilt shop told me you knew my mom when she first came to town. I'm trying to get some background about her, and I was hoping you might know a little."

"I can try. It's been a long time, you know."

"Right." She paused. "Do you know anything about a child who died?"

162

"Your sister," he said immediately.

A wash of icy cold poured down her spine. "My sister?"

"Sweetheart, you don't know this story?"

"No. I found a death certificate for her in my mom's stuff. That was the first I'd heard of it."

"Damn. I'm sorry." His voice was gravelly. "Your mom . . . I think that the loss messed with her head. She was hard to pin down, and her stories could be different one day to the next, but she didn't change this story about your sister. She died in a fire in California. A forest fire or something."

"But where was I?" Tillie cried.

"I don't know that part. I got the impression you were not there. Born later, maybe."

"Yeah." She peered at the screen. "Can you remember anything about her, then?"

"I'm not sure what you're looking for, kiddo." Now he sounded like an old guy.

"Me, either, honestly. But I feel like there's so much I don't know about my own mom. Like, I don't know if I have family somewhere or—"

"She always said she was from New Hampshire."

"And she said it was *my sister* who died?"

"Yeah."

She could feel his restlessness, or maybe she was projecting because she didn't know what else to ask. "Okay."

"Tillie, your mom had some problems, for sure, but I can tell you she was a good person. She loved you like you were the sun itself." He paused. "Maybe sometimes it's better to let sleeping dogs lie."

That sentiment again. "Maybe. Can I give you my number? Maybe you could call if you think of anything else?"

"I doubt I will, but you can leave your number."

She hung up, feeling more unsettled than ever. A sister. She had a sister. She'd died, and her mother never told her. Why? And why didn't she even get to have a name of her own?

Restlessly, she scanned her email, but there was nothing from Shiloh. Instead of dealing with anything in her real life that might actually be productive, she returned to the newspaper article about the Valencia firestorm, double-checking that there wasn't a second child listed. She remembered the settlement Jon turned up yesterday and texted him for the link, which he sent back immediately.

Doing ok? he added.

I mean . . . ok-ish. You don't have to worry about me. At least until tomorrow. Liam is leaving for England tonight. 😭 And then you leave tomorrow, right? This is going to be terrible.

I hate leaving you in this state. Why don't you come with me?

I wish. I'm already behind.

Let's have brunch tomorrow anyway. That place on 12th, Noon and Night? 11 a.m.

Yes. LOVE YOU.

I LOVE YOU MORE.

She copied the names from the settlement into a sketchbook on the table. There were seven, including her mother, and she started going through them one at a time to see if she could find links. She started with Facebook because it was the right generation, and she found three right away, all living in close proximity to the original fire. She DMed them separately. I'm looking for information about a woman who lost her daughter in the Valencia firestorm. If you remember her or the little girl, I'd love to talk to you. P.S., I'm family, not a reporter or anything.

In the meantime, she ran Google searches on the other names. Three more were deceased, which seemed like a lot until she realized they were middle-aged at the time of the fire, thirty-five years ago.

A ding alerted her to a private message on Facebook.

> I remember Arlette. We were good friends, and it was horrifying what happened to her daughter. How are you related?

She clicked "Reply" and hesitated, fingers hovering. Whatever she said might spook the woman since Tillie had no background and no idea if her mother had siblings or might have talked about that. Nothing. She needed unvarnished answers, so she opted for: I'm her cousin. My mom died and left her some sentimental things. Do you know where she is?

> I don't, sorry to say. It was a pretty bad time for all of us. Most of us scattered.

K. Thanks. One more thing: Do you know if she had another daughter?

> Not that I know of.

She sent a heart and a thanks emoji and peered into space. Where the hell was she when all this happened? She was starting to get a really bad feeling about it all.

CHAPTER
TWENTY-SIX

The donor Liam mentioned to Tillie was a woman. According to Krish, she'd donated nearly $50,000 to the foundation, most of it going toward scholarships and the travel expenses of those who couldn't afford the very high fees of the in-person workshops. He'd never spoken to her, and it wasn't such a terrible thing to be polite to people. It was part of the job.

She waited in the hotel restaurant, tucked away in a corner booth, and stood as he entered. Often, the donors were women in their forties and fifties, but Nikki Gonzales couldn't be more than thirty, and she was a knockout, blonde and healthy-looking, with clear skin unadorned by makeup. She was nervous as she offered her hand. "Hi, Liam. It's so nice to meet you."

"You, too," he replied, gesturing toward the booth, and sat. "I wanted to personally thank you for your generous donations."

"My pleasure." Her cheeks pinkened a bit. "I've gotten so much out of your meditations. I like imagining that others could get some benefit." She leaned close, and he found himself slightly trapped by the circle of the booth. Her leg bumped his.

"Yeah? Tell me about that." He moved away slightly. In other circumstances, he would have found her very appealing—she was just his type, or at least she would have been before he met Tillie, who wasn't that fit and not at all blonde, and yet . . .

"I was a mess before I started using your app," Nikki said, and rubbed her inner forearm, as if she'd been an addict. "It made all the difference."

"I'm glad. I share that history, as you likely know."

She nodded. Her hair fell down her arm in a shiny swath, which he observed as a fact, nothing more. "I do know. When I got clean and started my company, you were a role model in how to proceed."

"What's your company?"

"Oh, I'm just . . . an influencer. I'm a yogi, and a bunch of companies . . . well, a lot of products . . . I mean." She scowled. "Shit. I'm never this incoherent." She raised her eyes. "You're just a lot more compelling close up."

Her cheeks were pink, and her throat. She was crushing hard, which wasn't unusual, but he reminded himself to be kind and super careful in the way he extracted himself. With a chuckle, he patted her hand, as if he were an old granddad. "That's not important. Really."

She pressed her hand to his leg. "I don't want anything long term, or any of that. But what power could we unleash?"

He lifted her hand off his thigh and pressed it to her own. "Listen, Nikki, I mean this in the nicest possible way. Tell Krish to back off."

Her face fell. "I don't know Krish."

"Yes, you do." He threw bills on the table. "This isn't the first time he's tried this. But you're the prettiest by far."

"I really do admire you," she said.

She was so young, so crestfallen, that it broke his heart. "He's using you to get to me, but it's not your fault. Send me your influencer name, and I'll mention you."

"Would you? That would be so great."

He nodded. "It's all good."

CHAPTER
TWENTY-SEVEN

By the time Liam arrived at her apartment, the sun had come out. The day was so mild and beautiful that Tillie jettisoned her previous plans, and they took a train to the Staten Island Ferry. "This is one of the best views in the city," she promised.

He held her hand. "I'm just glad to be with you."

They rode outside on the ferry, enjoying the sunshine and the retreat of Lower Manhattan. The wind was soft, the setting sun lighting the water afire. He was quiet, taking in the view. Tillie sat next to him, pressing the sense of his form into her memory, already missing him. It felt foolish to let herself get so caught up in it. To try to be normal, she asked lightly, "What's your next city?"

"London," he said. "We've gone there a few times, and the crowds are really quite good."

"Will you see your friends? Or were they cousins?"

He leaned into her. "You remembered."

She smiled.

"Yeah. I'll spend a few days with my aunt. Technically, she's my mom's best friend, but I call her my aunt. Then we move on to . . ." He shrugged. "I don't even know where. Krish will tell me."

A dark expression crossed his face.

"Is everything okay?" Tillie asked.

"No. I had a situation with Krish today that made me wonder what's happening. He's overstepping in ways that I need to get under control." As if he regretted the harshness of this, he softened. "We've been mates since we were eleven."

"And?"

"He has a real gift for business, for all the parts that I don't want to deal with. He found the app designer, supervised the process, and got it all up and running." He looked down at their arms pressed together on the railing. "It's been good, really. I'm just not sure right now whether it's his vision or mine."

"That seems like a tough thing to sort out."

"I'm worried that the work might lose its center, that it's becoming more about personality and money than trying to help others find calm and joy."

"'In a troubled world,'" she quoted. "I looked up your website."

He half smiled. "That's Krish at his best."

"He seems very serious about protecting you and your image."

"No doubt." He pressed his lips together. "But you know that thing about power corrupting? I don't want to fall into that trap."

"Fair," Tillie replied. "I can see that might be a danger. Especially with your charisma."

"Am I charismatic?" he asked, leaning into her.

"You know you are. An aura the size of California."

"Thank you." He sighed. "Enough about my first-world troubles. How'd your day go?"

Tillie watched the city retreating. "I did some good work, and then I made some calls to see if I could find anyone who could give me any more information about my mother."

"Did you?"

"Not really." She thought about the thin clues. "But a man she used to date when I was little said he did know about the death of her daughter. He said that girl was my sister. But when I asked a woman in LA about it, she didn't know anything about me, a second daughter."

The weirdness welled up in her throat, and she felt suddenly, alarmingly, unmoored. She shook her head, trying to keep it together.

Liam looped an arm around her wordlessly.

"It's just so . . . disorienting," she said, "to think I know my history and then find out it's all a big lie. Or mess." Her throat was tight. "I really don't know what to do."

"You don't have to do anything," he said quietly. "Until you know the next step."

Ease moved through her body all at once, as if someone had pulled a plug in her toe and all the tense worry poured out. "Huh," she said, looking up at him. "That was pretty helpful."

He winked. "Just doing my job, love."

"Well, thanks." She traced a circle of words spiraling around his wrist in a stylized script. "What is this one?"

"'There is no real going back. Though I may come to the Shire, it will not seem the same; for I shall not be the same.'"

"More Rumi?"

"Tolkien." Liam smiled. "Krish and I discovered *The Lord of the Rings* at thirteen, and it was life-changing. We desperately wanted to be cast in the movies."

"Were you Frodo or Sam?"

"You're a fan!" he said.

She held out a hand, tipping it back and forth. "Sort of. It's a lot of boy-quest stuff. I was more of a Game of Thrones fan. Books, not the TV series."

"Always the book." They fist-bumped.

"Khaleesi?"

"Who else?"

"I never wanted to be a hobbit," he confessed. "Aragorn all the way."

"Of course." The sun blinked behind a row of buildings in the distance, covering them in gold, then darkness, then gold again. "Were you a big reader?"

"Hell, yeah. Still am. You?"

"We didn't have a television, and my mother believed in the library."

He laughed. The sound was slightly hoarse, deep. "We were such deprived kids, yeah?"

"So deprived. When did you get a computer?"

"Not until I was at uni."

"I got a laptop with money I earned myself, but we didn't have internet. I had to take it into town to an internet café. Remember that?"

"I do."

"Prime view of Lady Liberty coming up," Tillie said, standing. "Let's get some photos."

She showed him the gorgeous view of the Statue of Liberty from the ferry. They shot selfies of themselves hamming it up, and he let her take some of him in different lights and angles for her painting. He took approximately three hundred of her, which was both flattering and disconcerting.

They didn't get off the ferry, just looped back, and found a good vegetarian restaurant where they ate heartily, then walked the miles back to her apartment, talking. Time went so fast that she felt panicky when they got to her place—where there was no Jared, thank God. Liam looked up at the windows, where her lights were on.

"Do you have time to come up?" she asked.

"No. A car is on the way here now." He twined his fingers in hers. "And if I go up there, I'll cry."

She laughed softly. "That would do a lot for my heart."

"Do whatever you want with the painting. You can put it in your show if you like. I'll send you a release myself."

"That's okay. I just want it for me."

"I'll still send it." He stepped close, and their bodies touched lightly. "I hate leaving, Tillie. I really do."

"I hate it, too. That we can't even see where this is going."

"It's not over, is it?"

"Well, it can't really progress if you're traveling the world, can it?"

"We can text. FaceTime. Email." He curled his hand around her ear. "You can come visit when your show is finished."

The feeling of him leaving was a piercing hollowness in her heart. "Did you ever go to summer camp?"

"Sure."

"And fall in love? And then you promise to write each other, and you do for a little while. Then real life intrudes, and you drift away, and then the next year, you are a little awkward until each of you falls in love again. With someone else."

He was very still, those clear eyes beautiful even in the thin illumination of the streetlight. "This is not like that, Tillie. Nothing like it." He kissed her, a gentle kiss, sensual and so rich that she could live on it until she died. Everything in her years felt connected to him, cells to cells. "And I don't think you think it is, either."

When he raised his head, she saw tears gathering in his eyes, and it triggered her own, which were already too close to the surface. Then they were kissing and crying and hugging, and she would have done almost anything to keep him there. It was stupid, she thought, but it was also one of the best moments of her life so far, bittersweet and beautiful and awful.

"I am going to miss you like someone carved a piece out of me," she whispered. "It's crazy. I've known you less than a week, and it's like my whole life has changed."

"I think," he said, holding her head in his hands, "that we were meant to meet. And if that's true, we can trust that life will bring us what we need to be together."

She shook her head. "You're such a dreamer."

"Yeah," he said. "And you're a dream come true."

She laughed.

"Too much?"

"Yes. But I liked it."

A car pulled up, a black Town Car that was obviously his. Liam made a soft noise of protest and kissed her face all over, forehead and eyes and cheeks and nose and chin and then her lips. "I will miss you every second we are not together," he said. "But you won't be able to miss me because I'll be texting you constantly."

She hugged him, hard, to hide the rise of her emotion. "I can't wait."

And then he was gone, the car spiriting away the best thing that had ever come into her life.

Ever.

PART TWO: TSUNAMI

Faërie contains many things besides elves and fays,
and besides dwarfs, witches, trolls, giants, or dragons;
it holds the seas, the sun, the moon, the sky; and the
earth, and all things that are in it: tree and bird, water
and stone, wine and bread, and ourselves, mortal men,
when we are enchanted.
—J. R. R. Tolkien, "On Fairy-Stories"

CHAPTER
TWENTY-EIGHT
Wulfecombe

Clare had a long shopping list to carry into Barnstaple on Wednesday. Mostly, she shopped locally as much as possible, but it was time to stock up on various flours and staples, like the sunflower seeds and flax she used for bread, and the alternative flours she needed to make her gluten-free mix for her youngest daughter, who had a host of allergies and sensitivities. Clare had hoped she'd be able to heal them by the time Polly was grown, but she hadn't.

So Clare baked gluten-free for her, nut-free for one of her grand-children, and egg-free for the vegans. Not all in one bread, usually, but something for everyone, and they'd all be there for Liam's visit. She'd invited him to stay at the farmhouse, and he'd agreed happily. He would arrive on Sunday and stay for just a few days before he took off for his European tour. Clare had no doubt there would be many visits from the cousins who remembered him, and neighbors who were dazzled by his fame and beauty. It was like having a movie star in town.

But she was adamant about protecting him, too, thus the family dinner on Sunday, and a simple tea a couple of days later for the neighbors who wanted to drop in. She'd told Liam they'd all want self-ies. That was fine, he'd said, not bothered.

As she unloaded the flours and powders and bulk ingredients onto the cart, the woman and the clerk checking her out were gossiping, first about someone they both knew who'd obviously been caught red-handed having an affair. Clare sent out a kindly thought to the one who'd found them out and the two who'd been caught. It was never as cut-and-dried as everyone would believe. Life was less black-and-white than was comfortable.

In a little lag, Clare fished the last small bags from the back of the cart, brushing hair out of her face when the woman asked, "Did you hear about the bones they found in Wulfecombe? Surely, a murder."

The clerk tutted. "You've been listening to too much true crime, Nancy. It's probably some servant from the castle. Or some other poor being laid in their grave too soon."

"Murdered!" Nancy cried with some relish, and Clare saw that it was a game with them. "I heard it was a teenager, or maybe younger."

The clerk said, "My partner is with the police. They got the report back. A little girl, they think. Maybe seven or so."

Clare didn't realize she was staring so fiercely until the clerk said, "Sorry, is this bothering you? We'll stop."

"It's all right." She struggled to arrange her face, her chest growing tight. "I just think . . ." She looked at the groceries, which she would still need after all this. "I need some air. I'll be right back."

CHAPTER
TWENTY-NINE

On Saturday morning, Tillie sat at a sidewalk table outside Noon and Night, bathing in the milky spring sunshine, hoping to lift her spirits. A pot of daffodils bloomed by the door, and she could smell apple blossoms somewhere. Birds twittered and chirped and whistled in the short trees along the street. At the next table over, two young women with impossibly fresh skin wore halters as if it were July. She could see goose bumps on the arms of the one closest to her.

Once upon a time, that was Tillie, too. Now, in her late thirties, her thin sweater was not enough. Or maybe she was just cold from missing Liam. It had been strange to sleep without him last night, even if that was ridiculous. She had one text from him as he boarded this morning, well before she woke: I hate seeing the lights of the city disappearing, you with them.

She wrote back a long reply, then erased it. Instead, she wrote simply, Safe travels. I loved the past few days. Which seemed nice but not too overly needy.

Now, she glanced at the screen in her hand. No reply, but then he probably wouldn't even land for another hour or two. She typed: Hope you landed safely and all is well. I miss you already!

And then she felt like Jared and erased that one, too, then dropped her phone in her bag.

Jon strode down the sidewalk, a turquoise scarf looped around his neck, aviator sunglasses shielding his eyes. He looked the part of a successful artist, but then, he always did, probably had even back in Oklahoma. She stood to hug him, and he took off his glasses. "How are you doing, baby?"

"Good. Fine."

His expression was skeptical, but they sat down and ordered their favorites: eggs Benedict for Jon, a spinach omelet for Tillie. The hash browns there were fabulous, and they ordered some to split.

"So, is Lusciousness on his way?"

She nodded. "I was so trying to keep it light, but—" She struggled with the right image. "He hit my life like a tidal wave, and now I'm on the shore, and the wave is gone, and it's all just the same as it was before, only kind of wrecked."

"Oh, honey!" He took her hand. "You fell hard!"

"It's stupid." She blinked away tears. "I know it is."

"Is it, though? Isn't falling in love what we are supposed to do?"

"In five minutes?"

He lifted his shoulders. "I mean—maybe? For what it's worth, it sure looked like it was mutual."

"Thanks." She felt embarrassed by all of it. "I'm tired of talking about my life. Tell me everything. We haven't talked that much about the show, and it went so well!"

He was very quiet for a moment, his luminous eyes resting on her face. "Why do you do that? You're allowed to take up space, love. You can be needy and scared and lost, and I will still love you."

She ducked her my head. "I know. You love me. But I need to stop navel-gazing and thinking all about me, me, me. Will you help me, please? Let's talk about *anything* besides my life. What have you been reading? Bingeing?"

He measured her silently. Then: "Okay. I'm loving a book by Kacen Callender. It's dark but really good. I think you might like it."

She fell into the quick-slow rhythm of his voice, the cadence soothing in its intimate familiarity. He sketched the story, and she fell into the images he painted. It helped stop her attention from wandering back to her phone.

After they'd eaten, she asked, "All packed for Crete?"

"Please come with me. It's only ten days, and it will get you out of your head."

She was sorely tempted—the feeling of sunshine on her arms after the long winter. Having time to lie on a beach and swim in crystal-clear waters was very tempting.

But she shook her head. "You know I can't. This show has to get done." She narrowed her eyes. "And shame on you for tempting me at the runaway time."

He shrugged unapologetically. "I know. I just—"

"Don't want to go alone." She nodded. "I think you might enjoy it more than you think you will."

He sighed. "Maybe. I've just always had you or a boyfriend."

"Wait. You've never traveled alone at all?"

"No."

"You *have* to do it, then. It will be like a rite of passage. It will free you."

"I hope you're right."

CHAPTER THIRTY

Some hours later, Tillie found herself standing in the kitchen of her apartment. The kettle was boiling. A strainer full of tea was ready in a pot, and it smelled of cinnamon and orange, heady and rich, but—

When did she buy it?

A chill rolled down her body, and her hands began to tremble. How did she even get here? She'd hugged Jon, wished him bon voyage, and then . . .

Now, she was boiling water for tea she didn't remember buying. In a state of frozen horror, she stared at the boiling kettle, watched as it clicked off, and tried to piece it together.

What had she done? Where had she gone?

What the actual hell was happening to her?

She closed her eyes, took a deep breath, tried to feel for some sense of her actions, her journey home, where she'd gone. It was terrifying that she had wandered around the city in her amnesiac state. How long had it been? She'd left Jon around 1:00 p.m.

Light slanted through the high row of windows, about to disappear behind the building to the west. Her heart gave a single, hard thud. Way later than 2:00 p.m., which is about how long it would have taken to get home from the restaurant. She looked around for her phone, but her purse was across the room. Quaking, she turned her head to check the sunburst clock on the wall: 4:10.

Her legs wobbled, and she sank like a puppet to the floor. *Three hours!* Three hours wandering around the city without herself, Tillie without Tillie. She pressed her hands to her eyes, feeling panic swell through her body, squeezing the air from her lungs. The edges of her vision prickled, and she feared she would faint. Have a heart attack.

No. She thought of Liam telling her to breathe. In. Out. A long breath in, *one, two, three, four.* A longer breath out, *one, two, three, four, five, six, seven, eight.*

Again.

After a few rounds, she could think more clearly, but it didn't help. The three hours were utterly blank. Where had she gone? What had she done? Standing up, she looked at the bag of loose tea, and it had the sticker from the co-op she and Liam had visited together, the place that smelled of patchouli and lost time.

A tickle of memory rose through the fog. As they'd left the brunch spot, parting ways with a big hug, she had smelled a strong waft of patchouli and yeast, and thought, *That's an odd combination.*

The co-op was only a few blocks from the brunch spot where she'd had lunch with Jon. Maybe it was the smell that triggered her fugue state? She could imagine that she'd stopped by there to feel closer to Liam, relive a good moment, and then—

What?

Her phone. It tracked her path because she liked to keep track of her steps. The map followed her all over town. Jon thought it was creepy, but he had a robot in his apartment that listened when he spoke—and all the rest of the time—so he was one to talk.

The phone wasn't in the pocket where she usually kept it, and when she dug through her bag, remembering that she'd dropped it inside at brunch, she couldn't find it. She checked her sweater pocket. Usually, it was too heavy for that fabric, so she didn't carry it there.

It was gone.

She never lost her phone. It was here somewhere. She checked the bathroom, kitchen, studio, couch, bed.

No.

From her bedside table, she picked up her tablet and used it to ping the phone, listening for the series of dings.

Nothing.

Carrying the tablet with her into the kitchen, she poured hot water over the tea she'd already measured, and while it steeped, she realized that she was desperately thirsty. She poured a glass of water. Whatever she'd been doing, she was hungry, thirsty, and slightly sweaty, as if she'd walked a long time.

Well, yeah. Three hours.

The app offered a message: Phone cannot be located. Last location: Home.

Damn. The charge had been very low last night when she got back, but she'd forgotten to plug it in. The phone must have died somewhere before the locator pinged the restaurant.

Anxiety started roiling up from her gut. She should call Jon and—

Oh, wait. She didn't have her phone.

A faint Mylar line buzzed to life over her right eye. No! She couldn't get a migraine right now, not with a lost phone and a terrifying amnesiac episode, and her best friend on a plane to Crete and—

One thing she knew for sure was that this whole thing was getting out of control. She needed to talk to her therapist, pronto. Before the zigzag light took over her vision, she searched for the therapist's name in her contacts and sent a text through her tablet.

Winnie, I need help urgently. Having strange memory and migraine issues, even a panic attack. When can you talk?

It was only a few minutes before Winnie texted back. Can do a session in one hour. Phone or in person?

Zoom, pls.

Done. Sending link now.

The tablet would show her if anyone had texted her phone, but only if both were on the same system. Tillie and Liam were on different ones, so she couldn't tell if he'd tried. This added to her anxiety, but the aura was taking over her vision, so she stumbled into her bedroom. Setting the timer on the tablet for fifty-five minutes, she covered her eyes with a pillow to try to empty her head.

Surprisingly, she dropped off almost instantly, maybe worn out from walking so long. No dreams.

The alarm awakened her at almost the same moment the tablet dinged with a notice. She rolled over, testing, relieved to discover that there was no emergent migraine, just a little bit of a stiff neck.

The message was a text from Jon. **On my way, baby.** He added an airplane emoji.

Have so much fun! She typed back a dancing emoji.

She took a long swallow from her water bottle, then propped pillows against the wall and opened the Zoom app to connect with her therapist. The thought of her orphaned phone ribboned through her, as if she had physically injured herself, but if it wasn't locatable, it wasn't being used, either, so nothing dire would happen in the next hour. She imagined it lying on the floor of the restaurant, out of juice, hidden beneath a table or kicked into a corner, and it felt like her own body was lying there. She thought of the conversation with Liam about no television or computers when they were kids, and it seemed absurd that a phone felt like her body now.

But it absolutely did. She felt weird without it, like she was missing a kidney or a foot.

Before her thoughts went too dark, Winnie appeared on-screen, and only then did Tillie think to look at herself in the little window. It made her so self-conscious that she often left it off, but it was on from the last call she'd had. Her hair looked windblown, and any makeup was entirely worn away.

Winnie had seen her in worse shape. "Hey," Tillie said.

"Tillie! It was such a surprise to from you. It's been a while!" Winnie was in her fifties, maybe, with prematurely silver hair and a penchant for great lipstick. "What's going on?"

"It's crazy," Tillie said. "So crazy." She told Winnie about the painting, the strange bits of lost time, finding out she had a sister who'd died, the strangeness of the death certificate with her name.

Winnie nodded, listening, interjecting a question now and then, mostly clarifications. When Tillie reached the end—the strange business of walking around the city for three hours with no memory of it—Winnie sat quietly for a moment.

"Okay," she said, nodding. "Let me get this straight. It sounds like the painting triggered a push for your memories to surface, and the guardian portion of your brain that wants to keep you safe is pushing back to keep the doors closed."

"That sounds right."

"Almost exactly the sequence of events that triggered your problems in college."

She frowned. "No. That was just finals stress."

"Was it?" Winnie flipped back through a file on her desk. "I don't think so. The first episode, which was extreme depression and migraines, was triggered by a concert you attended, and you had several short memory losses."

"Wait. I did?" Tillie frowned, trying to remember. "I completely blocked that out, that I had amnesiac episodes that time, too." A clammy sweat broke out on her body. "Am I losing my mind?"

"I don't think so." Her tone was so matter-of-fact that it was reassuring. It was one of the things Tillie liked most about Winnie. No drama. Straightforward clarity. "But I think you are going to have to delve into those repressed memories, or these episodes will just keep getting worse."

She heard the ring of truth, and dropped her face in her hands. "Yeah. But how?"

"There are a number of therapies we can try. Are you familiar with EMDR?"

Eye Movement Desensitization and Reprocessing. It was a mental health treatment for dealing with trauma, Tillie had read. Her throat closed. "Yes. But what if . . ."

"What if?"

"What if something terrible happened, and I don't remember for good reason?"

"I suspect something terrible *did* happen, Tillie," Winnie said. "One part of your mind is protecting you from something it didn't think you could manage, and it has done its job. But you were a child then, and now you're an adult. If we go easy, I think we might be able to peel the onion without creating a crisis."

She was silent, thinking about the repercussions of opening a box she'd kept tightly closed her entire life.

"If you don't start trying to untangle this, Tillie, I'm afraid it will keep getting worse."

"Yeah." She took a breath. "Okay. I'm officially scared, and I need answers. How do we start?"

"Let's go back to the college episode, when we first talked. Do you remember what set that off?"

"I thought I did," Tillie said. "It was a rough semester. I was failing a class, and I couldn't get it together."

"According to my notes, you went to a folk concert. Do you remember that?"

"Not really. I mean, I went to a lot of concerts in those days. And smoked a lot of weed at them." She smiled. "Which probably accounts for some of the forgetting."

"Do you still indulge?"

She shook her head. "Makes me paranoid."

"That's probably better. You should avoid anything that alters your mental state for a while."

"Painting is mind-altering, but I have to keep working."

Winnie was silent for a moment, looking back at the notes in her file. "Hmm. You had a memory loss while painting then, too."

"What? Why don't I remember any of these details?"

"Protection, most likely."

"Do you have notes on what I painted then that caused a lapse?"

Winnie ran a finger down the page. "It looks like it was a cat."

Something plunked hard in her gut. "A cat. I don't remember working on cats then, like, ever. I was in a semiabstract stage." She could place herself in time according to the professors she'd been working with, and she'd been deeply enamored of a colorist who used abstracts to create mood. Jon had been in the same class, and it proved to be a keystone for him. "I was using big color," she said, reaching back. "Fuchsia and lime and—" A flash of the painting at Jon's gallery rose. "The painting that started all this is in those colors." She shook her head, feeling a headache starting to knock at her temples.

"That's interesting."

"And I've been painting this cat, like, over and over. I keep dreaming about him."

"Okay. That's good information."

"I can't stop painting these odd things, and I really need to focus on the things I'm supposed to be doing. I have a show in a few months."

"Okay." Winnie settled. "Do you want to get started with the EMDR?"

"Now?" she squeaked. "No, no, no. I don't have anybody around. My best friend is on a plane to Crete, and the guy I've been dating is in London. Anyway, he's tangled up in all of this somehow."

"You didn't mention him. How is he connected?"

"I'm not sure," she said slowly, "but I keep thinking that if he hadn't also been there that night I saw the painting, none of this would be happening."

"Yet."

"Right. I mean, I guess eventually things come out or . . . Do people ever keep things behind a paywall forever?"

"Sure," she said. "People manage all kinds of things in all kinds of ways. But in this case, your mind wants you to figure it out. Or at least that's how it looks from here. You almost did it that first time around but shoved it all back down. Now your mother has died, and you're processing all kinds of emotions."

"Yeah." Tillie curled her arms around herself. "My mom was still alive then."

"Yes. I also suspect that's the change here." She tapped her pen against her chin. "Tell me about the new guy. Do you think he reminds you of someone?"

"Not exactly? I just feel like I've always known him. Like, *always*, which is stupid, I know, and he's also famous, so maybe I've just seen him somewhere and filed his face away."

"Famous?"

"Not like a rock star or an actor. He leads workshops and things like that."

"I see." Winnie made another note. Looked at Tillie without judgment or conversation.

"So what do we do?"

"It's not going to happen fast, Tillie. I'd really rather meet with you in person as well. Is that possible for you?"

"Yes."

"We can also try some drug therapy, if you feel you need it."

Some part of her threw up a hand. *No.* She touched her chest in surprise. "No. Not right now, anyway."

"All right. You have twofold homework. I want you to journal every day as a general practice, preferably when you first wake up, and also whenever you feel anxious or worried. And I want you to keep a dream journal. Write down any dreams you have, and whatever emotions come up."

A little sense of panic fluttered in her throat. "I'm scared. What if I find out something I don't want to know?"

"We can do some hypnosis to help keep you from getting over-whelmed, if you like."

"Okay."

"We'll start that at our next session. Can you come in next week?"

"Yes, of course."

They scheduled an appointment. Winnie said, "You have my number. Text me if you need to. Are you feeling okay right now?"

Tillie tested her body. "I'm good."

"All right. I'll see you next week."

As often happened when she finished a therapy session, she fell back asleep.

And there were the girls, on the porch. With the cat, sitting between them. For the first time, Tillie saw that the place was a little shabby, and amid the flowers in the beds along the steps grew weeds. The girls played a game, maybe jacks, and their clothes were too big for them.

They were speaking a language Tillie couldn't quite hear—related but not exactly like a romance language, those fluid syllables. She strained to listen, and the words started translating in her mind, like subtitles on a movie, and she understood that she could do the same in return. In their language, she said, "Hello. What are your names?"

They turned, one hostile, one open. "That's our language!" the hostile one said.

"Sorry," she said in English. "What's your name?"

"Sunny," she said, "and this is my sister, Stormy."

"Sunny and Stormy," she repeated. "Who are you?"

The closed one gave her a look like she was an idiot. "We just told you!"

And then, as if a door slammed, she was back in her bed, staring at the ceiling, trying to capture the images rather than run away from them. The girls were dark-haired and skinny. Sisters, maybe even twins.

The language eluded her now that she was back in her usual mind, but wisps of it lingered, clinging like feathers. It was both familiar and not, as if it had been taken from another language she'd studied.

Mindful of her therapist's homework order, she got up and found a notebook to write down the dream. The subtitles made her laugh, and on the blank page, she drew the feeling of the syllables, lilting, and made it into an Arabic-looking format.

Sunny and Stormy. Sunny was her imaginary friend from childhood. Was Stormy the shadow version of that invention?

Then she asked herself if this could be the other Tillie, the one who'd died in the firestorm. Was it a snapshot of the pair of them at some earlier time? Was one of the girls her sister? It made her feel terribly sad.

Enough. The clock on the wall said 7:00 p.m. She really needed to find her phone.

CHAPTER
THIRTY-ONE

New York City

Noon and Night had transformed itself into a very hip bar for the evening, open to the warmish night. Well-dressed twentysomethings drank cocktails, a few of them standing outside to smoke. Soft jazz played on the speakers. Tillie stepped up to the bar. A young male bartender dropped a napkin in front of her. "What'll it be?"

"I don't need a drink. I might have lost my phone here earlier today. Did anybody turn one in?"

"I'll check."

She stood there. Nearby, a man leaned in to whisper into a woman's ear, his hand lightly stroking her upper arm. She suddenly missed Liam with a ferocity that was both surprising and unnerving. She was desperate to find out if he'd texted.

The bartender returned. "Sorry. They don't have anything in the lost and found."

"Is it okay if I check under the booth where we were?"

"Go for it."

The booth was occupied, of course, with a pair of women with heads close, having a deep chat. "Sorry to bother you, but do you mind if I check for my phone under your table?"

One gave her a weird look, but the other pulled out her phone. "I lost mine two weeks ago. It was such a pain." She turned on her flashlight and handed it to Tillie.

She crouched and shone the light under the table while the women lifted their feet. It was bright enough to illuminate the carpeted area connecting the booth to the floor. There was no place for a phone to hide.

"Thanks." She handed the phone back.

"Good luck."

The co-op wasn't far, but without her phone map, Tillie wasn't exactly sure where it was. She looked around carefully, remembering that she and Liam had been only a block or so from the train. She headed that way, trusting her gut to lead her. She turned right, down a couple of blocks, then left, and there it was, bright lights spilling out of the basement. Again, she felt the loss of Liam, the fact he'd been here and now he wasn't. It felt tragic.

Which was ridiculous.

A bearded man of about forty was ringing up a woman with a dowager's hump. Tillie pretended to be looking at the bulk items while he finished. He caught sight of her and lifted his chin, smiling in a friendly way. Tillie wondered if he'd waited on her earlier. Discomfort wiggled through her. How had she behaved? What had she said? It was horrifying not to know.

When the old woman exited, she headed for the counter, feeling weird and embarrassed. "Hi, I was in here earlier—"

"I remember."

Damn. "And I left my phone somewhere. I'm retracing my steps."

He made a little noise, holding up one finger, and reached behind the counter. "I figured you'd be back. It's dead, and I didn't have a charger, so I couldn't do anything with it until I got home."

Relief sent cooling waves through her body, almost shocking after the heat of the last few hours. "Thank God." She smiled. "And you. Thank you."

"No problem. I hope you find your sister."

Tillie froze, trying to work out what that meant. What she'd said. How could she ask for more information without seeming like a weirdo? But she couldn't think of a way, and just nodded. "Thanks." She headed for the door.

But seriously, this guy would never see her again, and she didn't have to please him or seem normal, but she really did need some answers. She spun around on her heel.

"Look, this is weird, but I'm having memory issues from . . . medication . . . and I know I was here because I brought tea home, but I don't remember what I said about my sister."

His brown eyes were concerned. "Wow. Are you okay?"

"Uh, that's a hard question to answer. Do you remember what I said?"

"Yeah, we talked for like five minutes about you losing her when you were a little girl and now you're trying to find her."

"I didn't say she was dead?"

"No. Is she?"

Tillie paused, trying to collate this information. "No. I *am* looking for her. Thanks."

He grabbed a piece of paper from the counter and scribbled something down. "If you need anything, just call or text. Anytime." His gaze was kind as he held out the paper. "I've been through a few things myself."

She realized that he thought she was an addict or something, and her face flushed. Although, why be embarrassed if he wanted to help, and honestly—

A roar filled her ears—embarrassment or confusion or both—and she snatched the paper and hurried out, phone clutched to her belly. She was anxious to get home and plug in the phone, but she was also worried about every single moment she'd be out in the world, fearing another dissociative issue. She flagged a cab, gave the driver her address, and let go of a breath.

My sister. She'd told the clerk that she was looking for her sister, not that her sister was dead. What did her memory know that she didn't? Were the lies her mother told even deeper than she suspected?

The tattered visions or memories that were surfacing gave her the sense that the two girls were sisters, and one of them was Tillie, but how did that fit the rest of what she knew—that her mother had a child who'd died in the Valencia firestorm and then moved to upstate New York?

It didn't make sense. None of it fit together.

A ripple of headache blipped across her forehead, and she immediately took a breath, let it out, and rubbed circles on her temples.

When the cab pulled up, Jared was sitting on her stoop. She blurted out, "What the hell?"

"Everything all right, miss?" the driver asked.

Tillie sighed. "It's fine, thanks." She ran her card, then grabbed her phone and stomped out of the car. "What are you doing here?"

"Hey, hold on." He raised his hands. "You told me to meet you here."

"What?" She closed her eyes, feeling her arms drop, her entire body droop. "When?"

"What do you mean, when? This afternoon. You texted me."

"My phone has been dead for hours. I lost it while I was shopping earlier."

Disappointment soured his features. With barely controlled fury, he smashed his finger against the app on his phone and turned the screen to face her.

Jared, I need help. Can you meet me at my apartment around eight?

You told me not to talk to you, and now you want my help?

Please. It's important. I'm scared.

What about Liam?

He left.

No games.

No games, I swear.

She stared at the words as if they would wake something up. Her heart thudded a warning, slow and hard. "I don't remember," she whispered. Because they'd been together five years and she maybe owed him something, she added, "I'm sorry. I'm having memory problems, and I can't remember what I wanted to talk to you about."

"You look like shit," he said, and did what he had always done—stepped forward and tugged her into an embrace that felt like a bulwark against the world. "It's okay. Let's get you upstairs and into a hot bath."

In the past, he would have done this for her when she'd had a migraine or a bad day. Helped her into the bath, washed her hair, brought her a cup of tea. One of the things she'd loved about him was his gentleness. In her fear during her blackout, that was probably what she'd yearned for.

But now that she was in her right mind, she knew she didn't want that. Still not with Jared.

Whatever else was going on, Tillie didn't want to give him the wrong idea. "Jared, I don't want to get back together."

His body tensed.

She pulled out of his arms. "I don't remember texting you. I'm sorry if I gave you the wrong idea."

He stared at her. "Memory issues? What does that even mean?"

She was too fried to even begin to explain. "I don't know."

They stood there, looking at each other, and suddenly he capitulated. "You know what, Tillie? Fuck you, and fuck this. Fuck everything. Don't call me again, for anything. Ever."

"Jared—"

"No. You're not going to use me and throw me away."

"I didn't mean to—"

But he was storming off.

Storming. Stormy. The hostile little girl looked up from her memory.

We are you, silly.

CHAPTER THIRTY-TWO

London

The workshop in London was only two days, plus an evening meet-and-greet the night before. Liam usually enjoyed this part—talking with people who shared his interests in meditation and spirituality, listening to their stories. They often had heart-wrenching, difficult tales to share, and he was humbled by the things people could leave behind them. Terrible things, sad things. Most people didn't start to walk the path to enlightenment without a big slap from life.

Tonight, he only wanted to go to his hotel room and wait for the phone to ring. He'd sent a dozen texts and two phone messages to Tillie, and nothing had come back.

He'd had harsh words with Krish on the plane over the incident with Nikki Gonzales, and his manager was now on his best behavior. He knew he'd overstepped, and was contrite, but Liam felt a certain arrogance from him that was unsettling. Liam would have trusted Krish with his life, but something had changed.

Money. That was the problem. None of the team had ever had any, and now they all had a lot. No matter what the intentions, that some-times shifted the dynamics of things. In Krish's case, a lot of people were depending on him—a brother in an expensive university in America, a sister with bipolar disorder who struggled to hold a job, aging parents. He'd never married, and although he didn't say so publicly in order to spare his conservative family, he was gay, with a long-term partner in Wellington, where they kept a house on a cliff above the Tasman Sea.

But it was one thing for Krish to worry about Liam, fear that he was going around the bend, and quite another to send in a beautiful girl to seduce him.

It was a mean, dark trick, considering how much Krish knew about Liam's struggle to learn how to have healthy relationships.

Liam didn't know if he could forgive it. Or maybe he could forgive it, but he couldn't forget. Which meant that Krish had to go. If that was so, how would the entire machine move forward?

And if it couldn't, was Liam using this situation to dismantle something he'd grown weary of?

As he circled the room, listening and shaking hands and accepting the loving embrace of the people there, he set the puzzle on a back table of his mind. He made himself focus entirely on the moment, the people here, the offering he could make right here, right now.

But he would have to make some choices. Soon.

In his pocket, his phone buzzed. Walking away from a little crowd, he checked it. Not Tillie.

Not Tillie.

Not Tillie.

A thread of doubt shimmered in the midst of his certainty. Had he gotten it wrong? Was Krish right? Was this just a repeat of a pattern he'd been employing for decades?

He caught his friend's eye across the room. Sober eyes. Knowing eyes. Until now, Liam had trusted him completely. He'd rescued Liam a half a dozen times, picking him up off the floor when he'd broken up with someone and gone on a bender, poured him into a shower and made him eat. The first time had been at age thirteen, when Belinda Tohu broke up with him after three months with no explanation. The last had been two years ago, when Melanie had grown tired of the demands of his career and decided she didn't want to be a part of it. He'd believed they would marry, and the breakup made him question himself, his choices in women, his ability to be real.

"Liam?" a voice said behind him.

He turned to see a young man, scrubbed and well tended, in a kind of uniform of loose pants and a tight athletic top that showed off his physique. "Yes, hi," Liam said automatically, and shook the extended hand.

"I'm Gregory Baker. Just wanted to meet you in person. I'll be in the workshop tomorrow, but I'm really happy to just be able to talk to you in person. Which I guess I already said."

Liam smiled. "Thanks." He forced himself to put aside the internal whirl to focus outward, on the people who'd come here to meditate with him, explore their inner world this weekend. He owed them his focused attention. "It's good to meet you. Tell me about yourself."

As the man started talking, Liam felt a buzz from his phone. And forced himself not to answer it.

CHAPTER
THIRTY-THREE

New York City

Back in her apartment, Tillie plugged in her phone, but it was so dead that it took a few minutes for it to go live. Relief flooded through her as the screen lit up at last. She gave it another couple of minutes and then opened the screen, relieved to see the number 13 by the messages. Two were from Jon, checking in on his trip. The rest were all from Liam.

2:15 p.m.—Landed. Didn't sleep much last night, so jet-lagged as hell. Can't wait to talk to you.

4:24 p.m.—Checked in to my hotel. Miss you. It's a big suite, with a gorgeous tub. We could swim in it!

5:10 p.m.—Hoping to hear from you soon. Thinking it's evening there, but I've been known to mix up time zones. Might not last a lot longer, but feel free to text. I'll see it in the morning. Xoxo

5:45 p.m. I'm out, love. Hope you're good. Business gets going in the morning at ten, which is insanely early there. Will be finished by around 5:00 p.m., then back at it for dinner at 7:00 p.m. But text me if you want. I'll be glad to see it whenever it comes in.

She was both disappointed and relieved—wretched that she hadn't been able to talk to him, but relieved that he'd texted. She checked the world clock and saw that it was 1:00 a.m. in London, but taking him at his word, she texted: Sorry! Wasn't ignoring you! I know it sounds lame, but I actually lost my phone! At five London time, it's noon here, so we should be good. LMK when you're free, and we can video chat! (And that's as many exclamation points as I'm allowed, I think.)

She sent it, and then it felt like not enough, so she took a breath for courage and typed: I miss you, too. A lot!! :)

And then she left her phone to charge and started walking circles around the studio. She wondered how to get herself back to herself.

There was really only one answer. She climbed into her painting clothes, turned on some decidedly unromantic music, and focused on painting. Not the angel but the gazelle girl. The painting was strong, and it absorbed her deeply—in a flow way, not a fugue way. She felt stable enough to allow herself to get lost in the colors and the music and the flow of just *making*.

When her shoulders and arms started to protest, she lined up the rest of the paintings side by side to figure out what might be next, what would help round out the series. It was unlike her to be stuck—there were usually more ideas in her mind than she could possibly capture on canvas—but she just wasn't seeing what the final three paintings should be. Actually, two, because one would obviously be the cat.

Across the worktables, she spread out charcoal drawings she'd made of the cat, and chose two of the strongest to pin to the bulletin boards. Using thick pastels, she sketched him again, one sleepy, one frisky, and one with the girl on his back, a basis for the actual painting, which she would work on tomorrow.

It reminded her of the cat Winnie said she'd painted in school. Picking up her phone, she texted Jon: Do you remember a cat painting I did the year I had my breakdown?

She put the phone down and looked at the paintings. What else?

She didn't know right this minute, and maybe that was okay. She glanced at the clock and wondered if was late enough to call Liam, but counting forward, it was still the middle of the night.

Giving up the day at last, she scrubbed her arms and hands, shed her paint-covered clothes, and climbed into a pair of sweats and a T-shirt. Nothing from Liam yet, of course. She imagined him asleep on thousand-thread-count sheets in a London hotel room and wished she was there with him.

Her unread email count was 6,209, which wasn't terrible for her. For a couple of minutes, she sorted the ads, unsubscribed, and erased until she got to the actual emails. One was from her gallery: How's it going? Can I see where you are?

Easy. Tillie turned on the overhead lights in the studio, then stood back far enough to capture all the paintings. She sent back an email with a long shot of the studio, paintings lined up conveniently. Getting there.

The gallery wrote back immediately. Shit! Love the witch! And the angel!

Tillie looked at the paintings, seeing what she hadn't: the transformed painting of her mother, the witch, was an excellent counter to the angel of Liam. She hadn't planned to use it, but maybe that wasn't really true if she'd sent the shot to her gallery with it fully visible.

She startled when a bell dinged with a new email, and she saw the header was from Shiloh.

> Oh, *that* painting!

> Hi, Tillie. Forest #21 is part of a series I did on the Devon coast. I don't have the photos handy (I only have a flip phone—I know it's weird but it keeps me present), so I can't tell you exactly where. But I was hanging with a woman who likes to surf, so it was north Devon, one of the little towns around Saunton Sands Beach. I want to say Croyde Bay or Braunton, maybe? There are a couple of others.

> One of the holiday villages along there. Hope that
> helps.

For the first time, a real break.

But Devon? That was kind of weird. Wasn't that where Liam was going to see his family?

A slight shiver ran down her arms.

She opened her laptop and called up a map, searching for Saunton Sands Beach, then zoomed in to the towns around it. There were a handful, greater and lesser distances from the beach. How to choose? Where to start?

She turned to her patchy memories. There was nothing in them about a beach or seaside. Only a forest. *A wood,* the girls in her dreams said, and it gave her hope. If they talked to her, it would be a big help.

Or else she was losing her mind, and she'd be on a wild-goose chase. Both were equally possible.

At this point, she felt she had no choice but to follow her gut. *Forests in North Devon,* she typed, and there were several, but not many close to the sea. She sucked on her top lip, mulling the choices.

One by one, she checked photos of various villages to see if any of them triggered a reaction. There were a couple of resort-style hotels, but most of the towns looked like every other English village she'd ever seen photos of—a central area with a square or a church, old buildings, a bookstore up a crooked road, and a bunch of houses that all looked about the same. Someone told her once they looked like that because there had been so much building in the fifties and sixties, as the country recovered from the war.

Which was staggering to think about, really. A nation so trashed by bombs that it was rebuilding for twenty years. It happened all the time, of course, was happening now, all over the world, but it was still awful.

Nothing in the village photos caught her eye particularly. Cloverly looked pretty, and there was a big hotel at Saunton Sands proper. She clicked on more photos of Braunton, then on Wulfecombe.

There, a photo of a mill whispered recognition. She clicked on others. An ordinary village, once again, a narrow street with a row of shops. One was painted yellow, with a mullioned window in front. A light-colored cat sat on the sill like a queen.

This one, her body said.

This one.

Her heart fluttered in her throat. She clicked around the rest of the village, picking up the little blue man in Google, dropping him in new places. A cottage with pink shutters caught her eye, but was that as a painter or as a memory? She was starting to lose perspective.

Something felt right about the village. Maybe that was enough at this point. The worst that could happen was that she'd be wrong, find nothing, and lose a few days of painting time.

Should she fly there?

It seemed completely insane, and it might also look like she was chasing after Liam, which was horrifying.

Truthfully, it was ridiculous to even consider. She didn't have time to spare, and she would have to go alone, but she wouldn't get her work done until she figured it out. It also felt strangely urgent, as if it had to be done *right now.*

Impulsively, she checked flights. Without giving herself time to back out, she booked one for the next day.

Should she tell Liam? Maybe not. Their connection was powerful and full of potential, and she didn't want to ruin the newness of it by appearing to chase him.

She wouldn't tell him. She'd figure out an excuse about why she was out of touch, and it was mostly while he was busy, anyway. She started to make a little chart of what time it would be in New York and how to stay on track with that, but her brain started breaking in three seconds, and it felt like out-and-out lying. She'd wing it.

Energized, she got up to pack.

CHAPTER THIRTY-FOUR

Wulfecombe

Clare left Levi sleeping in the darkness before dawn and quietly headed downstairs. A trail of animals followed her. George jumped up howling when he heard her, and she hurried over to give him some reassurance that it was only her. "Let's have breakfast, shall we?" He slurped a soft tongue over her inner wrist, and Clare bent to kiss him. "You're the sweetest thing ever," she murmured, pulling his ears through her hands.

George had been blinded by an accident with cooking oil, and his nose showed the scar tissue of that terrible day. It had fully been accidental, but his owners hadn't wanted to bother with a blind dog and asked to put him down. Instead, Levi adopted the sweet being, and he'd lived with them for nearly a decade. His world was the farm, and he knew where things were by smell and feel.

"Come, sweet," she said now, and he followed her into the kitchen. She fed everyone—cats and dogs and rabbits. The goats and ducks and geese were Levi's realm, and he'd take care of them when he got up.

As she started the kettle for her tea and pulled out a cutting board to start the vegetables, she felt a sense of *something*. Not quite a warning, but an alert as if the weather was going to turn. High seas ahead. She lifted her head and tried to gauge what she might need to do to prepare, but there was nothing more than the whispering sense of things on the verge.

Which was the natural way of the world, of course. Everything was always on the verge. She moved her senses over the beings in her world to see if she felt anything amiss—Levi, upstairs sleeping, with his sore back. Was it more than that?

No. And not the children, none of them. Sage and her baby, also fine, but—

Something. Something connected to Sage, then.

Was it the bones they'd found in the housing estate? She pressed a hand to her belly, gauging vibrations. Unclear. Maybe the bones, maybe not, but definitely something to do with Sage, her finally settled, happy daughter.

Protect her, she prayed.

Then she firmly planted a podcast in her ears, blocking out swirling strangeness as she chopped onions and turnips and potatoes and put them in to roast for a soup.

She sent out protective prayers, an umbrella over all the people she loved. *Be safe. Be happy. Be well.*

CHAPTER
THIRTY-FIVE

After nearly twenty grueling hours of travel—a flight, a quick sleep, a train, a long drive around narrow roads winding through thick woods—Tillie exited a taxi in front of the Green King Inn, an ancient building that leaned so precipitously toward the cobbled street that it seemed like it might fall over at any moment.

She wondered at her choice, paid the driver, and dragged her small bag behind her toward a thick door situated between two wide mullioned windows. She paused and looked around, asking her gut for any help it might offer. A vegan café stood down the road, and a fish-and-chips shop, and a bakery. She certainly wouldn't starve.

Inside the inn, it was dark and close and smelled of beer. The young woman behind the counter had a nose ring, and the ends of her hair had been dipped in red. "Hello," she said, friendly enough.

"I have a reservation."

She checked her in, four days, which was all Tillie had thought she could spare, and gave her a heavy key. "No elevator, I'm afraid. Take the stairs to the third floor, and your room is on the left. It's a nice one. You'll like it."

"Thanks." Tillie would have been glad to have a nap on a park bench. It was only midafternoon, but she was crashing hard. It was annoying. When she and Jon had done their world tour, she'd been proud of her adaptability—she never got jet lag.

She was out of practice.

The room was better than she'd expected. A big window looked out to the street, and the bed was generous. She dropped her bag, shed her jacket, and fell down on the pillows for just a little nap.

Which ended up being an hour. The buzz of texts woke her up, and she rolled over to scroll through them. Jon had arrived in Crete and sent a photo of gloriously blue seas.

Tillie sent one back of Heathrow. I just got to England.

Wait. You're in London? I'm crushed you didn't come with me! But I guess a lover is a bigger draw.

> :(I'm not in London. Liam is, and I didn't follow him. The painter from your show got back to me, and she said the house in the painting is on the west coast of Devon. Here to see if I can find it. Only a few days.

I'm worried UR there alone.

> Don't. I'm happy. I have the therapist in my pocket. All is well.

Is it, though?

> It's fine. Hey, did you get the text about a cat painting when we were in Hucker's class?

Yes. You don't remember that cat? It was a big painting, giant, and you painted it in two days.

I don't remember. Was it like the cat I've been doing now?

Now that you mention it, yes.

OK. I'm going to get to the bottom of this.

I am only a text away. ANYTIME.

Thank you. I promise I will text if I need you. Also, I promise to go somewhere with you after all this.

Deal.

Go have a cool drink, and eye the handsome men all around. Don't worry about me.

xoxo. Keep me posted, baby.

She'd sent Liam a text before boarding that left things a little vague. She didn't want to lie outright, but it felt ridiculous to tell him that she was coming to England.

Found out a bunch of new information. Will be traveling next twenty-four hours, but will catch up as soon as I can. Miss you!

He'd texted back several times:

Can't wait to hear all about it. Getting ready to head into the workshop. Hope you slept well. XO

Then: Tried to call but missed you. Will try later!

Later: Little window right now between lunch and the afternoon and evening session. Call if you get this.

That had been two hours ago. She rubbed her forehead and typed.

Sorry I missed you. Try tomorrow? I miss you. Really, really do.
Been some developments, and I want to tell you all about it, but
too long for texts.

Considering all that had happened, Jon's worry was not unfounded,
but she did feel fine. Excited, even. If she wanted to solve the mystery,
she'd have to get busy. She quickly unpacked, washed her face, and
headed out.

The day was bright with spring, but despite the weather, the street
seemed quiet for a Saturday. Both the bakery and the café she'd spied
earlier were already closed, and when she came across an Italian restaurant, she saw that it wouldn't open until 5:00 p.m. A small market
looked bustling, so she crossed the street, thinking she'd get some cheese
and bread and fruit, and eat it in a park near the river.

"Hiya," the clerk said, chewing gum, and dragged the packages over
the scanner. Then she frowned. "How do I know you?"

Tillie shook her head. She'd had some modest success, but it would
be very surprising if anyone here had heard of her. "I don't think it's me."

"You're American!"

She nodded. "Guilty."

"My mistake." But the woman tilted her head, peered through narrowed eyes. Shrugged, then handed Tillie the food. "Ta."

The sun was low, allowing a chill to rise from the ground, but her
body was happy to have some fresh air after so much travel. Walking
along the river with her bag in hand, she enjoyed the birds and the silvery ripples of the water, feeling at ease for the first time in ages.

At a low-lying spot, a scattering of people were gathered along
the banks, children playing in the shallow water, splashing each other,
laughing. Parents drank from plastic cups of wine and dangled their toes
over the short wall. A sign said WOLF FORD, and although she'd heard
of fords—places to cross a river—she'd never actually seen one. It was

so curiously old-fashioned that she decided it would be a good picnic spot. She settled on an empty portion of wall in the sunshine, took off her shoes to trail her feet in the stream, and opened her paper bag. The scent of pastry and paper rose, curiously evocative.

And as the cold water enveloped her toes, the world split.

"Sunny! Sunny! Do this!" A girl with long black hair spun around, splashing her hands through the water—

It was over before she captured much at all. Was it a memory? An *actual* memory? Did that mean she was in the right place?

She looked toward the buildings of the high street, wondering how to pursue these fragments of memory, how to get to the bottom of whatever was happening here.

In her pocket, her phone rang.

CHAPTER
THIRTY-SIX

The problem with Krish had been simmering for two days, but the trouble itself had been building to this point for quite some time. Krish had always seen the financial potential for the company, while Liam was more focused on the spiritual side, but that was always how it had been between them—Krish practical, Liam dreaming. It had been the pattern of their friendship long before Quiet was born.

Liam had avoided his friend through the workshops. They'd gone well, he thought at the end of the final gathering. It had been a very mixed group in every demographic way—age, gender, race, culture— which he liked to see and had been pushing for. The cornerstone population of the workshops was still a privileged set, well educated and monied. They tended to be generous as well, helping fund scholarships, of which there were many at every stop.

He'd just scrambled into his oldest jeans and a T-shirt when Krish knocked. "That went well, I think," Krish said.

Liam nodded, scrolling through the messages on his phone without looking up. His mother reminded him to text Clare; his oldest sister sent a photo of her dog rolling on his back; and then, Tillie.

Sorry I missed you. Try tomorrow? I miss you. Really, really do. Been some developments, and I want to tell you all about it, but too long for texts.

A swoosh of relief washed away half the tension in his body. He glanced up at Krish. "Something on your mind?"

Krish smiled tightly and closed the door behind him. He took the earphones from his ears. "You tell me."

"I'm not ready to talk about it," Liam said, punching in the time difference between New York and London. Only midday there. He'd call her straight away.

"Talk about what? You've been pissed off for days. Was it the veto of the painting that woman wanted to do? You know all the reasons it would be bad for the brand."

Brand. Liam sank into an armchair and wiped the weariness off his face. "It's not about the painting, but it is about Tillie in a way."

"I'm listening," Krish said, but his arms were crossed over his chest, and his chin was slightly lifted.

"You set me up with the donor."

"Yeah? And?"

"Because you wanted me to take her out, have sex, show me that the thing with Tillie is just another fling."

He lifted a shoulder. "Maybe. It didn't work, I guess, but you can't blame me for trying. We're at a tipping point here, and you want to drop everything for . . . a girl."

"Not a girl, and not *for* her, either. Bro, I keep trying to tell you this is not working for me, and it's my company, my idea. I don't want to think about branding or how many people we can pack into a workshop."

"That's why you have me. I've always been the one to deal with the hard stuff." He seemed to realize how it sounded and backpedaled. "Hard stuff, as in the things you don't like, the spreadsheets and marketing and donors."

"And branding," Liam said.

"Of course. You resist it, but branding is part of what we're doing here. You're offering a particular kind of experience, and people want to take part. I handle that end so you're free to do what you do—draw them in."

Liam had always known there was a fundamental difference in their approach. Krish was a numbers man, a scientist and business builder. He didn't even particularly believe in what Liam did. "The problem is that what I'm trying to offer is a connection to spiritual experiences, to keying into something bigger and better than any number. It's not quantifiable."

"The revenue says otherwise. It's definitely quantifiable. It's made both of us wealthy. Bought your mum a proper house, and mine the travel she wants to see her relatives, and my dad a car he's not ashamed of. What about those things? I know you understand that money is not just money. It's comfort and quiet and cleanliness."

"We have enough! More than enough. I need some time to collect myself, get some balance back in my life."

"By bonking some woman and falling in love and thinking she's going to solve all your problems. Again?"

"You're so focused on doing this your way that you set me up with a woman you thought would be my catnip, like sitting an alcoholic down with a bottle of whiskey." The anger dissipated as he spoke the truth. "That's not the action of a person I can trust."

"Overstating it a bit, aren't you? It didn't work. You've proved you've done the work. Problem solved."

"No. You betrayed me." He stood, feeling clarity. "You're done."

"Done?"

"You're fired."

"You're *firing* me? That's a laugh. The whole business will fall apart."

"I doubt it. There are a few very talented people on staff, but even if it's true, I can't be in such a close relationship with someone who

215

betrayed me so deeply." He held out his hand. "Give me your phone, please."

For a long, long beat, Krish stared at him, then handed over the business phone and walked out.

Liam called Yolanda. "Can you come down to my room, please? Do not let Krish into any of our spaces."

CHAPTER THIRTY-SEVEN

Wulfecombe

As she sat on a bench by the ford, admiring the river, Tillie tried to ground herself in her surroundings. She took out a tiny sketchbook from her bag, the little tin of watercolors, and a bleed-proof ink pen, and let herself fall into the easy pleasure of capturing the scene. The trees beginning to leaf out, the slant of sunlight, the children wading happily in what had to be very cold water, their parents on the banks, calling out to them. *Don't get your trousers wet. It's safe. Walk a little way!*

A sense of peace began to creep in, and she took a deep breath. Her previous memory made her feel like she was definitely close to getting the answers she'd been looking for.

Her phone buzzed. She picked it up and saw that it was Liam. He texted: I've just had a big fight with Krish. Can I call you?

Yes!

She glanced to each side to make sure no one would be bothered by her conversation, and when the call came through, she said quietly, "Hey. What happened?"

"I think I just fired him." He sounded bewildered.

"Wow. That's big." The sun spilled over the crown of her head, and she was so happy to be here, in this spot, that it was easy to be the encouraging one. "What happened?"

"He's been interfering in ways that are not okay," he said. She guessed by the sound of his breath that he was walking. "Just before I left New York, he tried to get a woman to seduce me."

A rumbling of disquiet sounded in the distance. "That's a weird thing to do. Why?"

"It's a long story, but he doesn't want me to get involved with you."

"With me in particular?"

"Anyone." He sighed. "This is not a conversation to have on the phone. I want to see you."

"What kind of conversation?"

"It's nothing. Well, it's something, but it isn't what—" He broke off. "You don't have to worry. I promise. Look, I can be on a plane in a few hours, be in New York by morning." He made a noise. "No, wait. I have to see my family. They're expecting me, so it'll have to be Tuesday or so. Can we hold off until then?"

She suddenly realized that she was never going to lie to him. How could she? "Well, here's the thing. I'm not in New York. I wasn't going to bother you, but I found out that the painting was done in a little town near the Devon coast." She took a breath. "So, I'm . . . uh . . . in England."

"What? You're here? In England?"

"I didn't want you to think I was chasing you or something, so I thought I'd just deal with this, see what I could find out, and then we could talk when you were done."

"Where in England?"

"In Devon." She looked over her shoulder as if to reassure herself.

"Wait. That's crazy. My family is in Devon. In Wulfecombe. Do you know where that is?"

A weird, twisting emotion swirled through her gut, her throat, welled in her eyes. "Liam," she managed in a hushed tone.

"What?"

"That's where I am. My feet are in the ford right now."

He was silent. Then: "This is getting really fucking weird."

"Yeah." She blinked, and tears rolled down her cheeks. Her emotion was pure terror, the kind of terrified that seemed unreal, like discovering that a haunted house was actually haunted.

"Don't leave," he said. "I'll be there in a few hours. Where are you staying?"

"The Green King."

"I'll be there soon."

"Okay."

He hung up, and she held the phone loosely in her palm, heart racing, then thudding, unable to make up its mind. What the actual hell was going on here?

The phone buzzed and showed her Liam's name. "Hello?"

"I forgot to say I really can't wait to kiss you."

A small laugh broke through the fear in her body. "Me, too."

"Tillie, this is—"

She waited.

"It's important."

"Yeah." She nodded, even though he couldn't see her.

"I'll see you soon."

It was impossible to sit there after that conversation. She walked aimlessly through the streets of the village, maybe half looking for the little house in the painting or maybe the yellow building that had looked familiar, or anything, really, that might jog her memory.

The light was still bright at 5:00 p.m., and she wandered up one lane and down another, admiring spring bulbs exploding from the beds, tulips and narcissi and a big patch of lily of the valley. She knew their names because her mother had taught her, and it made her feel close to Arlette to recite them.

She suddenly missed her so very, very much. Her funny croaky laugh, the way she'd put a hand to her upper chest when something was hilarious. She could be very funny, a master of puns and sly asides, and she had a friend in a crow who brought her presents of bits of glass or squashed bottle caps. She called him Reaper, for a Blue Oyster Cult song.

As if Arlette had sent him, a giant crow landed in the garden in front of Tillie and squawked. "Is your name Reaper, too?" she asked. It gave her a beady eye, squawked again, then flapped its wings and lifted off.

"Oh, Mom," she said aloud. "What is this all about? Couldn't you have left a letter or something?"

She thought of Jon's question. *Are you sure you want to keep going down this road?*

She was suddenly not at all sure.

CHAPTER
THIRTY-EIGHT

Liam rode to Devon in a Town Car. He texted Clare on the way out of London to let her know he was coming. She sent back a smiley-face emoji. Can't wait to see you!

He sat in the back with headphones tuned to the most calming music he could find, easy synthesizer and piano and flutes, mostly. He used them as background for the meditations in his workshops, and they worked now to ease his sense of agitation. He listened to the music, watching the landscape pass by the windows, and counted breaths. Whenever his thoughts urgently intruded—*What have you done? How will you move forward without Krish? How the hell is Tillie in Wulfecombe?*—he started his breath count over.

Halfway to Devon, he took out his phone and texted his mentor: Bhante, I have come to a crossroad. Can we speak soon?

Just the act of typing it out gave him a sense of calm. He could hear Bhante's voice, calm and full of humor, giving him back a piece of wisdom Liam most likely already had within. And in a moment, a text came back: Yes. Remember, too, that everything has a beginning and an ending. Make your peace with that, and all will be well.

He texted back a grateful-hands emoji and leaned back. The surprise was not that he'd parted ways with his old friend, but that it had taken so long. Krish had no connection to any spiritual practice, which was fine in the world (or not fine, but not his business), but it was impossible to run this business without that deep grounding. Going forward, Liam would correct his mistake. His team should be as serious about the goal of the work as he was: not money, although there was no problem with wealth, but love. Love as a practice, as a method of living in the world. Approaching everything with a spirit of friendliness.

A conundrum, really, if he thought of Krish. He still felt anger over the betrayal. It would take time to work through his feelings of injury.

The car delivered him first to Clare's farmhouse, where he would be staying. When Tillie said she was at the Green King, he'd almost changed his plans, but Clare would be wounded, and in truth, he wanted to be in the house with his family, to soak in the nurturing he would find in those walls, amid the wounded animals and the smell of baking bread and his auntie's warm arms. He wondered how he'd let so long a time lapse without coming back here.

Clare herself came out of the house when she saw the car. She was tall and lean, her black hair short and spiky. "Liam!" A trio of dogs came with her, a beagle with a tumor on his nose whose ears dragged the ground, a clearly blind Lab, a little almost-hairless thing with healing wounds on its back. Clare flung her arms around him and hugged him, the gesture so welcome that Liam found himself sighing, letting the hard day fall away.

"I'm so glad to see you!" he said.

She pulled away, her hands on his arms. "You're even more beautiful as an adult than you were as a child. You look just like your father, you know."

"Do I?"

"A clone," she said. "The minute I saw your mother with him, I knew I'd lost her."

It made him feel oddly emotional. "Never lost her."

"No, not really, of course."

A woman, short, with skin the color of teak and a baby on her hip, waited on the step, grinning to show a space between her two front teeth. Liam inclined his head. "Amelia, is it?"

She held out an arm. "We are so happy you're here, cousin!"

He bent to hug mother and child, and the baby giggled, grabbing Liam's hair. "Who's this, then?" he asked, disentangling the chubby fingers.

"This is Teddy."

Liam pulled a little fist to his mouth and kissed it.

"Come on," Clare said. "Let's get you settled."

She showed him to his room, tucked under the eaves, with windows looking out toward her greenhouse and the roofs of the village below. The bed was covered with a white candlewick spread and piles of pillows. "D'you remember this room?" she asked. "Your mum stayed in here. Not that you spent any time here at all."

He laughed. "True enough. We were all off building forts and trying to avoid being stolen by fairies."

She nodded, inclining her head. "Something on your mind, love?"

Startled, he swung around to look at her. "How did you know that?"

She placed a hand on his upper back, gestured for him to sit down. "I have some gifts of my own, you know. Even as a boy at the most vigorous age, you were a sensitive. You felt all the ghosts and knew all the secrets."

"I don't remember that."

"Do you want to talk?"

He took a breath, measuring her open expression, the pale blue eyes. He remembered that she was a spiritual leader of some kind, one of the New Thought arms that had emerged from the late 1800s— Divine Science or Unity or one of those. Sinking down on the bench by the window, he said, "I've met someone. In New York, just a week ago, but it's been . . . intense from the first day. I had to come to England for the gig in London, and she's been trying to figure some things out, so she stayed in New York, but then—"

He halted. It was just too strange.

"But then?"

"She came here. To Wulfecombe. Independently."

"Did she look you up or something?" Clare asked, frowning. "A bit stalkerish."

"No, it's not like that. She didn't come to find me. She came because something else brought her here, and now I think it feels fated between us, but I've had some problems in this area, falling in love too fast, too hard, and I don't want to mess up again."

Clare was silent for a long moment. Then she said, "Of course you fall in love hard. You love everything. The grass and the moon and pie and the people in your world, and the women who move you. It's such a beautiful gift, even if it sometimes hurts you."

He looked at her, feeling very close to tears. It had not occurred to him, even with all of his work over the years, to simply accept that he fell in love because that was how he operated. Not because it was a flaw. He gripped her hand. "I'm so glad to be here."

"It was meant to be," she said with a little smile. "Now, she's in town, here?"

He nodded.

"Go get her and bring her to supper. It'll just be us—Levi and me and whatever cousins can come."

"I will." He stood. Turned back and hugged her, feeling so grateful to be with people who loved him. Him, Liam, who had been a boy and would one day be old. "Thank you."

CHAPTER THIRTY-NINE

Sage let herself into the shop late in the day. They'd closed early, when the foot traffic died with the weather and there was no point in standing around. Sage had wanted to get home and roast vegetables for the tart her mother had asked her to make for lunch tomorrow.

She'd done that task, and found herself still restless. Paula was holed up in her studio, working in a fever on a new clutch of songs. That was how she always worked, in big bursts of wild productivity, then long stretches of fallow time. She'd promised to emerge for lunch tomorrow with Liam, which was the important thing.

Left to her own devices, the ingredients for the tart ready for assembling in the morning, Sage walked in the gloomy day to the shop. A few figures wove around the edges, shapes but no details, like a painting, and it gave her a little shiver.

The shop was quiet, only Sage and the ghosts from the centuries. She'd thought of a selection of chocolates she wanted to bring to lunch, and now set about collecting them. She'd already assembled a box of the fruit-based chocolates her mother liked, and the cherry cordials, which were a particular specialty Sage had created just for her mother's delight. They'd eaten Christmas cordials for years, and Sage had come up with a few variations: cherry and black pepper, cherry and ginger, and her own favorite, cherry and saffron.

Those had already been gathered, along with the caramel treats Paula loved. Sage had no way of knowing what Liam would like, but her gut led her to citrus, lime, and coconut, and a strange little banana and bitter chocolate that people either loved or hated.

Hmm. Not quite finished. She let her hand hover over various flavors. Nothing over the usual favorites, pistachio, vanilla, and raspberry. There was a little more energy when she neared the chai and white chocolate, stronger still when she crossed the turmeric and ginger, and then her best invention so far: a concoction of rosemary and sage ganache with pecans enrobed in white chocolate colored blue and topped with glitter. It was unusual and delicious, and she was quite proud of it. She placed them in a box with the ones for Liam, and then let herself tune in to the subtle energies of the chocolates themselves. What else wanted to go with her?

The blood orange caramels, a few traditional truffles dusted with cocoa powder.

Anything else? She moved her hand in the air above the rows, hearing the leaping pleasure of candied violets and the deep, sophisticated voice of Mexican chili and dark chocolate.

The baby danced. Sage nestled the chocolates into a beautiful box, feeling a kind of exquisite joy that could sometimes steal upon her in her sobriety, a feeling she'd never understood or known to exist before, except maybe long ago in the days before her sister was lost to them.

She allowed herself to feel it, all of it—the baby, the creation of her hands, the cool air of the shop. Everything, so beautiful.

She didn't pray, but she sent out a thank-you. For now. This moment. Her life.

Today.

CHAPTER FORTY

A thick fog seeped into town, and Tillie feared she would get completely lost. She headed down the hill, thinking she'd gone uphill for most of the way, and when the material of the road turned from tarmac to cobblestone, she let go of a little breath. At least she was in the right area. She followed narrow sidewalks along the fronts of shops, mostly closed. A man in a red coat stood out across the street, and she thought she recognized a shop window she'd passed earlier.

But the road dead-ended against a wall, and she turned around, walked down the other side of the street, stopping when she got to what she thought was the high road, and then headed—

Instead of winging it, she opened the map on her phone, centered herself, and looked for the Green King. Two blocks over. She crossed back across the narrow street and followed the line to her hotel.

A ghostly shape emerged from the fog, and Tillie saw a cat with thick striped fur and a long tail. It mewed at her, and she bent to pet him, but he ran toward an alley. "I was only going to be nice to you," she said. He paused and looked over his shoulder, then disappeared into a hole she couldn't see.

In one of the stories Tillie had loved as a child, she would have followed the cat and discovered a mystery, but at the moment, real life had mysteries enough without adding another.

As she straightened, a shimmer of gold paint on a window caught her eye. Words were painted on the window in an understated gold script. *Rosemary's Chocolates.* A painted cat, looking serene and clever, sat beside the words.

Tillie felt dizzy. "That cat," she said aloud, and touched it on the glass. Blue eyes and tan fur and a long, striped tail.

In the distance, she heard someone call, *"Rosemary! Where are you?"*

She switched apps and shot a photo of the cat. This is the cat I keep painting, she texted to Liam.

A sharp pain arrowed through her temple, and she shook her head. *Get back to the hotel, have a drink of water, maybe a little nap.*

As she came around the corner, a figure appeared out of the gloom. A tall, fit man with shining hair. He smiled as he saw her, and Tillie couldn't help launching herself in his direction, flinging her arms around his neck, feeling the dampness of his jacket, the drips of water from his hair, his solid, safe self.

"Oh my God, I'm glad to see you," she said against his shoulder. His arms were tight around her waist, and then he was kissing her, and whatever might have been wrong with the world was okay.

~

Her room was at the top of the hotel, a small suite with a gigantic claw-foot tub and windows that overlooked the now very rainy street.

She drew Liam down to the sofa under the window. "Let's call for some tea, and you can tell me everything." She realized that he wore only a coat over street clothes. "Where are your things?"

"I dropped them off with my aunt." He picked up the phone and ordered tea for two, then sat down with her. "She wants me to bring you back for dinner."

It seemed such a normalcy in the middle of the strangeness of everything that had been happening. She felt a little awkward sitting with him there. She couldn't quite figure out what to do with her hands, or her eyes. It seemed that a lot had happened, and all of it was strange, and suddenly, she was glad to have something to do that was so very normal—go to dinner at her boyfriend's family's house. Family, period. "I didn't bring many clothes, but that sounds great."

"Good." The tea arrived, and Tillie let in the woman from the front desk. She settled the tray on the coffee table, shooting a glance toward Liam. "Aren't you that meditation guy?"

"Guilty," he said, and held out a hand. "Liam Redfern. You are?"

"Tammy O'Malley," she said, her cheeks going pink. "Nice to meet you. I really like your app. I listen to it every day."

"I'm glad you like it," he said, and Tillie loved the way he turned his entire focus on the young woman, his hands loosely laced between his knees.

"Well. Anyway. Enjoy your tea."

"Thank you," Tillie said.

"Tammy," Liam called, pulling a pad of paper off the table to scribble an email. "Take this, and send me a note, and I'll see that you get a copy of one of the books, yeah?"

"Oh, wow. Thank you, Mr. Redfern."

She slipped out, alight with pleasure. Liam said, as if apologizing, "It's not always girls, I promise."

"Even if it was, I wouldn't mind. They're allowed to be a little dazzled by a famous, beautiful teacher."

"Beautiful?" he echoed.

"You know you are," she returned, and poured tea. "I bet this will actually be decent."

"No doubt."

When they both held a cup in their hands, Tillie said, "Can we talk about how weird this is? It's kind of freaking me out. Like, we just met by accident at that gallery, and then we have this wild connection. Then we split up but we just *happen* to land in the same tiny little town on the Devon coast?" She shook her head. "It's really creepy in a way."

"Well, but let's think about it." He raised a finger. "The gallery thing was timing, right? You were there to see Jon's work, and I was in the hotel across the street. That happens." He paused. "Actually, I saw you from my window. You helped an old woman who fell. Do you remember?"

"Yeah." She half smiled. "I gave her my umbrella."

He curled his palm around her knee. "People are not often kind, especially in bad weather. When I saw you run into the gallery, I decided to come meet you."

She narrowed her eyes. "Really? So you were stalking me."

"I was intrigued."

"She gave me a crystal, the old woman." Tillie hopped up and scrambled in her purse and brought it back to the bed, dropping it in his hand. "Maybe it was a magical talisman."

It was red and pink, with black weaving through it, and it had weight. Warmth. He closed his fingers around it and looked at her. "Maybe it is. Maybe it brought me to you. Maybe it brought you here to find out what happened to you."

"Maybe. I don't really believe in magic."

"You've said that before. But your paintings are all about magic, about looking through the current illusion to the reality that lies beyond."

"That's true." She frowned. "But why bother with a pair of lovers when there is so much wrong in the world? I mean, if magic is that powerful, why not fix the really big stuff, like making sure all children are in safe, loving homes, and wives don't get murdered by their husbands?"

A lock of her dark hair trailed around her long neck, and he reached for it to buy space to feel where this was going. "So as long as there is bad in the world, there can be no good?" he asked gently.

"No." Her eyes looked very bright. "No, that's not what I meant. Just . . . if magic is aligning things, or the Big Spirit in the Sky is answering somebody's prayer, why wouldn't it be something important?"

He took her hand. "What if we met so that we can heal each other and make each other better, and then we go on together to make the world better all around us? Maybe not the whole world, not every child fed or stopping all the evil that exists, but what if we make life better sometimes for some people because we are together?" He kissed her fingertips. "What about that?"

She stared at him, tears running down her face. "Where did you come from?" she whispered.

"I reckon it was a magic spell."

"I'm falling in love with you," she said. "I mean, for real."

"Me, too. But you already know that."

She realized that it had the weight of something she could trust. "Maybe." She sipped the sweet, hot tea. "Tell me what happened with Krish. Did you fire him?"

"I did. We don't have to talk about that now, though. Let's focus on you and what you're trying to find."

"But I don't even know what that is, and you've spent a lot of time helping me. Give me a chance to be present for you."

"Fair enough." He paused. "I fired him."

"What will that mean for your business?"

A flicker of uncertainty crossed his face. "I dunno. He's been the linchpin, honestly." He brushed grains of sugar from his fingers. "I've been thinking about it for a bit, but he really crossed a line a few days ago, and he's been manipulating me in other ways, too. I owed him a lot, but . . . I think that debt is paid now."

"Who will do the work he was doing?"

"There's a woman who's been with us a long time, almost since the start. Yolanda. I reckon she can do the job, and she'd welcome it." He paused. "But I might be ready to change this business model, anyway. The travel is too much. I don't want to live my life on the road."

"I can understand that."

"Anyway, that's catching you up. Let's not talk about anything work related for tonight. Did you find anything interesting today?"

"Not really. I had a ripple of something at the ford, but it was brief. I was hoping to find something substantial, but I haven't yet."

"Something in particular?"

"Maybe the house in the painting. A forest . . . but there's no forest around here that I have seen."

"Clare, my aunt, has lived here most of her life. She'd probably know where it was. I do know they've done some clearing and building."

She nodded, a whisper of yearning running over her nerves. She wanted to tell her mother about him, about this strange quest she found herself on. She wanted the spell of strangeness to be broken.

Or did she? What if when she found the answers, the spell around Liam was broken, too? What if the quest left her even more alone than she'd been before?

CHAPTER
FORTY-ONE

They weren't expected for another couple of hours, and Liam wanted to have a nap. Tillie curled up with him, glad for the company, but she only dozed. Something restless kept chasing itself around her mind, showing blips of a dark wood and then a cat, a chocolate bar layered with oranges, a child opening her hand to show a perfect chocolate with the stem of a cherry sticking out of the top.

When she sat up an hour later, all the noise that had been swirling around—an almost whisper, the snippets of pictures—was gone.

It was, she realized, the first time her brain had been silent since she'd seen the painting that first night.

To give herself some space to enjoy it, she took a shower and washed her hair, wanting to look good for her meeting with Liam's family. She let it dry naturally in soft waves, and left it loose.

Looking at herself in the mirror, she peered into the background behind her, seeking some answer she hadn't turned over, as if she were a being in one of her paintings. It wasn't a particularly appealing mirror, a plain, modern bathroom style, but she remembered the oval in the other room and, wrapped in a towel, went to stand in front of it.

The mirror had a baroque frame, imitation gold leaf, and it was old enough to be a little discolored in places. With her wet hair and towel, she stood in front of it with a sheet of plain paper, just the room

instructions turned over to the blank side, and a pencil she took out
of her purse. Looking beyond her reflection in the mirror, she held her
hand over the paper and waited. What could be there? What would be
there if she painted this mirror, this face, this place?

She saw a forest. A cat wandered out, that very big cat she'd seen so
many times now. He moved without hurry, and sat to lift his nose to
the air. A woman slid between the shadows, the witch from her fugue
painting, skinny and sharp. She glanced over her shoulder and saw
Tillie, watching. For a long time, she only looked at her, then slipped
into the forest. The cat licked a paw.

Without rushing, Tillie sketched the scene, waiting to see if anything else appeared. An orange rolled out of the shadows, and she heard
laughter.

And that was all.

She looked at the sketch. *Soon,* it seemed to say. *Soon.*

~

They walked to Liam's aunt's house. It was no more than a mile down a
country road that had houses on one side, meadows and undergrowth
on the other. Tillie could see through the row of trees lining the road
that sheep grazed in a series of rolling hills. Cars came by every so often,
but not many, and they made room for the walkers.

The house was down a smaller lane. A hedge provided a fence, but
over the top, the roof and windows of the highest floor were visible.
"That's not what I was expecting," Tillie said.

"It looks better on the outside than on the inside," he said.

As they came up the lane, a dog howled. "I forgot to tell you there's
a motley crew of misfit creatures," Liam said. "Levi is a vet, and they
have all kinds of critters."

Tillie laughed. "How wonderful!" The dog, a shiny black Labrador
with a big head who was clearly blind, waited for them. He nuzzled
Tillie's hand and whined in sweet greeting. She got down low and spoke

to him in a soft voice. "Thank you for that, sweetheart," she said, rubbing her hands over that giant head. He groaned and licked her face.

"He is never like that with anyone," a man said, coming out of the house. "You must have the touch."

Tillie stood to greet a tall man with reddish-brown skin and a thick beard. "I don't know about that," she said.

"You must be Levi," Liam said. "I'm Liam."

"I know who you are, lad. They've been all atwitter waiting for ye." He shook Liam's hand, clapped him hard on the shoulder.

"And this is Tillie," Liam said.

He enclosed her hand in both of his, peering intently at her. "Tillie, is it?" he said as if it wasn't the name he'd expected. He looked over his shoulder at Liam, then back. "Remarkable. Come in, come in."

Tillie didn't quite know how to respond to that, so she simply followed them up the rest of the walk. Flowers grew on either side, just now putting out green shoots.

A gray cat with half an ear wandered out to see what was going on, and Tillie greeted her. Right behind her came another cat. Tillie froze. She grabbed Liam's hand. Pointed.

"Who is this?" Liam asked, leaning down to scratch the cat's ear.

But Tillie felt a wildness as she bent down to pick up the big solid animal, white and light brown with a tiger-striped Siamese mask. He happily melted into her, bending his head to press his nose to hers. She closed her eyes. She *knew* this cat. How was that possible? Tears rose in her eyes, and she kept her head down to hide them, the cat purring low against her hands.

"This is River, one of the local breed," Levi said. "They're unique to the area, maybe a mix between somebody's pet Maine coon and a local Siamese or Ragdoll that spawned a new breed. There are dozens of them, and they're good pets, good mousers." He scratched the cat's back. "Aren't you, love?"

The cat meowed, and Tillie let him down, feeling off-kilter but also intrigued. The cat followed them into the house.

They went in through a back door, Levi leading. "Look who I found!" he called out.

A trio of women were gathered around a big, freestanding butcher-block counter, backlit by a large window that looked out to the fields. Tillie had to blink to see anyone at all. The one closest to her had long blonde hair and red cheeks, and Tillie recognized her instantly as Paula Davies. A little flush of pleasure ran up her neck. "Hi."

Liam said, "That's Paula, which you already know—she's a fan." He stretched out a hand. "Me, too. I'm Liam."

"Oh, that one American fan," she said with a laugh. "I've wondered who that was, buying my records over there."

Tillie laughed. "You're too modest. I love the music. I paint to it all the time."

An older woman, very thin and long-limbed, said, "Wow, your voice," and Paula said at the same time, "You sound exactly like Sage."

"Sage?"

"Me." The woman was haloed by the light, so Tillie could only see the nimbus of light around her hair and the curve of a belly. "Is that how I sound?"

"Bro," Liam said, and Tillie picked up the slightest disturbance from him, an alert or concerned note that made her look up at him. He stared at Sage, then looked to Tillie, and shook his head.

"What?" she asked.

He put a hand on either shoulder, warm and heavy, and walked her to the other woman's side.

Tillie looked at Sage. Sage looked back at her.

And here was the mirror she'd been staring into earlier, a woman a few years older than she, with sharper cheekbones and more lines around her eyes, but the same face otherwise. The same dark hair, though Sage wore hers shorter. The bodies were different, because Sage was pregnant and Tillie was not.

"You're American?" Sage said.

"Yes." She had the strangest urge to lift a hand to the other woman's face, as if to affirm it really was so similar. They stared and stared, and Tillie felt a roar starting up far away, the echo of the feeling she'd had this morning, and yet the migraine aura didn't come back. The cat wound around her feet.

"I'm Clare," said the third woman. "I'm Sage's mum." She was tall and lean, her hair going silver in single strands. Tillie had a sense of a mountain lion, powerful and sharpened by years of hardship. Her eyes were clear and all-knowing, and Tillie felt a strange, deep pang somewhere in her intestines.

She *knew* this face. Those eyes. A pain slid between her ribs, burst in her chest.

"Where were you born, love?" Clare asked gently.

Tillie started to answer, and then realized nothing she knew about herself had thus far proved true. "Los Angeles. I think." She was trembling, very finely, all over her body, as if she'd liquefy. The only thing anchoring her was Liam's hand. "She died, my mother, a few months ago, and . . . and . . . I don't know, honestly. Maybe New Hampshire?"

Clare said, "Sage, say something."

"Los Angeles, I think," Sage repeated.

The accent was different, and it didn't really sound the same to Tillie, but the room went completely silent. Tillie felt a sucking sensation, the rolling back of the waters of the ocean as it was sucked into itself, revealing the base of the sea and stranded animals and wrecks never seen before at such a depth.

But just now, it was pulling back and back and back. Clare's eyes filled with unshed tears. Sage stared at Tillie as if she'd burn a hole through her. Tillie shrank back into the wall of Liam.

Abruptly, Sage reached for Tillie's arm, and turned it over to reveal the delicate inner flesh. She pressed her index finger into the deep divot in the hidden place midway between wrist and elbow. "How did you get this scar?" she asked, raising her eyes, and up so close, they were exactly the same eyes Tillie saw when she leaned in to put on her mascara. The same color of iris, the same layered bits of yellow and green amid the blue, the same slight dip on the inner corner.

"I don't remember," she whispered.

"It was a rock," Sage said. "You slipped down the hill and landed on it."

Clare made a soft sound. "Impossible," she whispered, and took Tillie's other hand. "After all this time," she said, nearly airless. "Rosemary."

Tillie backed away, pulling out of their grasp. "I don't understand."

"You don't remember?" Clare said, and her eyes filled with tears.

"Remember what?" Tillie asked, the ocean sucking back and back and back.

"I remember," Sage said. "I remember everything. You're my sister. My twin. We thought you were dead." She whispered, "All this time, we thought you were dead."

And even though she'd been searching for the answer to questions that made no sense, Tillie couldn't take this in. Not this.

She stared at the two of them, unable to think of what to say.

A sense of panic rose in her chest, and she suddenly turned on her heel, broke away from the group, and ran outside, her breath far away, vision prickling at the edges. She tried to haul in air, but her heart was beating too fast, too fast. She couldn't breathe. She was going to die.

CHAPTER
FORTY-TWO

In the garden, Tillie bent over, bracing herself on her knees. She felt Liam approach and wanted to push him away, but she didn't have the strength. He placed a hand on the top of her back.

"You're not dying," he said. "Remember? Let's breathe in. One . . . two . . . three . . . That's right. Out one . . . two . . . three . . . four . . . five . . . six."

She coughed, stood up. Pushed away. He was part of the insanity. She strode through the grass, paced back. "Why did you do this?"

"I didn't. I swear."

"It's impossible. It's all impossible."

He waited.

Tillie covered her eyes, howling. "I don't know how to think about this. I don't remember anything. Wouldn't you think I'd remember when I saw them?"

"You don't have to make sense of it all at once."

Tillie thought of Arlette, laughing when a raven stole her earring. Singing when they played games in the fields or planted seeds in the greenhouse. Thought of her laughing, with one hand on her chest. Her heart burned. The panic returned.

"That's not my mother," she said, pushing away from Liam. "They're mistaken. I'm not the person they think I am."

"Okay."

"You're humoring me," she cried. "Like a frightened horse. But just because they want it to be true doesn't mean that it is." She paced through the grass, agitated, and paced back, her hems gathering bits of seed.

He simply stood there, hands at his sides.

She stared at him as if this was his fault. "How would that even be possible, Liam? You know? Like, we just accidentally met at the gallery, and then we had this wild affair, and now I'm here—were you part of this, like some weird scheme to get me here?"

"No," he said again. "I swear." He held up his hands in an oath.

Her eyes filled with tears. "What about my *mom*? My *real* mom?"

She stared back at the house, as if there were dragons within, unable to move in any direction.

"Hey," he said quietly. "What if we just see what happens? You don't make any choices or alliances or believe anything."

She waited.

"You were looking for answers, yeah?"

She nodded.

He held out his hand. "Shall we go in and see if we can find some?"

"Okay." She placed her hand in his, her smaller fingers enfolded in his own, and let him lead her back inside.

CHAPTER FORTY-THREE

Tillie was only slightly steadier when she went back into the kitchen through the back door. All three women looked up. Tillie paused to look at Sage and Clare, taking her time, looking with her eyes and her artistic eye to see that yes, she resembled them, and Sage looked older but wore her same face. Undeniable.

And so undeniable that Sage knew about her scar.

Clare easily could be her blood mother. Physically they looked alike, too, enough that her artistic brain offered her a visual of two kittens with a mama cat, all the same fur and eyes.

"I'm sorry," she said. "I just don't know . . . I feel so . . ." She gave up and flung up her hands.

"Why don't you come sit down," Clare said quietly. "I've put the kettle on. We can have supper, just as we'd planned."

Tillie sat down. Sage was next to her, and her hands were on the table. Tillie's hands, long and slender, with short nails. Tillie settled hers beside Sage's. "They look the same." She touched her thumb. "The nails are exactly alike."

Sage nodded. "You have a dimple on the opposite side." She smiled to show hers, on the left. Tillie's was on the right. "Like parentheses."

They looked at each other. Tillie assumed Sage was seeing the same things she was, the ways they were the same—eyebrows the same shape, the width of their shoulders, the terrain of their mouths, a fuller upper lip than lower. Tillie looked at the baby bump.

It was a safe-enough topic. "When is your baby due?"

"June 15." She rested her hand on the swell. "Do you have children?"

"No."

"Tillie is an artist," Liam said. He'd settled across the table, next to Paula. "Quite well known, actually."

"Really?" Clare brought mugs and spoons to the table. "What kind of art?"

"Painting. Realism mixed with fantasy elements, like people who are part animal."

"A lot of Green Man stuff," Liam said. And to Tillie: "It's a big thing around here."

"I'm going to look them up right now," Paula said. "If that's okay."

Tillie nodded. She kept looking at Sage, her nose and the exact line of her ears. "I don't remember *you*, exactly," she said by way of apology, "but I've been drawing you ever since I was very small. You were my imaginary friend, Sunny."

Sage closed her eyes, and she clutched Tillie's hand. "Imaginary."

"I'm sorry."

Paula, on her phone, said, "What's your last name?"

"Morrisey."

Paula typed it into her phone. "Oh, here you are. These are great! They could illustrate my songs, couldn't they?"

Tillie felt that part of her was a hundred million miles away, but she wanted to be at least polite. She nodded.

They all fell silent for a long moment. The air felt heavy. So many things to take in.

Clare said, "So, what do you remember, dear?"

Tillie took a breath. "Nothing, really. I didn't remember anything before—" She paused, and it seemed like a lot to explain. "Let me start at the end. My mother died five months ago, and I started getting these headaches. And then, a week ago, I saw a painting that must have triggered memories. It's a house with a porch and two girls and a big cat. Giant." She pointed to the cat sitting by the Aga, cleaning his face. "Like that cat."

Levi, who had been quiet, said, "I told her he's from the local clan."

Clare smiled, a little sadly. "We had one when you were little. He was called Joey, and you were very attached."

Tillie closed her eyes. A whisper came alive, and she thought of the dream she'd had of him. "Joey. I remember him stretching from my chin to my knees, with a very soft purr. He was so big."

"He was a normal cat," Clare said gently. "You were just small."

"Ah. Of course." She realized that Liam, too, was very quiet.

"When you started remembering, what happened?" Clare's voice was soft, so it didn't feel like she was being pushy. "How did it all lead you *here*?"

"I tracked down the painter, and she told me she painted around here. Would that porch be around here somewhere? I wanted to find it."

"It might have been the Beach Lane house," Clare said. "That's where we were living when . . ." Her throat closed. "You went missing."

"But what happened?" Tillie asked. "When? How old was I?"

"You don't know any of this?"

"No. My mother—" She hesitated, but how could she change that? What could she say? "She said I had a head injury." She drew her fingers through the white streak, illustrating. "I don't remember that at all. Or anything before it. I did have a broken rib, which I only know about because I had an X-ray once for something else, and they saw the scar."

Sage said, "We were playing in the woods, and I lost you. We all started looking, but—" She swallowed. "We didn't find you, only a sock by the river. They thought you might have fallen into the river and been swept out to sea, or maybe eaten by animals."

Tillie stared, trying to imagine how that was for them. "What a horrible story," she said, but it was awful in the way that hearing a story on the news was. She wanted to feel more of a connection—to the history, to the people looking at her with such longing—but she didn't.

Not even to Sage. She should have felt some connection to her actual twin, shouldn't she? "But how did my mother find me? Take me to America? I just don't get it."

"We have no idea," Sage said.

"Who is your mother?" Clare asked. "What's her name?"

"Arlette Morrisey."

Clare covered her mouth, the other arm bent over her belly. "Arlette," she echoed. "Oh my God."

"You knew my mother?"

"She was not your mother!" Clare cried with agony. "She *stole* you from me. She was my friend, and she moved after you were lost, but I never put the two things together."

A hollow ache filled Tillie's chest. Her throat was tight with all the words she didn't know how to say.

"Arlette was looking, too," Clare said. "And then she had a big family emergency and had to go back to America. We never saw her again." She deflated, her shoulders rounding forward. "I can't believe she just *took* you."

Tillie bowed her head, as if she'd had something to do with it.

"One of the things that started this quest was that I found a death certificate in my name that was for a little girl who died in the Valencia firestorm."

"The little girl. Tillie. Yes." Clare seemed winded, and her husband took over the task of making tea.

He poured strong dark brown tea into her cup, and then pushed the sugar toward her. "Drink, love."

She obeyed, stirring sugar into the tea. Sipped. Steadied herself.

It was something Tillie had done every day of her life, squaring herself with reality. Something about that stung, that she'd never seen it.

And all of it rushed in—that she'd had a big family and a sister, a twin, and could have grown up here, instead of alone with her mother out in the middle of nowhere. She could have had this family. Siblings and a father and—

Her breath caught at the intensity of longing.

"She was a mess," Clare said. "Just—" She shook her head, looking over to the middle of the table for the rest of the story. "Not okay. Not all there. I don't think her baby had been gone very long, maybe a year or two, and I felt pity for her, as any mother would have. She loved to spend time with you, both of you, and I let her babysit many times."

"I remember Arlette!" Sage cried. "She had the most wonderful songs!"

Tillie said, "That's her. She loved to sing."

Another long silence fell. Liam said, "Maybe let's take a little time, absorb all this, and come back together tonight or something, huh? What do you think?"

Tillie looked at him gratefully. Pressed a hand over her diaphragm. Nodded.

Sage reached for Tillie's hand. "Don't disappear, okay?"

And for some reason, it was easier to look at her than Clare. "I promise."

"Clare?" Levi said in his kind voice. "Are you all right?"

She nodded, looking at him. "I'm sorry," she said. "I have to . . . process all of this."

CHAPTER
FORTY-FOUR

They'd met at the Laundromat, of all places. Clare had to drag bedding over from the small house she rented. The girls had been infected with a stomach bug, and she wanted the big machines to sterilize their sheets and pillowcases. They busied themselves with a pair of rag dolls they loved, a gift from someone Clare couldn't remember when they were first born, moving back and forth between their own language and English. The language had begun to fade the past six months or so—they were leaving it behind with sucking thumbs and the blankets each had dragged around since toddlerhood. It was time, she supposed. They'd turned four in March and would start school in September.

She was struggling to fold a quilt when a woman came over and said in an American accent, "Let me help you with that."

Clare was grateful, and the two began chatting. They were close in age, and judging by Arlette's free-flowing blouse and the amulet she wore around her neck, of like mind. They got along immediately, laughing at the same things, sharing a love of the same music and a pleasure in the joys of gardening. Clare had been quite lonely since leaving her mean-hearted husband behind in Barnstaple, a move her mother had disapproved. She'd left behind her friends, too.

Arlette was traveling after a terrible tragedy, trying to find some way to live her life. For quite a while, she didn't discuss what that was, but one night after some spaghetti and cheap wine at Clare's house, she spilled the story. Clare clutched her daughters tight to her that night, happy for once that they only had the one bed to share.

In her warm kitchen so many years later, sitting in silence with Levi at the table after everyone left, Clare bent her head into her arms. How could she have missed the fact that Rosemary—not Tillie, never Tillie, how could she ever call her that name?—had been *stolen*, not washed away by the fast-running waters of the creek that fall?

They'd had rain for days on end, and the girls had gone out to play during a rare break. Only Sage had come back, hysterical, her sister lost. When she led Clare back out into the forest, the ground had given way on the bank, and one of Rosemary's socks had been found nearby.

Lost to the water.

They'd combed the woods, and called for her, and teams had gone out to sea to look for her body, but she'd never been found. Rosemary was gone.

"How did I miss the fact that it was Arlette? All this time?"

Levi said, "You trusted her."

"Did she really help us look? That seems so bold. And surely, Rosemary would have protested."

"Maybe. Children do what they're told, don't they? And she knew her, so maybe she just trusted that she was supposed to follow directions."

"The girls never stayed with her one at a time."

"She probably had a good explanation."

Clare sighed, pressing three fingers to her chest. "I feel so guilty. And so furious."

"You couldn't have known, Clare."

"But my poor girl, lost forever. Lost to her sister, to me." She shook her head. "How can she not remember?"

"Meg doesn't remember her mother. She was six. Tillie was younger, wasn't she? And to survive, she'd want to forget."

"It breaks my heart. For both of them." She looked at her husband. "And she seemed so aloof, didn't she? Like she wasn't sure about us at all."

"Consider it from her side. It must be overwhelming. Give her some time."

"I suppose." She spread her hands, looking at her rings, her nails, which were like her daughters'. "I wonder how Sage is doing."

"I'd wager she's making chocolate, working it out." He touched her knee. "Perhaps you should bake some bread for supper."

"Yes. That's a good idea." But she felt winded. Empty.

He stood and held out his arms. Clare let herself be enfolded in his warmth and good smells, in the solidity of his presence. "Things will work out," he said, his voice rumbling into her ear through his chest. "You're strong."

"Mm." She just melted into him, letting go of everything else. "What would I do without you?"

"It would be miserable," he said.

She couldn't dredge up a chuckle, as she was meant to do, but she leaned against him and sighed.

CHAPTER
FORTY-FIVE

Sage was indeed in the kitchen of her shop. She'd left Paula and gone straight there. Unlike her mother and her sister, she was not conflicted. Her mood was one of the purest joy.

All these years she'd punished herself, diving into the relief of addiction to assuage her guilt over losing her sister, and now, here she was. Sage was absolved. Her sister had returned.

But to work through the things she couldn't say aloud, the things that had tattered her soul and made her weep long in the dark, her hands knew she needed to make chocolate. She listened, letting them lead the way. First a ganache, made with extra-rich cream and the best chocolate, melted with a few shavings of orange, then walnuts. She let it cool, then rolled it into balls, rolled the balls in walnuts, and set them in rows to go through the tempering machine. She started it up to let the chocolate warm, taking pleasure in the scent rising out of it, richness and promise, the darkest of the dark chocolates she made, 70 percent Belgian couverture.

In her belly, the baby slept, and Sage sang to her, a lullaby she remembered only by humming. It had no words, but the tune shaped around memories of her sister, calling up visuals of the child she'd been.

Rosemary had been the leader between them, ten minutes older and a half inch taller, always. Rosemary was the one who'd spun fairy stories about the woods where they played, and created a cat kingdom just beyond the river.

Movement at the front of the shop caught her eye. Through the door, she saw a figure in front of the plate glass window. Not unusual, of course. People loved chocolate. But the person lingered, peering inside. Sage wiped her hands and walked through the darkened front room.

It was Tillie, her face framed by the arch of the gold lettering, *Rosemary's* a crown over her head, *Chocolates* a smile over her chest. She simply stood there, looking.

Sage located the big skeleton key that still fit the old-fashioned door, and unlocked it. Stepping out into the damp day, she said to her sister, "Why don't you come in?"

Tillie nodded. Sage stood back, holding out a welcoming hand to direct her through the door, and followed her, relocking the door and pulling the shade. The gloom was not thick but very quiet, even the ghosts holding their breath as Tillie turned, arms loose, and took in the room. "It smells heavenly in here."

"Come into the kitchen."

~

Tillie followed, caught in a magnetic field that surrounded her sister's orbit. The light was good here, pouring in through mullioned windows to the back and from overhead lights hanging from a high ceiling. The age of the place was plain, with the bricks and the ancient floors. Without asking if she could, she sank down on a stool before a big butcher-block counter and took it all in. A machine hummed quietly nearby. Rows of white molds were stacked nearly to the ceiling over another pair of machines. Racks held trays of finished chocolates in different shapes and sizes. Sage looked like a fairy from an old children's book, with her short hair and big eyes. Tillie's mind offered up a vision of winged fairies, pale colored with iridescent wings.

"How are you?" Sage asked. Her voice was kind. But also, it was resonant, with a kind of depth Tillie never associated with her own voice. "Kind of a lot of information, right?"

"Oh, I don't know. Only that my entire life is a lie." She lifted her hands, dropped them to her legs. "How do I—how do we—do this?"

Sage smiled gently. With deft fingers, she arranged a trio of chocolates on a little plate she took from the dish station and set it before Tillie. "Chocolate often helps."

"Does it?"

"I brought some to Mum's house, but we didn't get a chance to sample them. Something told me to bring chili-infused. What do you think?"

"Oh yes," Tillie said. Sage pointed to a square on the plate. Tillie picked it up and took a nibble. She was indifferent to chocolate for the most part, but this was something more than just chocolate. It melted instantly on her tongue, as if joining the molecules of her mouth—chocolate first, then bright sprays of dark chocolate, then a finish of heat. She closed her eyes, reveling.

A table covered with pastry, a bowl, cups, and spoons. Cooking. Windows fogged with steam. A woman singing, flour puffing up in the air as she flipped it over. Chocolate. Peppermint. Oranges. Christmas.

She opened her eyes. Sage worked small balls of chocolate into a bed of dark-brown powder—cocoa powder—and lined them up on a small pan. There was no hurry about her, no judgment, no pressure at all, just a cloud of calm that made Tillie feel calmer, too. She looked at her sister's face, finding her own features slightly askew. "We're twins," she ascertained.

Sage nodded. "You're older by ten minutes, but I see now that I look quite a bit older. It's a little disconcerting."

"How old were we when I . . . disappeared?"

"Four and a half."

"Do you remember?"

"Remember you? Yes, of course."

"Remember when I was lost."

Her expression collapsed. "Yes. It was the worst day of my entire life."

Tillie bowed her head. "I hate that I don't remember."

"Maybe it's a blessing."

"I guess." She nudged the place where the hole lived in her memory, feeling the hollow. She picked up another chocolate, this one shaped like a tiny Bundt cake.

"Let it just melt in your mouth," Sage said.

Tillie did. It started dry and a little bitter, then softened until it was only the purest taste of chocolate she'd ever known. Again, she closed her eyes, but this time, there was no picture, just the wonder of the taste, filling her, transporting her. "How do you do that? I don't even like chocolate all that much."

A Madonna smile touched Sage's lips. "You won't remember, but there's a family story about a cake a neighbor made, a torte with layers of ganache." She frowned, looking off into the distance. "Maybe it was Arlette who made it! That would be so weird." She shook her head. "Anyway, I almost drowned in that cake. And I can still remember how deep and wild that chocolate tasted. It was incredible."

Tillie found herself relaxing, letting go of some tension in her body that had bunched her shoulders up to her ears.

Sage continued. "I had a pretty substantial meth problem."

"They don't really come in small, do they?"

Sage laughed. "True enough." She rolled a chocolate in the powder. "I was gone for about eight years, living in Barnstaple and London. And one day, a woman was kind to me and gave me some chocolate at a shop." Rolling, tapped lightly, set aside. "I can't even imagine how I looked, like some skinny girl monster with no teeth. But her shop reminded me that there were other things in the world. I didn't get clean right then, but it started then."

"I'm sorry that happened to you."

She looked away. "I'm okay now."

"And married to my favorite folk singer," Tillie said. "I'm not kidding. I adore her."

"She is wonderful. Truly." She rolled the last chocolate. "She looked up your art online and showed us. You're amazing."

"Thank you."

"All those mirrors," Sage said. "Eerie, isn't it?"

Tillie's mouth dropped open. Mirrors. "Oh my gosh. Mirrors, mirrors everywhere." Her eyes filled with tears.

Sage rounded the table. "May I?"

Tillie nodded, and her lost sister wrapped her thin arms around her and held her while a tidal wave of grief swept over her.

But she still didn't remember.

CHAPTER
FORTY-SIX

Liam took Tillie back to the hotel, and when she left, he paced with his sense of unsettledness, rounding the room over and over until he recognized the insanity of it. He lived the confrontation with Krish over and over, seeing it from all sides. He saw the expression on Tillie's face when she looked up to him and said, "What about my mom?" and he knew she didn't mean Clare, her newly discovered mother.

The unsettledness was also over the realization that he'd recognized Tillie because he'd known her twin as a child, not because she was a soulmate. It made him ache somewhere deep, that this time he'd been so sure, and once again, he was wrong.

And if he was wrong about the sense of connecting souls, maybe he was wrong about Krish. Maybe Krish had been right all along, that Liam had no judgment in these matters. He fell in love too fast, too wildly, for it ever to be real.

But he thought of Tillie's quick mind, her metaphorical grasp of the world, her strength enduring everything she'd faced, and he felt a million layered things. Love and protectiveness and admiration and sorrow for her losses, and lust and satisfaction and yearning and contentment. He felt that she made him a better version of himself. He thought of holding her in the night, her hair streaming over them both like a silken blanket, and the emotion he felt in those moments and how it anchored him to himself in some strange way he couldn't articulate. He thought of the first sight of her, crouching down to help an old woman in the rain, leaving her umbrella—embodying kindness. He'd gone down to the gallery to find her. Even right now, he longed for her company, as if he'd found an extra arm and now needed it.

It wasn't like it had been with Opal. She had dazzled him physically, and he was enthralled by the sex. That happened to people all the time. Human beings were wired for sex and for wanting a lot of it with the possible mates who triggered the chemical response genes insisted upon.

Which was the scientific angle of soulmates, he supposed.

With Tillie, yes, he wanted her physically. He wanted to *mate* on some visceral level that meant children and families and all of that unfolding into the future. On some deep level, he loved that she was from his mother's village, that their bloodlines looped back and forth through time, their ancestors probably going back to the Bronze Age. He imagined a Tillie at the dawn of Stonehenge, laying an offering on the stones at the solstice, and it gave him a shiver.

Standing at the window, he looked down to the street and watched the rain make patterns on the pavements. He wished he had someone to call, to talk things out with. Krish had been his only close friend for a very long time, and maybe that had been part of the problem, too. He'd leaned on him too much. And maybe Krish had grown greedy as well.

That, too, was a thing that happened. It just did. Humans were wired to want more and more.

Leaning on the casement, he brushed a hand over his chin, feeling prickles, and took a breath, centering himself. What was here now? Could he stand just in his body and be aware?

He took a breath, let it go. His thoughts chased themselves around his mind: Krish, Tillie, India, the workshops that had grown so crazy and out of control. He let them whirl round and round.

Standing in his body, he felt his empty belly. His arms were cold from the draft off the window. He had a little ache in his midchest that might be missing Tillie, or sadness over the loss of the cheerful lunch he'd been anticipating. Perhaps he should return to Clare's. She must be so devastated by all of this. And Sage, too, although of all of them, she'd been the calmest.

He left the window and sat down on the big chair, wrapped a blanket around his cold shoulders, and settled in for meditation. Muddy waters, left to stand, would clear. He sat for an hour, sat in the moment and his body.

As he sat, the water cleared at last. He saw that he loved his work, truly. Loved the people who came to practice with him. Loved seeing their joy when they discovered moments of peace. He loved the love inherent in spiritual work.

Love. A sense of expansion struck him. Love like a wind or a breeze, love blowing over mountains and rivers and oceans. Love settling on him in a bar in Auckland when he saw a girl as pretty as a fairy. Love rising from a crowd at a workshop like pink steam, filling the air with a fragrance of peace. Love in the offerings, love in the app, love in Clare's kitchen and love in Sage's chocolates. Tillie's paintings and the light in her face when they made love, and the way he felt doing simple things, like eating with her.

We are all soulmates.

He saw her bending to help the old woman up, saw himself helping her up the stairs to her apartment, saw her ex in despair on the steps. Love, love, love, love.

We are all soulmates.

When he finished, he stood and opened his laptop.

What did he know for sure?

He loved the workshops. He genuinely did. The people, the pleasure of helping them find their way. He loved the big groups sometimes, and he loved the financial rewards of the app.

What he didn't love was being on the road all the time. It was draining and left him out of touch with himself. He needed a home base. His people around him.

Maybe here.

He opened his laptop.

To: Yolandatk@gmail.com
From: LiamRedfern@gmail.com
Subject: Meeting?

Do you have some time this week for a deep talk?
We should discuss how to move forward. Text me
some times that work for you.

He sent the email, and then crossed his arms and tested his feelings about Krish.

To: KrishnaTK@gmail.com
From: LiamRedfern@gmail.com
Subject: Re: Meeting

If you haven't left England, let's have a meal in
London next week. I'm not sure what I'm doing with
the business, but I can't see a world without you in
my life.

He paused, hands on the keys. That felt wrong. Although it was painful, he needed to walk away from Krish, at least for now. He hadn't been a proper friend for a long time. He could love his old friend but also set boundaries. Maybe they could create a new relationship in the future, but that time was not now. Because Krish had overseen much of the creation of the business, it would take some time to sort it all out.

Aside from the business, Liam would miss him, his oldest friend. He didn't know how it would feel to be completely out of touch.

But after so much time and so much work, so many hours working through his own character, Liam trusted himself at last. He trusted *himself*. That centered place said he needed to walk away from Krish for now.

He moved the message for Krish to the trash.

Tillie texted him. I might need some time alone. Do you mind going back to Clare's without me for now?

He worried about her being alone with such a big load of information, thought about her panic attacks and the migraines and—

She was a grown woman. She'd been managing her life just fine. She didn't need rescue. She needed to sort herself out, work through everything.

He, however, needed to be around people, and his people were in that house on the hill. A little part of him wondered if they, too, needed space and time, but his need for human company was rather too large to ignore. He stalled a little by calling his mother as he walked up the hill. She answered on the first ring. "Lucky for you I've been up with a sick goat," she said.

He couldn't believe he'd forgotten to check the time. "Hi, Mum. Just needed to hear your voice."

"Oh, that's not good. What's going on, son? Aren't you in England with Clare?"

He realized she would know this story. It hadn't just happened to him, to Tillie and Clare and Sage. "I am. And there's a lot to tell. Do you have a minute?"

"Always. Let me make a cup of tea."

So he spilled out the story, about meeting Tillie and all the coincidences, and then the fact that she was Clare's lost daughter everyone had thought was dead.

"Well, no one would believe you if you told this story anywhere."

"Right?"

"And the woman, Tillie. Is she important to you?"

"It's new," he said, like an adult. "But yes, I think she is."

"Another soulmate," she said with a droll tone.

He didn't take offense. "Well, it does seem fated."

She laughed. "In this case, you're right. Get off the phone. I need to call Clare."

CHAPTER
FORTY-SEVEN

Tillie stared at the ceiling. Liam had gone to Clare's, leaving her to the hotel room. It just seemed too hard to talk to anyone. She considered calling Jon, but even that seemed too much. She closed her eyes and let everything swirl through her.

A twin. Who *smelled* just right.

A living mother who felt like a stranger, but looked like her. All this time, she'd known she didn't look like Arlette, but she'd assumed she looked like her father, the father she didn't know, would never know.

Instead, she belonged to these people, this family, this place in the far west of England. Again, the image of a cat and two kittens came to her—Clare and Tillie and Sage.

Clare and *Rosemary* and Sage.

She had a blood mother, one who had other children and a husband. If Tillie had not been stolen, she would have grown up here, with a twin and other siblings and a father—really, a whole village. She had been so lonely at times as a child. So lonely and outcast and alone with Arlette and her mental issues.

But now what did she do? Who was she if she wasn't Arlette's daughter? Who would she be now, going forward? It made her ache to try sorting it out, and she didn't know whom to talk to. Not her therapist. Not any of her "new" family.

Drifting, she thought of the cat. It had been strangely crushing to realize it had once been alive, with a name, and now no longer existed. It took him away from her in a way that seemed ridiculous.

Good grief. She was a mess. She looked at the time change to Crete. RU up?

Three dots.

Three dots.

Three dots.

Tlak tmrw?

She laughed at the typo. Must be having fun. xx

Even a glancing connection with Jon made her feel like herself. Which led to knowing what she really needed right now was to paint.

Urgently, she got up and looked on her phone for an art store. A shop was open for another twenty minutes a couple of blocks away, so she braved the rain with an umbrella borrowed from the front desk. She'd just get a pan of watercolors and a sketchbook and work out some of this confusion.

Hardly anyone was out, understandably. She followed the directions on her phone a little way off the high street to a narrow lane where the leaning buildings blocked some of the rain. It was quieter here, with echoes of time coming off the walls, and she lowered the umbrella, struck with a sense of familiarity. She passed a home with a slightly crooked door, violets in a pot nearby the step, and in her imagination saw a mouse wife with a little apron.

Prickles ran up her neck. The imaginary creature was both familiar and not, and very clear. She could see the little painted toenails, the vague shape of legs, the flowered apron. A book she'd read?

Three doors down was the art shop, and she hurried to the door, hoping she was still ahead of the closing. Lamplight glowed within, yellow and welcoming, and she ducked in, setting off a bell.

An older woman, thin and dressed in the working clothes of an artist, poked her head out. "Closing soon."

"Thanks. I just need to pick up a few things."

The woman stepped out of the room, a perplexed expression. "Sage?"

"No," Tillie said. But she didn't have the energy to explain. "Do you have watercolors? A tin and some brushes, maybe?"

"Yes, of course. In that corner by the window." She came out from behind the counter, as if to show her.

Tillie raised a hand. "That's all right. I can find them."

"Of course you're not Sage. Your hair is too long." She shoved her glasses down on her nose. "But it's remarkable. And your voice is just like . . ."

Tillie stopped hearing her. She moved through an archway into an alcove by the window, smelling dust and paper and the waxy presence of crayons, and her body was entirely, completely swamped with memory.

She was smaller, which she only knew because she looked up toward the top shelves, which held the pastels she desperately wanted. Her mother said she couldn't afford them, but another person came forward, offering a note. "Let me, Clare," she said. "The child has a gift."

Hope spilled through her. The pastels would be hers. The paper, too.

Sage took her hand. "Will you share?"

"Yes."

The woman had followed her into the alcove, and her face had gone white. "It's you, isn't it? Rosemary. You loved it here so much."

"My name is Tillie," she said, but there was a breaking, a sense of something coming, that tsunami pouring over the defenses she had built.

She remembered. Sinking down in a chair, she felt the breaking waves and could do nothing to stop it. All at once, the empty place in her memory filled to the brim and overflowed.

She remembered Joey, the cat, purring next to her, and her whole heart swelling with love as vast as the sky. She remembered sitting on a sofa with her mother, Sage on the other side, their hair still wet from their baths as Clare read a book in her lively voice, giving the animals all voices of their own. The mouse wife and fairies in the forest and hares and wolves and all the other beings who had made their way into her work.

The memories she thought might drown her simply washed through her, settling back into their places. Some thin, some bright. She saw Sage playing by a stream, eating across the table, playing dolls behind a chair somewhere.

She heard Sage crying out, "Rosemary, where are you?"

She took a breath. "I'm here," she said. "I'm Tillie, but I am also Rosemary."

The woman sank down next to her and took her hand. The grip was strong and cool, bracing. "Welcome home, child."

From the back wandered a cat, a big cream-colored Siamese with crossed blue eyes. He meowed a welcome, too, and jumped in her lap as if he belonged there.

Tillie bent her head and kissed him, and even as she did, and claimed the old lost part of herself, she felt a burning longing for Arlette. She wanted to tell her mother the story of finding her other mother, of finding these cats, of discovering she had a place in the world that felt so very, very right.

Even if her mother had been the one to separate her from it.

The shopkeeper peered at her. "But where have you been all this time?"

Smelling the fur on the cat's head, she said, "A woman stole me," she said. "And took me to America."

The woman was silent. "We always said it was as if you were stolen by fairies."

Tillie nodded. In a way, she supposed it had been just like that. She thought of her mother, gardening so cheerfully, stirring a pot of soup, laughing in the way that she had with her hand on her chest, so tickled with herself.

She felt she should be angry with Arlette, but she couldn't find that emotion amid the grief. She only missed her. She would always miss her.

And yet, it was good to be home, too. At last.

CHAPTER
FORTY-EIGHT

The family was gathered in the living room of Clare's house when Tillie returned. It was only Clare, Levi, Sage, Paula, and all the animals, scattered around the room. A fire burned on the hearth.

Clare held out her hand. "Will you sit with us, Tillie?"

She felt Liam look at her, and she gave him a slight nod, then joined Clare and Sage on the sofa. Clare sat in the middle, Sage on the other side, their hands clasped together. When Tillie sat down, Clare continued to hold her palm up, and Tillie hesitated, then gave in. Clare had long white fingers and neatly shaped oval nails. They were Sage's hands, and Tillie's. That was a thing she'd never had before, seeing her traits in the body of another person. She felt both resistance and comfort in that recognition as the two long-divided parts of herself began to come together. A little wail somewhere deep cried her other mother's name, and yet, she saw something in this mother's eyes that felt real and true. Recognizable.

It had been such a long, long, strange day, after a long, long, strange week. She was tired to her bones, and had a great many things to think about, but she didn't feel off-center, or lost, or any of the things that had undermined her. The memories that had returned were only tatters and bits, but they were like rocks, mooring her to this place, these people.

Clare held the hands of both of her daughters. "I know you must be very, very tired, Tillie," she said. "I promise not to keep you long before we feed you and send you to sleep, but I have a little story to tell you, if you can bear it."

Tillie nodded. For the first time, she let herself really look at Clare, at the sharp nose and dark hair. At her temple, the skin was thin enough to show the veins beneath.

"The Evelys have been a part of this village for centuries," Clare said. "Some say since before William the Conqueror, though I have my doubts it has been that long. We've been farmers for the most part, ordinary village folk, and happy to be so. We were not complete here in this generation without you, and I just want to welcome you back into our fold. Maybe it will never feel quite like home, but I hope it will feel like *a* home. We want you, and we are glad you're found."

An opening creaked through Tillie's soul, and she saw how Clare had been in her paintings, over and over, through the years: an owl, a coyote, a bobcat. Her throat ached with the possibility, suddenly untenable, that she might never have realized that simple truth.

"We don't expect you to love us right away, or come to terms with everything, but we are here for you. Take as long as you need."

A tear spilled over her cheek, and Sage said, "Mum sandwich?"

And Tillie knew what that meant. She leaned in and let her sister and her mother embrace her. She smelled home in Clare's shoulder, and her sister's hand touched her head, and although she had so many, many, many things to think through, she felt moored, too. "Thank you," she whispered.

The moment ended, and they got up and went to the table, where a spread of fresh food and pie and big goblets of cider waited. Liam sat next to her, and Sage on the other, and they feasted.

And later, Liam curled with her in his bed and said, "I think I have to finish the European leg of the tour."

"I think you do," she said, brushing a finger over his knuckles. Light shone in through the window, illuminating his bright hair.

"And you have to finish your show."

"Yes."

"I hate the idea of not sleeping with you every night."

"Me, too," she said. "But I think if the universe or whatever worked this hard to get us together, we can probably trust that it's going to be okay."

"What would you think of coming here to live when we get through this round of stuff?"

Tillie paused, testing it.

He brushed his hand through her hair. "It is fast. I understand if you're not ready."

She made a soft noise. "But I am. It feels like so much has been lost that it would be almost criminal not to see where this goes."

He kissed her, visibly moved. "Yes."

They wove their hands together, and Tillie rested there, in the space he made for her. Time spun out ahead to a thousand moments like this, resting together as the world turned around without them, and she took a long, easy breath.

"You're going to be an auntie."

"I am!" Tears filled her eyes. "I was so alone as a child, Liam. I know you can barely imagine, being one of six, but it was always just my mother and me, away from town. I made up siblings and cousins and a father who was away on a journey."

"A journey?" he echoed with a smile.

"Well, I didn't want him to be at war or anything."

He nodded. "Now you have a giant family. And more to come. There're a lot of us on my side, too."

She hadn't even thought of this. The swell of longing rose so high and hard that she had to bury her face in his chest. Liam gently stroked her hair. Kissed her part.

When she had settled again, he asked gently, "Do you think you might want to be a parent eventually?"

"Not too eventually," she said. "I'm not exactly a spring chicken."

"Oh." He sighed, curling closer. "That's fine with me. The sooner the better." He kissed her shoulder. The tip of her ear.

Tillie closed her eyes, suddenly wishing again she could tell her mother—who would always be her mother, no matter what else transpired—about all this, about Liam and finding her sister and Clare. She wasn't mad at her, at least not right now. That would likely come as her memory filled in and she had more time to process.

But Arlette had been a broken, mentally ill woman, who'd stolen her, yes, but had also given her a good childhood and a strong foundation.

"I'm thinking so much of my mom," Tillie whispered. "I wish you could have known her. She wasn't a bad person. She really, really loved me."

"I believe that."

"I still miss her so much." Grief, never far away, circled back and filled her. "I wish I could tell her about all of this. About Sage and Clare. And you."

"I feel so sorry for her," Liam said. "Losing her daughter."

"Yeah." Tillie stared into the dark. "I wonder how she did it, got me back to the US."

"I think that's why your name is the same as the child who died."

"Oh!" The puzzle fell into place. "Of course." She frowned. "I wonder when my real birthday is."

"Will you want to change it?"

She thought about it. "Maybe I'll have two birthdays."

"Grand solution." His voice sounded slower. He'd had a few hard days, too. She should let him sleep. Turning into the fragrance of his chest, she closed her eyes. "Good night."

He kissed her head. "Good night."

CHAPTER
FORTY-NINE

Wulfecombe

Six months later

The day was September warm, sunlight pouring down on the small church that was almost always too cold. Clare had been waiting for this day for nearly three months, and she'd written the ritual herself.

Rituals mattered. People needed them to mark time and enormous events, to connect with each other and their community. Weddings and funerals were the prime example, of course, but other moments mattered, too. Christenings and baptisms, coming-of-age ceremonies like quinceañeras and bar mitzvahs, graduations and birthdays. She loved and studied ritual, and had performed dozens of types over the years.

This one needed to encompass both sorrow and joy, loss and new beginnings. She'd studied and thought, and rewritten several times, and thought she'd come up with something beautiful.

The church, built an unimaginably long time ago, with priests' names carved on a stone tablet as far back as 1140, was festooned with flowers supplied by the entire village—enormous dahlias and late roses wound with baby's breath and yellow daisies. Sunlight shone in the windows.

Her family sat in the front pews. Levi and the daughters he'd brought with him, Meg and Amelia; the boys they'd made together, Ben and Arthur, tall and good-looking like their father, with the Evely blue eyes. Next to them was Paula, glowing with her nascent pregnancy, though few knew it yet. Sage held Clover, the plump baby who'd been born with her mother's calm nature, and Tillie sat next to them, rubbing Clover's toes. Then Liam, causing a stir with his beauty and his fame, holding Tillie's hand. Jon, Tillie's best friend, was there with a slim Greek man. George, the blind dog, had been adorned with a flower collar.

Clare had flown to New York over the summer for Tillie's show. It thrilled her to travel on her own, to see her daughter's life and meet her friends. She'd been dazzled and proud to admire Tillie's paintings, seeing herself in them, and the girls as children, and even Arlette, who'd caused them such pain. There was a painting of the twins, peering into a mirror, showing past and future, and an owl/mermaid something that was breathtaking.

But her favorite was the enormous painting of a Wulfecombe cat, big and muscular and somehow cheerful, flying through the woods with a girl on his back, a girl who was laughing in utter joy as her hair flew out behind her. Joey and Rosemary, long ago.

And now.

"Today," she said to the gathered number, "we're here to welcome back our lost daughter, Rosemary Tillie Evely Morrisey. Tillie, will you come up first?"

Tillie walked to the front, and Clare tied a long red ribbon around her wrist. "Now Sage." Sage carried her daughter with her, and Clare wrapped a pink ribbon around each of their wrists.

She followed with more ribbons of different colors for the family sitting in the front row, green and yellow and bright blues, and they all stood in a circle, waiting. The boys looked skeptical, but she forgave them. They were doing it.

When all were assembled, Liam, too, she wrapped a white ribbon around her wrist, and looped it around each of the others. "Love binds us even when we can't see it, even when one of us is lost," she said, and began to weave the ribbons all together in a particular way, one to the next to the next. "We are renewing our family bond in front of the community, to declare that the past is remembered but doesn't claim us, that we love one another as we are now."

In a bit of magic, she wound the center ribbons into a simple wreath and held it aloft. "We are family, now and forever. May it be so."

Clare looked at Tillie. Tillie looked back.

"All is well," she said.

"All is well," Tillie said.

"All is well," Liam said.

"Bah, bah, bah!" Clover cried.

They all laughed, and kissed. Clare held her daughters' hands, one on either side. A pain, the loss of so many years with her child, would always live within her, but life was never everything a person wanted.

But it could be good. It could be sweet. It could be so very rich, right in this very moment.

Right now.

ACKNOWLEDGMENTS

Ahriana Platten, the author of *Rites and Rituals: Harnessing the Power of Sacred Ceremony*, was in my thoughts very much in this book. Thanks for the hours of deep conversation about life and the beautiful rituals you've designed for me and my family. Much love, my friend.

Many thanks to Kevin Shaw, chocolatier extraordinaire and the proprietor of Coastal Mist Chocolate Boutique & More, for taking time a week before the busy season to sit down with me to share his journey and answer a million questions about making chocolate—and sent me away drunk on the heady taste of salted-caramel drinking chocolate. I highly recommend his original and delicious chocolates, which you can find online at https://coastalmist.com. Any mistakes are entirely my own.

I spent many hours lost in the beauty of writing, fairy tales, and magic at Terri Windling's excellent blog, *Myth & Moor*. Tillie is named for the lovely dog who was her companion for a long time.

Thanks to my husband, Neal, who picks up the slack when I get lost in the worlds of my writing, who walks dogs and does the shopping, does dishes, reminds me to get outside and breathe when I'm getting too much in my own head, and listens to a million iterations of the stories as I work them out. My world is so much better with him in it.

ABOUT THE AUTHOR

Photo © 2009 Blue Fox Photography

Barbara O'Neal is the *Washington Post, Wall Street Journal,* and *USA Today* bestselling author of more than a dozen novels of women's fiction, including the #1 Amazon Charts bestseller *When We Believed in Mermaids, This Place of Wonder,* and *The Starfish Sisters.* Her award-winning books have been published in more than two dozen countries. She lives on the coast of Oregon with her husband, a British endurance athlete who vows he'll never lose his accent. To learn more about Barbara and her works, visit www.barbaraoneal.com.